This page left blank

The War

A Mirror Gate Chronicle

The fourth book of Shaméd the Wizard

Written by
TJ Boyer &
Elizabeth Ajamie-Boyer

Copyright © 2009 by Timothy Boyer & Elizabeth Ajamie-Boyer
Rev: 01
Authors: TJ Boyer & Elizabeth Ajamie-Boyer

Website: https://mirrorgatechronicles.wordpress.com
Email: tjboyer.author@gmail.com

Cover art: Shutterstock

First paperback printing, 05-23-2011
Second release date: 2018

ISBN: 9781520211848

Table of Contents

Chapter One 6
Chapter Two... 14
Chapter Three.. 21
Chapter Four 26
Chapter Five.. 49
Chapter Six.. 63
Chapter Seven 77
Chapter Eight 88
Chapter Nine 97
Chapter Ten... 108
Chapter Eleven.. 121
Chapter Twelve 140
Chapter Thirteen 150
Chapter Fourteen... 155
Chapter Fifteen.. 163
Chapter Sixteen... 170
Chapter Seventeen 184
Chapter Eighteen... 193
Chapter Nineteen 203
Chapter Twenty... 216
Chapter Twenty-One.. 227
Chapter Twenty -Two 235

I would like to say a special thanks to all of you who helped me get the Mirror Gate Chronicle books into print. Without the help from so many family and friends it would never have been completed.

Here is where I put a big hug and kiss, and thank you to my lovely wife, Elizabeth who starting with book 3 I get to add her as coauthor. She has put up with me as I sat in front of the computer writing the stories.

I have been asked to explain some of the items, worlds, and characters that are in the stories in more detail. I will be putting together a book very soon that will have more information about the characters, such as who helped me create them, their physical descriptions, and the items they use. I hope to have art work of the characters and the items. Until then, I hope this book will help explain more of the background of some the people in these stories. It should give you, the reader, a better understanding of them.

Also, there will be a book detailing the lives of the Thorns, where they came from, their history, their culture and much more.

If any of you have thought of drawing pictures of any of the characters, please do, and send them to me. I would love to see your interpretation.

As always, if you have any thoughts about any of my books please email me or go to my web page

storiesbytjboyer@yahoo.com

www.mirrorgatechronicles.wordpress.com

Chapter One

Shaméd entered the world room. The only one there was Benn. He was standing near the MA-TED working. Benn saw him enter.

"Good day, Lord Shaméd."

Shaméd walked over.

"I did not know you were working this shift?"

"I am just covering for Reklan. He had something to do and will be back soon. Is there something you need? Are you ready to go back to ZMEDWT873? I just sent Mordock there. By the way, have you seen the data on that man? His genetic make-up is amazing. He has over thirty different species in his DNA."

"Yes. I knew about Mordock after the first time he came here. I have even seen what he really looks like. As for leaving, no. I just wanted to see if you have heard from Rae or Nakobee?"

"Let me check."

Benn turned back and started tapping the letters and numbers on the table in front of the small MA-TED. Shaking his head, he re-entered the numbers and letters, then turned to face Shaméd.

"I am sorry, but it seems there is something wrong with the MA-TED. It says Rae is out of touch and so is Nakobee. I can understand Rae being offline - he has done it before. However, Nakobee has no way of disabling his tracker, not since it was fused into his chest. If you want I can have it checked out further to find the problem."

"That is not necessary, I just..."

"Wait, there is a message coming in from Nakobee."

Benn turned a knob on the table and Nakobee's words and voice came through.

"This is Nakobee. I am with Rae and we are in a city called Na-Car. Can someone please inform Shaméd we are here and waiting for him."

"How did Rae get on ZMEDWT873? I thought he was still on his own world."

"He was sent there a few weeks ago to help Nakobee. Send a message telling them I will be there in a few hours."

Shaméd turned and walked out of the room. In the hallway he heard Benn calling Nakobee. Shaméd called out to Rednog the world.

< "I need to talk to you about Rae." >

< "What do you need to talk about?" >

< "Who authorized Rae to have garments made by the Thorns?" >

< "I did when I discovered he was a descendent of the first king on his world. We have known for a long time that we needed someone with that genetic makeup to activate the chair throne. It is the only way to the hidden rooms. Once below we would have access to the data that is stored there and to the satellites around that world". >

< "Is that why his training was changed? You and the others decide to train him to be a puppet king on his world?" >

< "There are no others. I took the information from your mind and went further to confirm it. When it was confirmed that he was indeed genetically linked to the first king, I made the needed changes to Rae's, Jym's, and Jon's lives to make sure they would be able to someday return and rule. In doing this it will help us find the information we are searching for and it would help them with their world". >

< "You did this all by yourself, you did not tell anyone? Why?" >

< "That is obvious. The people on their world are dying, and in less than three generations all human life will

be gone. Since those boys have come here, that world has had four world-wide plagues. Each one nearly wiped the human population off that world. We do not know how the plagues were stopped, only that each time the population was down to about half when the sickness finally stopped. Each plague was slightly different, and each one was about a hundred years apart. Rae is the closest or possibly the only one who can save them. Moreover, it is what you wanted to do, is that not true?">

Shaméd stopped walking and leaned his back on the wall, looking around making sure no one was there.

<"I found out he was heir to the throne when we rescued the people that were kidnapped and the other slaves on his world. He was the grandson to the king of that time. Because he was not there, his cousin was crowned king. I was not going to manipulate his life or force him into becoming king. I was just going to show him that he would be the best choice for his people.">

<"And now you can. There have been six kings since Rae and the others left their world. Almost four hundred years have passed. The people on that world do not realize the danger their world is in. You left Rae on ZMEDWT873 so he could get further training on leading people and tone his fighting skills. I was enhancing his training - sort of fine-tuning it to what he would need to be a leader. Of course, I also made sure nothing major would happen to him. That is why I had Urick manufacture clothing for him, making sure he stayed alive to reach the main goal. Urick and a few others know about Rae, too. They are willing to help him however and whenever he needs it. This includes returning to his world to help him become king. After you go see Terrine and Téral, you might want to go to ZMEDWT873 and have a talk with Rae and Nakobee".>

Standing there in the hallway, Shaméd thought about the conversation. He knew Rednog was correct; he was just angry he was not included in the planning.

"Ok, I will go and talk with him and send him back."

<"No, you need to keep him there and place him in charge of the army that fights the Nanzorbans at the ravine bridge. It will build his confidence and show him that he is ready. Not only that, it will help stabilize the war effort. Remember each one of those kings will want their own person in charge. It would be better to have someone neutral. After that is completed, you need to take him home and make him king.">

<"You already know the outcome of the war. What about the rest?">

<"I only know the outcome of the one against the Nanzorban army. I figured based on the data I have you will need to leave during the fighting. You will only be able to transport near the island, not on it. You will walk to the ruins and search it. We are sure the mirror and other artifacts are there. When you find them, you should be able to transport them, yourself, and your crew out of the building. I can tell you if you do not transport out before the Demons notice the power surge you will not be able to transport. You will have to get outside the building before you can use the PTD, and you will have to fight your way out.">

<"Then we will have to move fast. Using the war to help cover my transporting to the island should help. I will return to the world room and head back now.">

<"No. You need to go see Terrine and Téral who have been waiting for you. They both have visited you as you slept this last year. The woman loves you and you need to tell her how you feel.">

<"I don't know if I should. What would happen to her if I die in the upcoming battle? She would be hurt even more. I don't think it would be right.">

<"What would not be right is not telling her. You helped her and her son when they were in trouble. Every time you returned to this world you see her. She can feel your love even if you do not tell her. What I am going to tell you only one other being knows. Terrine is like you. What I mean by that is, she is half human, and the other half is unknown. Unknown as in, we do not know what race she is. But we do know it is the same race as yours. That also makes her son, Téral, of mixed breed and part of your unknown race. If we never find your race, then you need to know there are others like you. Go to her now. When this war is over the two of you can take some time to be together. There will be time before you have to help Red.">

Shaméd stood there; he could not believe what he just heard - Terrine was like him? He could not hide his feelings from her anymore. The world knew about them. That meant others did as well.

<"Thank you for telling me.">

Shaméd headed off to find Terrine. He would tell her how he felt - that he wanted to spend his life with her and Téral. They would become a family.

Shaméd walked to Terrine's room and knocked. The door opened and Téral was standing there. When he saw Shaméd he yelled and jumped up into his arms.

"Shaméd, you're awake. Did you know mother and I went to see you every day? Nogar said it was ok, so we would sit and talk to you. When did you wake up? How long can you stay? Do you want to see what I have learned? I can move a chair. Lord Nogar and Master Kereel are teaching Enomis and me how to move it. And they have helped me learn how to better control the thoughts I hear.

Nogar says I remind him of you when you were my age. I told him I want to be just like you when I grow up."

"Téral, give Shaméd time to come inside and relax. Just because he has been sleeping does not mean he can stand there holding you all day."

Shaméd looked at her - he caught a flash of thought. She was happy to see him. His heart fluttered and he was a little concerned about how to tell her how he felt. On the walk there he went over it in his head. Now standing in front of her looking into her green eyes, he was dumbstruck. He walked into the room and used his foot to close the door. Putting Téral down, he stood there looking at her as she walked up to him stopping a foot away. He could smell her; she smelled like flowers and it made his mind swirl.

Terrine looked at him, stepped back, smiled, then moved closer to him.

"You look like you have been working. You went off world. You went back in time and rescued your friend Loorn. You were there two weeks and now you come here to see us. You were not going to come here, were you?"

"Are you going to let me talk? Or are you just going to keep reading my mind?'

Shaméd looked down into her eyes as he spoke. She stood there looking back up into his eyes, a smirk on her face.

"I will be quiet. I want to hear you say out loud the words that I see in your mind."

"Then you will hear them. Terrine, the first time I saw you I felt something for you. I did not know or understand what it was. I have never had such feelings before. It has taken me a long time to long to realize that I love you and that I want you and Téral to come live with me. I am asking you to be my wife, and Téral to be my son, if you both will have me."

Téral stood there as Terrine turned away from Shaméd. He stood there looking from her to him, trying to figure out why his mother was not answering Shaméd. He knew she loved him, he had read her mind a hundred times. She was always worried when he went off world. She was afraid he would not return.

Terrine turned back to face Shaméd.

"I have tried to not think about the feelings I have for you. I did not want to be hurt if something should happen to you. I did not love my husband. It was an arranged marriage. But I did grow to care for him. I helped him in his business. I could read the minds of the people that he did business with and I told him when they were lying or were thinking of cheating him. As time went on his gambling habit grew. He started to lose, he was angry at me because I would not go with him to read the other's minds when he played cards. I told him I would help in the business, but I would not help him cheat others out of their money. He started losing and after a while we were in over our heads in debt. That is why he died. Men came to the farm late one night. They dragged him out of the house and killed him. I tried to keep the place going. No one would work or do business with a woman. Meeting you and coming here has changed our lives. Téral has grown stronger and the people here are helping him and I learn to control our minds."

"I know you have been hurt, I have seen into your mind and I want to protect you. I don't want you to hurt anymore. I promise when I return, if you will have me I want to marry you. We can go anywhere and start our lives together. We can be a family."

Terrine held up her hand her finger touched his lips.

"You would never be happy leaving here. The people you love and care about are here. If you want to marry me, I accept. We will live here among your family and friends."

Shaméd leaned down and kissed her. Téral let out a yell.

They both jumped and turned to see what was wrong.

"What is wrong?"

Terrine knelt down toward him.

"Nothing. I am just happy that the both of you finally decided to tell each other you love each other. Now we can be a real family."

Terrine reached out and grabbed him giving him a hug. Then she pushed him out arm's length.

"Ok, you go play. Shaméd and I need to talk, alone."

"Ok. Shaméd, will you be here when I get back?"

"I am afraid not. I have to go help some friends. I will return soon, though."

"OK,"

Running to the door, he opened it and ran out, slamming it behind him as he went.

"I do not have much time to talk. I have to go and get a report from Rae. I left him back on your world six months in the past. I think he will be upset with me for not telling him that was the plan. But when everything is over we will sit and talk. You need to go to Elizabeth and ask her for help in planning our wedding. I know she will want to help. I will tell Nogar and the others."

"I know you cannot stay. You have known Rae a long time. He will have figured out you did what you did for a good reason."

"That's just it. I also have to tell him he has to return to his world and become king. The people there are dying, and without our help they will all die within a few generations. If Rae is their king, he can ask Nogar and the council for help. And since he knows about us, they cannot refuse."

13

"Then you must go. Help the people on my world to be safe. If you need to go help Rae become king on his world, go and help him. I will be here waiting for you."

Shaméd reached out and took her into his arms and hugged her. He kissed her for a long moment then looked into her eyes.

<*"You are the one who will make me complete. I have always known I was missing something, and now I know it was you. I love you with all my heart and soul. As the One is my witness I will return and we will be married. I will make you happy and we will have many children."*>

<*"We can talk about the many children, after we are married and you live though the first years of raising one."*>

Laughing, Shaméd gave her another hug. He kissed her again, and then let her go and walked to the door. He turned and looked back at her.

"I should have spoken sooner about how I felt about you. I will return as fast as I can. I will do everything in my power to make sure the coming war does not last long."

Stepping out, Shaméd closed the door and headed back to the world room.

Chapter Two

Shaméd walked into the world room. As he entered Benn looked up.

"That was fast."

"Yes. I have discovered that I need to go back now. Please focus on Rae and Nakobee so I can leave."

"I can do that. Here they are. Wait a second and the room will appear in the IDG."

Shaméd walked over and stood in front of the IDG. The image went from his reflection and the world room, to a swirling mist. The swirling began clearing, a wall and table appeared, and Rae and Nakobee were sitting at the table playing cards.

"Thank you, Benn."

Shaméd stepped through and Rae and Nakobee looked up as he entered the room.

"That was a fast two hours. I knew the time on this world was different but not that different."

Rae tossed a card on the table. Nakobee looked at it, and took one from a stack that was laying there.

"Rae, we need to talk. Would you two stop for a while?"

Without looking at Shaméd, Rae watched Nakobee move his cards around in his large hands.

"Oh, we need to talk alright. Do you have any idea what Alora and Marcel were trying to do to me? After we set things right and her father was back in charge, they both were trying to get me to stay."

Nakobee looked up at Shaméd a big grin on his face.

"I believe their true intentions were that Rae would marry Alora. Duke Marcel openly gave them his blessing. He said he would like nothing more than to step down and let them rule his land together. She definitely wanted to marry him. She became very attached to Rae during our little adventure there."

Nakobee looked back at his cards. He rearranged them in his hand three times, then he laid all but one on the table, the last one he tossed face down on the table next to the pile. Rae looked at the cards on the table, then up at Nakobee. He tossed his down.

"We are done, you win. As for Alora wanting to marry me, I told her I would not and could not. I had to get back to my own home. Besides, she is weird. She has this strange notion her people are from another world. Once we got things settled, she had books brought to me to prove her point. They had stories about how they traveled this world

15

in a large metal ship that could travel between the planets. They believe there were many ships, but that they somehow got separated and lost and landed on this world. She had no real proof. She said the main documents were in the city that her people made on the other side of this world. However she and her people believe it to be true."

"That is very interesting. Would you be willing to tell me what you did after I left you there?"

Rae looked at Shaméd, pushing his chair around so he would be facing him.

"Ok, when you told me to go and stay with the Duke and Alora, I ran all the way there. I passed Jon and told him you were coming and to get ready to leave.

When I got to Marcel he was pushing at the wall. The wall opened and he and Alora entered. I tore a piece of cloth off so you would be able to find the door. I know you did not find it and you beat me to the outside and left us there."

Rae stopped talking and reached inside his shirt to pull out the amulet hanging around his neck and placed it on the table beside him.

"I have a good idea. Most of the time the amulet was active. Why don't we just let it tell you what happened. If you need more information Nakobee and I can fill in the blanks when it was not working."

"That might be a good idea, and I would like to know why and how it was not working."

Shaméd reached into his satchel and pulled out a rectangle metal shaped object. It was 12 inches long, 6 inches wide and 1 inch thick. Shaméd placed it on the table between them. On top of the object were small letters, numbers, and other symbols.

Taking Rae's amulet, Shaméd placed it into the small opening on the top of the rectangle.

"I have never seen that before. What is it?"

"There are only a few available. It is used to check the amulets off-world. It is what I used to keep tabs on you and Mordock."

The amulet began to glow blue. The blue glow projected up expanding 18 inches before stopping. As the light cleared a picture of Rae, Nakobee, Marcel, and Alora appeared, they were standing in a cave. Then they heard the voices.

"Shaméd sent me to stay with you. He said you would need my help. Is everything ok?"

"Everything is fine. Marcel found the secret passage. I am marking it so the others can find it. What was all that noise back there?"

"It seems the solders are being attacked from behind. Shaméd is going to cave in the tunnels so the soldiers cannot follow us.

"Marcel, could your people be attacking the solders?"

"No. It is probably the Trackels."

"The Trackels? What are the Trackels?"

Rae and Nakobee stepped inside the tunnel. The door began to make clicking sounds as it slowly shut. When it closed, the rock Rae marked with a cloth pushed out and fell to the ground.

"I told you about them. They are the creatures that dug most of the tunnels. They are a large bug-like creature. They can talk, well sort of. They understand and speak our language a lot better than any of us can theirs. My great-grandfather found them, and after learning how to talk with them, worked out the deal between us."

"These are the creatures you mentioned earlier?"

"Yes. They are a very pacifist group. They must have been really provoked to have attacked the soldiers."

"Okay, never mind about them. Let's get going. We can wait for Shaméd and the others at the cave opening."

Marcel and Alora turned and started walking away. A few minutes later they heard a muffled sound like an explosion. The tunnel shook, dust, and dirt filled the air.

"What was that?"

Alora stumbled; Rae reached out and caught her, pulling her close and keeping her from falling.

"Shaméd must have tried to stop the soldiers again." Nakobee answered as they all pressed closer to the walls.

"It sounds awfully close. If he is not careful he could bring down the whole mountain, or reactivate the volcano."

"Volcano?" Nakobee looked at Marcel then Alora.

"This whole mountain range is one big volcano. There are hot springs and lava flows throughout the valley where we live and farm. It has been silent for many years. But if there were a big enough explosion, it could make life here very unpleasant."

Rae and Nakobee stood there looking at Alora. Shaking his head, Rae pointed down the tunnel.

"We need to keep moving. The faster we get out of these tunnels the better. Nakobee, you take the lead."

Nakobee moved forward and the others followed. After several minutes they noticed the glowing rocks were starting to dim. Without any warning, the lights from the rocks they were holding went out.

"We really have to hurry. Either something happened to Shaméd or he is already outside."

Nakobee started moving faster, the others close behind. They had to stop twice and take a break, but finally they came to the end of the tunnel. They now stood staring at a wall. Again, Marcel started feeling around. He grunted, and then the wall started to move.

"Here it is. We only have a couple hundred feet to go and then we will be out in the open."

Nakobee pushed the door open and stepped though, followed by Alora, Marcel, and then Rae. As they moved away from the door, it slowly scraped across the floor and shut.

"You would think we would have seen that when we entered."

Nakobee pointed at the floor where the ground was scrapped away.

"With the passing of time and the spiders coming and going, it had smoothed out. That is why we did not see it. Let's keep going."

Nakobee again took the lead. An hour later Nakobee, Marcel and Alora, stepped around the bushes into the sunlight. They all looked around.

"It looks like we beat them here."

Marcel walked over to a rock and sat down

"No, they were here and left."

Rae walked out from behind the bushes. Alora looked at him, her face in a frown.

"How do you know?"

"I found a note in the cave addressed to me. They could not wait. The note says Nakobee and I are to help you take back your kingdom. When that is completed, we can make our way home."

Rae started walking down the path.

"Why would he not have told us that is what he wanted us to do?"

Nakobee walked up behind Rae as they headed down the trail.

"Because he knows I would have said no. Now I understand the things he told me about getting their place back. He said there were two ways to take back this place; one took too long and too many people would die. The second way he said was faster and fewer lives were lost. We, you and I, are the faster and better choice. So now we go get re-supplied and head back in there. The sooner we get this done the sooner I, I mean we, can return home."

Alora and Marcel did not hear Rae's words, but they could tell Rae was not happy about being left behind.

It was dark when they reached their old campsite. Once there Rae looked at them.

"Let's get our supplies and move up into the rocks. It will be easier to defend. As we eat we can talk about how to handle the soldiers and priests that are still there."

Rae checked the horses to make sure they were ok. Nakobee helped Rae take the supplies out of the tree. Everyone helped carry them up the mountain where they found a small clearing surrounded by boulders. There they stopped and made camp.

As they sat around the campfire eating, Marcel sat his plate down and looked over at Nakobee.

"You and your people are very handy in a fight. Too bad the others are not here to help you."

"We will not need their help. Rae and I should be able to handle what soldiers remain. Of course, with the help from your people, it will go a lot faster."

"I am glad you have such high esteem of your abilities. I am pretty sure my people will help you remove the vermin that are running around our home."

"I do not boast. I am just stating a fact. You saw how Rae fought the other day. He, alone, killed over fifty men. I watched him in a battle on my homeworld. He did more killing than any ten men. When Rae gets started fighting, he is almost unstoppable."

"Nakobee that is enough about my so- called fighting skills. We both know that I am not that good of a fighter unless the rage takes over. And we will both make sure that does not happen. Now Marcel, about your people, when we get back inside we need to gather them together and find a safe place to hold up. Then we can start attacking the enemy."

"That will be no problem. There are a lot of large caverns where my people can hold up. We can even get the

Trackels to help. If they truly were the ones fighting the soldiers then they know we need their help. They are very resourceful creatures."

"Yes, I am sure they are. Let's all get some sleep. Nakobee and I will take turns watching."

Rae stood and began cleaning up dinner. Alora walked over and took the dishes from him.

"You go talk with Nakobee. I can clean up and put the food away."

"Thank you."

Rae walked back over to Nakobee.

"I will take the first watch. In about four hours I will wake you and you can take the last four."

"That sounds good to me."

Nakobee turned and walked over to his pack, unrolled his bedding alongside a boulder, then stretched out and went to sleep.

Chapter Three

In the morning they climbed up the mountain and reentered the cave. They made four torches. Rae handed two lit torches to Marcel. Rae lit the other two, then handed one to Nakobee. With the torch in hand he entered the cave. Rae found the secret passage within minutes of entering the cave.

"That was fast, how did you know where to look? I have been through here at least a dozen times and I always forget where it is."

"I remember things like this."

"Remember, Father, his friends said he was a thief. He has to be good at what he does, or Lord Shaméd would not have left him here to help us."

Rae looked at Alora and gave her a smirk.

As the rock swung open Nakobee entered first, Marcel second, then Alora, Rae entered and watched as the door swung shut.

"Ok, let's head back to wherever you think your people are hiding. I just hope Shaméd did not block us completely out. I am not looking forward to having to climb up and over this mountain."

"We won't have to do that. There are other ways we can go. We passed several tunnels and they all will lead us back to one or more of the large caverns. And if we don't find one, we might find the Trackels. They will help us."

"Yeah, if they are not too mad at humans. Otherwise we just might get eaten instead."

"No, they won't eat us. Trackels do not eat meat. At least I don't think they do! They eat dirt and whatever they dig out of the mountain." Marcel looked at Rae.

"Ok. Let's just get going."

Nakobee started walking. Time is not easy to measure when you are walking in the dark and in a cave. They walked a couple hundred feet around a bend and entered a large cavern.

Nakobee stopped as the others caught up with him. When Rae entered the cavern he started to draw his sword but after seeing the smiles on Marcel and Alora's faces, he stopped.

"This is great. We found the Trackels. They can help us get to my people faster. You stay here while I go talk to them."

Marcel handed Alora his torch, then he walked forward. Nakobee moved closer to Rae.

"Do you see them? They look like giant bugs. We have insects that look like them on my world, except they are the size of my thumb."

"Yes, they do look strange, but remember we have seen many strange life forms. I have been on over a hundred worlds and some of the intelligent life that I saw

22

has been strange. Let's just hope these Trackels are friendly.

Marcel came walking back with a very large bug beside him. It stopped a few feet away as Marcel kept walking toward Rae.

"You can put the torches out. The light hurts their eyes. They are bringing us some glow moss. It will give us the light we need."

Nakobee and Rae both dropped their torches to the ground and kicked dirt over them. Alora also put her torches out. As the fires went out the cavern lit up with a soft green glow. Two bugs came walking toward them. They were carrying sticks that were glowing green on top. One stopped in front of Rae and held out the glowing stick. The other walked over to Nakobee and did the same. Rae reached out and took his at the same time Nakobee took his.

"Thank you"

"U r wel com."

The bug stood there staring at Rae. Rae looked over at Nakobee then back at the bug.

"You can speak our language! That is very interesting."

"I not good. I young. Not be with humons much. U teach me?"

"Are you asking me to teach you how to speak my language?"

The bug moved its head up and down and its two upper set of legs, arms, or appendages wiggled as it stood there.

"U teach me humon words, then I be able to read humon books."

Rae looked over at Nakobee to see if he could get any help. Alora and Nakobee just stood staring back at him. Nakobee smiled and nodded his head yes. Rae looked back at the bug then he noticed that the other bugs were moving closer.

"Yes, I could teach you. However, I will be a little busy with trying to rid the mountain of the bad humans that are here. So I might not have very much time."

"I be with u all time. I watch and learn. Not be in way and help if you need, I there."

Rae rotated his head then shoulders. He closed his eyes and took a deep breath, and then opening them he looked at the bug.

"Ok, you can be, I mean, come with me. I will teach you the words of humans. Do you have a name?"

The bug stood there then turned its head back toward its people. There was a long blast of squawking and squeals, from him and the others, before it turned back to face Rae.

"U give me humon name. Humons not can say my real name."

"Ok, I give you a human name. But not now, I will have to think of one. Here is the first lesson for you. We are humans, not humons. Marcel, can we go find your people now?"

The bug moved back as Rae stepped passed and walked over to Marcel. He noticed the bug was mumbling the word "human" over and over again. It stayed four feet behind Rae.

"Oh, the Trackels already found them. My people are in another cavern not far from here. Your new friend there will take us to them. He and his sister will be traveling with us."

Marcel pointed to the bug that was standing next to Nakobee when he said sister.

"You can tell their sex? And how do you know that is his sister?"

Rae stood there looking from one bug to the other.

"Because the big one over there the green and yellow one, and holding the long curved stick, told me. He is the king, and he was hoping you and Nakobee would help teach his children. The boy is the oldest and next in line to be their king. His sister will be leaving in a year or two to go to the other mountain and marry the eldest son of that tribe."

"There is more than just this group? How many Trackels are there?"

"As far as I know, there are only about three hundred. In this mountain there are only a hundred or so. The others live in the mountains to the east and west of here. Humans outside of my land don't like them, so whenever they see them they hunt them down and killed."

Rae looked at the bugs. They were all standing there staring. He could not believe that if humans hunted and killed them why they would want to learn how to speak and read the human language let alone help?

"Take u to others now?"

The bug moved alongside of Rae as it spoke and used one of its upper legs to point to the other side of the cavern.

"Yes, please take us to the others."

The bug moved off with his sister by his side. Rae watched it walk away. Nakobee walked up next to him as Alora and Marcel started following the bugs.

"Shaméd would have loved to be here for this meeting. He likes meeting new people."

Rae looked up at Nakobee when he said the word people.

"Yeah, people. This just keeps getting better every minute. I wonder what more exciting things are in store for us. Well, let's get going."

Rae's mind was trying to figure out what kind of bug they reminded him of. Nakobee had said they looked like one back on his world. Only that one was smaller, about the size of his thumb.

Their bodies had what looked like a hard shell on their backs. When facing them he saw their body was long and thick. They appeared to be able to walk upright or down close to the ground. When it stood in front of him he saw what looked like four legs and four arms. As they walked away he saw the two set of legs moving in union. The head had two very big eyes, and just above what could only be their ears were antennas. There were small slits on the face just above the mouth where the nose would be. And its mouth, when it was talking to him, made him just a little uneasy. The teeth he saw were scary. There were a lot of them, and they all looked like they could cut though a tree as easy as he could bite into a piece of bread.

It did not take long to reach Marcel's people. They walked down a tunnel for a few minutes then came to another cavern. When Rae and the others entered the cavern the people saw Marcel and called out to him.

"Lord Marcel! We are so happy you are safe and have returned to us. When will we go and take our home back?"

Marcel waved at them and tried to calm them down as he greeted each and every one of them. Alora was greeted the same way by the women. They were giving her hugs and as Rae and Nakobee moved in among the people Rae saw the children.

Chapter Four

The cavern was filled with supplies. The people, once free, had not wasted anytime. They had returned to the castle and raided for supplies as well as setting others free.

Rae and Nakobee stood off to the side as Marcel and the others talked. Three men were doing the most talking. They sat across from Marcel and Alora. The one on the left was the oldest. His name was Robert. He had a long gray beard and hair, and appeared to be in his late sixties. The one in the middle was called Fredrick, in his early twenties, he had a short brown beard, and his hair was cut short. The last man was Samuel, he was of middle age, and his beard and hair was peppered with gray. Samuel looked at Marcel.

"After we were locked up we thought the worst had happened to you. No one knew where you were or if you had escaped. I told everyone you had escaped and went to get help."

"Samuel, stop kissing up. Lord Marcel, how are we going to take back our home? With the Trackel's help we might be able to chase them out. But without any weapons we don't stand a chance of keeping them out."

"Fredrick, we were able to set all of you free with the help of these two men and their companions. Their companions have taken the leader of the fanatics away. And with the help of these two men, we will take our home back."

The three men looked up at Rae and Nakobee. The older one nodded his head. Samuel sat there staring.

"Only two men? How can they help? We will need at least a hundred, maybe more to route those crazies out of our home."

Marcel smiled and pointed first at Nakobee, then at Rae.

"Believe me when I say the soldiers do not stand a chance against these men. I saw them fight and they are very good. They took out over a hundred men on their own, during our trip here."

"If you say they can help then we believe you. Samuel, you will be silent and let Lord Marcel tell us what has transpired on his journey outside and how long it will be before the King comes here to help us."

Robert leaned back and stared at Marcel, waiting.

Marcel sat up straight and looked at each of the three men's faces. He was getting nervous; he looked over at Rae. He saw the people start gathering around. Rae started to move closer, the bug moved with him. Stopping, Rae looked at it and pointed to the ground.

"You stay here."

Rae then went and stood behind Marcel.

"Lord Marcel was busy trying to convince the King to come to your rescue. But the King is busy with other matters. There is a war brewing. This cult has dozens of priests out in the land causing trouble. That is why *my* Lord came here to help. He captured the leader, Krakdrol, and has taken him away. He has left me and my friend, Nakobee, here to help. We have experience in this sort of thing. I promise you we will have these soldiers out of here within a month. What we have to do now is gather weapons and Nakobee and I need to learn the lay of the land. And I mean tunnels when I say land. We need to know every secret way to get into and around the castle. We will cause so much trouble the soldiers and their little wizards will not sleep and within days be arguing with each other.

I can see you have already begun gathering food and that is good. We will need more. What I would like to do is remove all the food and stores from the castle so the enemy will have nothing. I know you have farmers still working the fields. We will need to get them all inside the tunnels. When they are safe Nakobee and I will begin the real fighting. If you have any soldiers here we will need their help."

"You are coming across like you are in charge. Lord Marcel is our leader and we will do as he says."

Samuel stood as he spoke, his finger wagging at Rae.

"I..."

Marcel stood and faced Samuel.

"Rae speaks on my behalf. I have given him control of my soldiers and my kingdom as long as there is a threat. He has the experience and I trust him. I expect the council to give him their support as well."

Samuel looked at Marcel. He felt the cold stare coming from him. Samuel bowed his head and without speaking sat back in his chair.

Rae looked at Marcel who nodded at him, then sat too.

Rae looked at the council members.

"I was going to say I was not taking any authority from anyone. Nakobee and I are trained in this sort of thing. And yes, you are right, we are mercenaries. However, you will be happy to hear we are here helping you for free. So no matter what you think of mercenaries, be at ease with us. We are only here until the followers of Krakdrol are captured or dead and all of you are returned to your homes. Lord Marcel, with your permission Nakobee and I will leave to begin our search of the tunnels."

Robert, Fredrick, and Samuel all looked at Rae, then at Marcel as they waited for him to respond.

"Yes, you both may go and begin your work. We will start making groups to organize the food and other belongings. When you return we should know how many of my soldiers are left and where they are being held captive."

Rae turned around as Nakobee moved off toward the tunnel right behind the female bug. The other bug was still standing where Rae had told him to stand. It tilted its head.

"I move now?"

"Yes. You will lead us through the tunnels that will take us to the castle."

The bug's antennas wiggled and he moved off after his sister with Rae right behind him.

They walked for what seemed like miles through twisting and turning tunnels. They would stop and the bug

29

would point to the wall. Rae would move closer searching it until he found the handle that would open a small door that opened into a room or a hallway.

After finding five such doors, Nakobee walked up to Rae.

"Have you noticed them stopping and digging into the walls? They are eating the dirt or whatever they are digging out of it."

"Yes, I have noticed. And I have not seen them drink anything."

Rae stopped walking and called out.

"Hey Bu... Buddy, come here."

The bug stopped turned and looked at Rae then walked back to him.

"We no go where u want? Buddee my name?"

"Yes. Your name is Buddy not buddee. It means friend. And no, you are taking me to all the right places. I just wanted to ask you and your sister a question."

"I.. Buddy-friend? You like me?"

Rae stood there trying to figure out what to say next. He saw Nakobee give a little smile before he got it under control.

"Yes, I like you. You are different, but I like you. What I want to ask you is I have seen you eating from the wall. Are you hungry? And do you ever drink?"

Buddy stood there his sister came walking up next to him they looked at each other and in a low squeaking began talking. Then they were silent, Buddy looked at Rae.

"Sister wants to know if you can name her. And yes, we are eating, but it is to help find location and remember where we are. Each location taste different."

Rae looked at Nakobee then at Buddy.

"You are speaking a lot clearer. How is that?"

We listen to you speak and see your words so the more you speak the better we learn. What do you mean by drink?'

Rae was taken aback by all the words and then Buddy asking him a question.

"I wanted to know if you drink water. See here?"

Rae reached for his flask and after opening it he took a drink then offered the flask to Buddy.

Buddy took it and raised it to his face. He poured a little of it on what would pass as his hand. Then he raised the flask up to his mouth and poured some in.

He handed it to his sister. She took it and did the same thing, then handed it back to him. Buddy, using both sets of hands, returned the flask to Rae.

"You honor us in the sharing of the liquid of life. We will now always be of you."

"I am not sure what you mean by that last part. But I am the one honored for your help. The offering of water was just one way of showing that. How do you go so long without drinking?"

"We drink of the ground. There are places in the mountain with pools of the life liquid. But we can go a long time between visiting them."

"So you do not carry it with you like we do. That is interesting. We will have to change that once we begin fighting. We will be moving a lot and you will need to carry water with you. We can work on that later. Do you have any idea where Marcel's soldiers are being held captive?"

The two began talking in their squeaking tones, Buddy pointed to the left.

"Sister believes they are down there, where death is."

"Death? You mean they are all dead?"

"Not dead. It is where humans take things to hurt before killing."

The realization came over Rae. These creatures really were pacifists. They did not understand the killing and torture that humans did. But yet, here they were helping. Shaméd really needed to be here to meet them.

"I understand what you mean. Humans call it a dungeon. It is not a good place. Can you show us the way?"

"Sister will stay here. The smell is bad and she cannot understand why humans do things that they do. I will take you."

Buddy began walking forward, but his sister moved off to the side and sat. That was when Rae and Nakobee noticed the shell. When she started to sit her shell moved up her back, it began folding in on its self-exposing her lower half so she could sit on a rock.

Traveling several hundred feet, Buddy stopped and pointed to the wall. Rae moved close and looked for the secret handle. He found it quickly and opened it slowly. Nakobee drew his sword, and Buddy moved back as Rae drew his sword. Stepping out into a hallway, and moving a few feet in each direction, Rae and Nakobee began looking around. They returned a few seconds later as the door closed behind Buddy.

"We can open it from this side, right?"

Buddy tapped the wall.

"Here is the handle to open door."

"Ok, lead us to where the soldiers are being held."

Buddy walked passed them. Rae looked at Nakobee.

"Have you been able to hear them walking?'

Nakobee looked from Rae to the back of Buddy.

"Now that you mention it, I have not. They are very light on their feet."

"Yeah, another creepy thing - giant bugs and light on their feet. All we need next is another giant snake. That would make my whole year."

Nakobee laughed as Rae moved fast to catch up to Buddy. He whispered when he got closer.

"Buddy, there are no giant snakes in these tunnels are there?"

Buddy stopped, tilting his head he looked at Rae.

"Snakes? Do you mean worms? Or tunnel dragons?'

"Tunnels dragons? Are there dragons in this mountain?'

There was what sounded like chipping coming from Buddy as his head and body shook.

"You are not afraid of dragons are you?"

"Were you just laughing at me?'

"Laughing, a noun, it means: a time of great fun and enjoyment, or something that gives fun and enjoyment. Or in this case, to find something funny or amusing in an event or a reaction to what happened to another creature. I am sorry, friend Rae, yes, I was laughing."

"Why were you laughing?"

"Your body gave off a similar odor like it had when you first saw us. I believe it was fear or maybe…"

"Ok, don't say anything more. Let's just go get Marcel's men."

Nakobee leaned toward Buddy.

"He does not like snakes; dragons are fine - snakes no."

"Snakes are good. I mean taste good. We hunt them for food as well as the spiders that live here."

"I thought your people do not kill"

"We do not kill for the reason humans do. We only kill for food or in our defense."

Rae coughed. Buddy moved forward as Nakobee turned to keep an eye out behind them.

After passing the third turnoff, Buddy stopped and moved to the side of the wall.

Rae and Nakobee could hear voices. They were coming from ahead of them.

"There are four men in the cove ahead, they are what you would call guarding the cells."

"You mean there are four guards up there? How do you know there are only four?"

Buddy tilted his head. "I can smell them"

Nakobee pointed toward the sounds. "We can take them."

"No, we do not want them. We want the others in the holding cell. There are more coming, from behind us. It is better to move in another direction"

"And how are we going to move in another direction?"

Rae was going to say more but Buddy began digging and within seconds there was a hole where the wall was. It was three feet wide and six feet high. There was very little dirt on the floor.

Nakobee and Rae looked at each other and then just followed Buddy into what appeared to be an adjoining tunnel.

They moved fast going about two hundred feet before Buddy stopped.

"Men here. I can free them, then we can move down there to get the rest."

Without waiting Buddy began digging again. Rae and Nakobee moved away as the dirt was pushed back behind him and tossed at them. Five feet in the wall crumbled away, and Buddy stepped into the cell.

Buddy stood there facing twenty men. They had heard the digging and moved to the far side of the room. When Buddy entered they began to move forward. They moved faster when they saw Rae and Nakobee enter.

"Who is in charge here?"

A large man stepped forward.

"I am Sergeant Jones. Who are you two and are Lord Marcel and Lady Alora safe?"

"They are fine. They are back with your people and the Trackels. We are here to set you and the others free. My name is Rae and this is Nakobee and that is Buddy. How many more of you are still here?"

"They have killed over a hundred men and women. There are at least a thousand men that did not get captured. They are hiding out on the other side of the mountain."

"How do you know there are a thousand men that made it?"

"Because they have come here to try and set us free, but as you can see they have not succeeded. Whenever they try ten of our people are brought outside and killed. So they stopped trying. If you plan on rescuing us, then you need to take us all."

Rae looked at Buddy

"Buddy, can you go dig out the others? We need to get them and get away fast."

"Buddy can get others. You take these back the way we came."

Sergeant Jones turned to Rae.

"It might be better if I stay with Buddy. We all trust the Trackels but seeing a human will help in his rescue."

"Then go with Buddy and the rest of you follow Nakobee."

Buddy and Sergeant Jones moved out into the hallway and turned left. Nakobee and the others followed and turned right. Rae went to the door and checked the lock making sure it would not open without a lot of effort.

Rae caught up with the others. As they drew closer to the hidden door, it opened. Nakobee stopped and with his sword out waited for the attack.

It did not happen. When the door opened out stepped the female Trackel.

"How did you know we were coming?"

"Smell you, I could. Come, Buddy said."

"Take these men back to the others."

The female moved back inside the men followed Nakobee entered after the last man and watched them disappear down the tunnel.

Rae stood by the wall. A few minutes later he heard footsteps then he saw a couple hundred men and Buddy coming toward them. The men moved pass entering the tunnel. Buddy stopped and stood next him.

"Did you have any trouble?

"I had no trouble. The soldiers that these men killed had trouble. Four soldiers came through the hole I made. These men made sure they did not make noise or get away."

Rae had seen some of the men carrying swords and knives and he wondered about them.

"Good, I am glad you did not have trouble. Let's go, we have a lot of work ahead of us. More people to free and more enemy soldiers to get rid of."

Rae entered the tunnel with Buddy right behind him. Buddy closed and secured the door and the two moved off to catch up to the others.

Walking into the cavern Rae and Nakobee saw the soldiers they released being greeted by the others. Marcel was sitting at a table with a group of people and standing across from him was Sergeant Jones. Rae and Nakobee walked over stopping a couple of feet away - close enough to hear but not to interfere.

"Sergeant Jones, I am sorry that so many of your men were killed. I should have listened to you and Lieutenant Pike when you said not to let those priests inside our mountain. For your commitment to me and our people I am promoting you to captain. I expect you to pick out your men to fill in the ranks. I heard some of the men got away and are hiding out on the other side of the mountain. I have asked the King of the Trackels to send some of his people to find them and have them brought here. They should be here in a day or two. You should go and get some food and rest and later you can start organizing with Rae and Nakobee, here, to take back our home. Rae, Nakobee, if you would step close I would like to introduce to you Captain Jones."

"We have met. Buddy here dug through the wall to release them and the others."

Marcel looked from the bug to Rae.

"So you have given him a name. That is good. Buddy, is a very good name. Your father will be proud of you and your sister. Both of you have done us all a great service in freeing our people."

"It is my honor to help fellow believers in the Father and Son."

Rae and Nakobee both looked at each other when Buddy spoke of being believers of the Father and Son.

"Yes, we are all family here. Now, Captain Jones, go get yours and your men's wounds taken care of, then get some food and rest. We can talk more tomorrow."

The Captain snapped to attention, saluted then turned and trying not to show it, limped away.

"He is a good man and I should have listened to him and Lieutenant Pike when those evil priests showed up. Oh well, that is in the past. Now what are your plans?"

"First, we need to get a count of how many men you have and what supplies we have. I need some paper and some help in tallying up all the supplies. With the help of Buddy, Nakobee and I will search the tunnels and the mountain. By the time your men show up I will have a plan for you and the council."

"I trust you and Nakobee. Take whatever you need and when you are ready let me know."

Rae gave Marcel a slight bow, turned, and headed for where he and Nakobee had stored their supplies. Buddy and his sister followed a few feet behind.

When they reached their packs they both bent down to go through them.

"What we need is food for two days. Then Buddy, you and Rose will take us to search the tunnels."

Before Rae was done talking, Buddy, and his sister where chirping and squeaking in their own language, their antennas wiggling fiercely. Rae and Nakobee stopped digging through their bags at the same time. They both turned to look.

"What is wrong?"

Rae stood and faced Buddy.

"I asked, what is wrong? You two are acting weird."

Buddy stopped, tilted his head his sister did the same. They stood there looking at Rae with their heads tilted to the right. Buddy pointed at his sister then Rae. She took a step closer.

"You me name. I now am friend of Rae. I sorry if we discouraged you. I executed you giving me name."

Taking a deep breath then letting it out slowly Rae tilted his head in the opposite direction.

"You mean distracted us. And I think you meant excited, not executed."

"Words new still to me. I learn more from you?"

"Yes, you will learn more words. We were just worried that something was wrong."

"What rooz mean?"

"Rose not rooz. It is a flower that grows on my world, I mean homeland. Roses are usually red, pink, yellow, or white and they give off fragrance that people like. Our women love to grow them and to have them."

"Name good."

Rose straightened up and moved behind her brother.

"Ok, if we have that taken care of. Nakobee, are we ready to go?"

Nakobee reached down and grabbed Rae's backpack and tossed it to him, then reached down and picked up his own.

"I will take that as a yes. Then let's get going. Buddy, you, and Rose lead the way. I want to know every way into and out of the castle. Then we can look for other tunnels."

Buddy moved off toward an opening. The others followed.

They walked for two hours only stopping when Rose or Buddy would touch or point at the wall. Rae and Nakobee would look until they found a lever that opened the secret door.

"Ok, we need to stop and rest. We can continue after we sleep for a few hours. Buddy, do you and Rose sleep?"

Again they both tilted their heads. Rose spoke.

"Sleep to rest the body. Yes, we sleep. We take what humans call naps. Rest for short times. Once a cycle we all sleep the big sleep for one full turn of the big moon."

"You hibernate. That is interesting. What would happen if the volcano erupted during your hibernation?"

"You ask if mountain open and let its hot blood flow through the tunnels. What would happen to us? If the guards did not wake us in time we would all die."

Rae and Nakobee stood there looking at them. They sat and leaned against the wall.

"So you leave some of your people awake to keep watch. And if they do not wake you in time you would die. Does this bother you just a little?"

Buddy and Rose had moved across to the other wall and after their outer shells moved up they had sat.

"Bother us? How would it bother us? We would be dead."

"I mean does it not bother you that you might die when you are hibernating? I think that would bother me."

"Why would it bother you? You would be asleep and not know you died. And then we would be with the Father and Son. That is where we all want to be when we are dead."

After taking a long drink from his flask Rae took a bit of bread.

"It will take some getting used to - you and your ways. Nakobee, you take the first watch wake me in two hours."

"You two sleep - we watch. Rose and I only rest a short time and humans need to sleep more than Trackels."

"If that is what you want to do then it is ok with us."

Rae and Nakobee took out their bed rolls. Nakobee stretched out.

"If you need some food or a drink help yourselves. The extra canteen is there, and there is bread in that bag next to it."

"Thank you, friend Rae; we may drink of the water but nourishment we do not need at this time."

"Ok, goodnight, or at least I hope it is night. For all I know it could be the middle of the day. I have sort of lost track of time in these tunnels."

Rae stretched out and covered his head with his blanket. He heard Rose speak softly.

"It is night, friend Rae. The second moon is just rising. The sun will be up in six of your human hours."

Smiling under the blanket, he moved his back closer to the wall.

"Friend Rae, friend Nakobee, time to wake up. We need to leave. There are enemy coming this way."

Rae tossed his blanket off, rolled, and was in a crouching position with his sword in one hand and a knife in the other. Nakobee was sitting with his back to the wall and let out a chuckle.

"Buddy did not say the enemy was here only that they are coming."

Rae glanced from Nakobee to Buddy and Rose who both had jumped back at his movement. Standing up, he put away his sword and knife. Rolling his shoulders up and around, then his head in a circle, his back, and neck popped.

"I am sorry if I startled you. I have always been a little jumpy. How far away is the enemy?"

Tilting his head to the right, Buddy took a step closer to Rae.

"They are moving slow, should reach this point in an hour."

"An hour away, and you can hear them from that distance? Your people must have very good ears."

Both Buddy's and Rose's bodies both shook and they made clicking sounds. Rae was about to say something when Buddy spoke.

"We sorry for laughing, but we did not hear them. We felt and smelled them. We hear with our ears like humans, only close."

"How did you feel and smell them? Do they smell that bad?"

Nakobee had moved close to stand next to Rae as Buddy was talking.

"We feel everything in the mountain. We eat of the mountain and we feel it move and feel what happens inside and out of it. They stink of fire and smoke. They carry the fire on sticks and the smoke we smell."

"That is bizarre about the feeling thing. I do understand about the fire and smoke. Ok, we can talk more about how you feel movements inside the mountain later. Can you lead us to an outside door? I want to start exploring the landscape outside."

"When you are ready there is a door to the fields just a hundred of your steps down there."

Buddy pointed down to a side passage that branched off from where they were. Rae and Nakobee packed their belongings. With their backpacks on Rae looked at Buddy.

"Please lead the way."

Buddy moved forward. Rae, then Rose and Nakobee followed last. Buddy stopped after a couple hundred feet. He pointed at the wall. Rae and Nakobee moved forward to search for the lever. Nakobee found it and pushed. The door slowly slid open, and bright light flooded the cave. Rae and Nakobee closed their eyes, and quickly covered their faces with their hands.

"It is bright after being inside with the green light. My eyes got used to it. Nakobee, we need to remember this the next time we go outside."

"Yes. I have spots floating around my eyes. I am glad we do not have to fight, it would be very difficult to see."

Rae moved out to stand next to Buddy and Rose. They had both walked by when Rae and Nakobee were blinded.

"Does the sun not hurt your eyes?"

"Our eyes inside shields have. Slide over and cover when we go outside. Protects us."

"I would like that."

Nakobee was moving slowly as he spoke, his eyes were blinking rapidly to adjust to the sun shining down on them.

"What time of day is it?'

"It is the first hour of sunlight. We have come out facing the sunrise. When you can see you will find the humans are out working the fields and the enemy are watching them."

Rae and Nakobee moved over to a boulder. Standing beside it, they looked out over the vast fields. They looked to the north then south then east. They could see the mountain range circling around the field. Then they saw the road that ran around the outside of the fields and the main one that ran down the middle. Below them they saw lava flowing out from a crevice down the wall and disappearing into a pit.

"This is a very big and old volcano. I see the steam from many hot springs around the valley. Marcel said there was only one way into this valley. And you had to maneuver around lava pits to get in. This would be a very good place to live and hide from the outside world. The only problem I see is what happens when the volcano erupts."

"In my life it has never let out its fire more than a little at a time. My father was little when it broke open and let out so much fire that the valley was gone. That was many years before Marcel people came here."

"Marcel's father came here over a hundred years ago. How old is your father?"

"Father is very old. He has lived a long time, over a thousand cycles."

"How old are you and Rose?"

"We are the youngest of father's children. Rose is younger than me by ten cycles. I have seen twenty cycles."

There was a sound from above, then rocks tumbling down around them. Rae and Nakobee both jumped aside drawing their weapons. A soldier slid passed them a few feet. They heard the laughing and voices coming from above.

"Stupid idiot. I told him to watch his step. You two go down there and see if he is alive. The rest of us will keep going. We will meet you down below. I hate this place. It is hot, sticky, and the air stinks."

Buddy and Rose both moved back against the mountain when the man fell passed them. Nakobee, then Rae moved away so the two men climbing down would not see them. They passed without even looking in their direction.

"Should we kill them? We might as well start now. I do not think it will matter if these three come up missing."

Nakobee looked at Rae as he spoke.

"I will go after them. You take Buddy and Rose and move off in that direction away from the soldiers. We can meet below."

Rae put his sword away and silently moved off after the two men.

"Friend Rae would kill those men for no reason?"

"Rae kills because there is no other way. These men only know death and killing. And if we are to set Marcel and your people free from being hunted down and killed by them, this has to be done. Believe me if Rae can find a way to stop the killing he will. I have been with him in many fights. He is very good at killing and when it is over I have seen the pain it causes him. Come on, let's get going."

Buddy moved off with Rose, Nakobee close behind.

Rae heard the conversation and blocked it out of his mind as he moved closer to the two men. As they made their way slowly down toward their fallen comrade Rae stayed out of sight but crept nearer. It was not difficult to stay hidden from the two men. The mountain was covered with large boulders and deep chasms. When the two men reached their comrade one of them kicked him. There was a groan.

"He won't be able to walk down by himself. Let's just kill him. We can tell the Sergeant he was dead when we found him."

"Might as well. He did not want to be here anyways. He is too young and was always saying these priests are evil and we should not be helping them. He should never have become a mercenary. He is too weak."

The man drew his sword. As he raised it, Rae tossed his first knife. It entered the left side of his throat. The man fell forward gurgling as he fell. The second man tried to turn around to see where the knife came from. He never made it.

Rae grabbed the man's chin twisting it back and up as he twisted to the left as hard as he could. At the same time the knife in his right hand penetrated the neck slicing through the spine. The man was dead before he hit the ground. Wiping his knife off on the dead man's shirt he bent down to the young man on the ground. He laid there staring up at Rae. Fear showed in his eyes.

"I will ask you some questions and you will answer them truthfully or die. Do you understand me?"

"Yes, I understand. When you kill me please do it as painlessly as you can."

"I will not kill you if you speak the truth. What I want to know is how many soldiers are here, and how many priests?"

"The priests have two hundred of their own men. There are two thousand mercenaries. More were to arrive the other day but they have not come. The priest and their men have become even more cruel and evil. I think it is because of the missing men and what happened yesterday."

"What happened yesterday?"

"Their half-elf god was taken. He was captured and many of their own soldiers were killed trying to rescue him. The priests began torturing captives. But they are now all gone and we were sent out to try and find them. We were told if we do not find them we will take their place. I was scouting out front and was trying to sneak away, but I slipped and fell."

Rae sat back and looked at the young man laying there. He was just a boy, about sixteen years old.

"What is your name and where do you come from?"

"My name is Alex. I come from Kaloon. I have no family and was sold as a slave to a merchant. The ship was attacked by mercenaries and I was given the choice of joining them or dying. As you can see, I chose to live. I don't know if that was a good choice since it seems I am destined to die."

"You will not die, at least not by my hand. I believe your story, and I will help you leave. Right now we need to see how bad you are hurt and get you to a safe place."

Rae went over to the two dead men. He took their swords, belts, and a few other items. Removing his knife from the soldier, he cleaned it and put it back into it the sheath on his left arm then went back to the youth.

"Ok. This is going to hurt a lot. I am going to use these to make a splint for your leg. Bite down on this belt so you won't scream."

Taking the two swords, Rae placed them, still in their sheaths, on either side of the young man's leg. Then he gently took hold of his foot and without saying anything pulled and twisted it straight. The boy flinched but with the belt in his mouth no sound came out. Tears poured from his eyes. Using the belts, Rae wrapped the two swords as tight as he could around the leg.

"Ok, that should hold until we get you to some real help. Give me your hand and we will start down the mountain."

The kid raised his left hand and with as much help as he could muster, he stood. The climb down was slow, since they had to move between the rocks looking for an easy way.

Before they reached the bottom Buddy came out from behind a boulder.

"Friend Rae, you did not kill the enemy?"

The boy jumped back and tried to scream. Rae slapped his hand across his mouth as he pulled the kid to the ground. Pinning him down, Rae whispered into the boys' ear.

"Be quiet. This is a friend. He will not hurt you. As a matter of fact, he and his people are pacifists. They do not believe in killing like humans do. Buddy, if I had not seen you before you stepped out I could have hurt you. You need to be more careful."

"I knew you saw me. I felt you coming and would need help. If you want I can carry the enemy."

"He is not an enemy. He was trying to escape from them. I will explain to you later how some humans are forced to do things they do not want to do. For now, let's get moving. Where are Rose and Nakobee?"

"Sister Rose and friend Nakobee are down below under the trees with some growers."

Rae looked at the young man.

"Ok, now if I remove my hand you will not scream. If you do then I will have to break my word about killing you and that will not be good for you or me."

The boy nodded his head up and down. Rae took his hand away and the boy laid there looking up at Buddy.

"I did not know they, I mean, I did not know you could talk. We have been ordered to hunt your kind down and kill you. We were told you are dangerous and would sneak in at night and eat us as we slept."

Buddy made the little squeaking sound as his body shook.

"Humans are funny. Why would we sneak in at night to eat you? If we wanted to eat you we would hunt you all the time then eat you."

His body wiggled and there was more squeaking. The kid grew tense and his eyes got big. Rae was just about to say something when Buddy spoke,

"Buddy only make joke. That would be wrong and against the teaching of the Father and Son. Come, friend Rae, and I will take you down so the others can help you."

Buddy moved closer and with both of his left arms reached out to the young boy. The boy never flinched as Buddy took hold of him. They got to the bottom faster with Buddy's help.

As they came walking up to a small stand of trees, Nakobee stepped toward them.

"You brought us a prisoner? I though you did not believe in taking prisoners? But, I like what you did with the swords - a very good way to bring us more weapons."

"He is not a prisoner. His name is Alex, he was trying to escape. He was forced into this way of life. We can take him inside and leave him so the others can take care of him. Have you found any information?"

They walked to a tree and sat the boy down so he could lean against it. Turning, Rae faced the farmers.

"How can we help you besides getting rid of the mercenaries and priests? Do any of you need food or medicine?"

"We are in no need of food or medicine. We have all we need. The soldiers only bother us when we do not work as fast as they think we should. We are in touch with our own soldiers. They have sent word that Lord Marcel has returned and we will all be free in a few days. You two are the ones who came with Lord Marcel?"

"Yes. We came with Lord Marcel and it might take more than a few days to get rid of the soldiers and priests. We need to scout out the best places to capture or attack them and not get any of you hurt."

"We will not be hurt. They have already tried but the fairies will not let them hurt us."

"Fairies? What are fairies?"

Rae looked at Nakobee who just stood there and shrugged his shoulders.

The farmers looked at each other then stood there staring at Rae and Nakobee.

"You do not know what fairies are? Where have you lived that you have never heard of fairies?"

"Believe me when I say I have never seen fairies. And I have been places and seen things you wouldn't want to see, but no I have never seen these fairies you speak of."

"Then young man, you just need to look out at the fields, you will see them.

Rae moved out to the edge of the trees and looked out at the field. He saw men and women working and what looked like little birds flying in among them. They were going from plant to plant. Rae turned and with a smile on his face he looked at the old man.

"You mean the bees and small birds flying around the fields? We have birds and what we call honeybees where I come from."

"Those are not bees. Some of the fairies that do not have their own wings fly on the backs of small birds much like men ride horses. No, young man, those out there you call bees and birds, are fairies and they help us take care of our crops."

Rae stood there smiling and just nodded his head.

"Ok, old man, you can call them whatever you want. Right now we need to return to Marcel and give them our plan."

"We have a plan?"

Nakobee stood there still looking out at the field.

"Yes, I think I have a plan. And it should work as long as we can get Marcel and his people to agree to it."

Chapter Five

"We need to get back inside and talk with Marcel."

"You know Lord Marcel well? He only let's those that are family or close friends say his name without Lord first."

Rae looked at the old farmer who had spoken.

"Yes, I know Lord Marcel very well. He has given me control over his soldiers so I might be able to reclaim his and your land. I hope to do this quickly so I might return to my own home."

"I see. Well if there is anything I or my people can do just send a message to me. My name is Frank. I am the head of the farmer's guild."

Turning around, Frank waved at the other three farmers waiting under the trees. The four walked out toward the field. Within minutes they were surrounded by little birds and what looked like large bees.

"Look how close, those bees, and birds are getting to them."

"They are helpers. The fairies work with the humans."

Rae and Nakobee looked at Rose. She was staring off at the four men walking.

"Fairies. I have seen a lot of mythical creatures in my life and travels. But I have never seen fairies. I suppose there could be fairies. Let's get going. Rose, do you and Buddy know a faster way back into the mountain? I don't want to have to climb back up to the place we came out. It will be too difficult for Alex."

Buddy was sitting next to Alex. Rose looked over at her brother; they both began talking in their language. After a few blasts of their squeaking, Rose turned to face Rae and Nakobee.

"Brother say I may take you to the door that is down the round road. The hurt one should be able to make it there."

"You will take us? You make it sound like Buddy is not coming with us."

"Brother will go up to make sure the bodies you left are hidden. He says if left there they will stink and enemy will find them and may try and hurt the field people."

Nakobee and Rae looked over at Buddy who was now standing.

"That is a very good idea. I should have thought of it. Buddy you are very wise. We would not want the farmers hurt because of us. Nakobee, you help Alex; and Rose, you lead the way."

Nakobee walked over and with one hand reached down and grabbed the front of Alex's shirt, pulling him up to his feet. They walked for over an hour when Rose turned toward the mountain.

Suddenly, soldiers came screaming out from behind the boulders where they were hiding. The screaming is what killed them, and saved Rae and the others.

Rae with lighting reflexes drew and tossed two knives. He dropped two men. Nakobee dropped Alex and drew both of his swords and rushed the oncoming soldiers. His screaming must have startled them because some of them stopped in their tracks. Rose picked up Alex and scurried over to some rocks. After placing him down, she moved back out to the fighting.

Nakobee killed four men, and was pushing five other men back toward the mountain.

Rae, using his sword and long knife, held off the men rushing him.

One man, then another, fell from Rae's swift movements with his sword as he parried left and right. More men came toward him. He spun around to block a man that had moved up to his right. The man never made it. He dropped to the ground minus his head. Seeing this, three soldiers screamed and tried to run away but they were not swift enough. Rose ran among them using her second set of hands like knives and killed them.

Rae saw it all and so did the men he was fighting. With terror on their faces they began to move away from Rae and Rose. Rose just stood there watching after killing the three men. Her head twisted and turned back and forth looking at all the dead bodies.

As fast as it started, it ended. Fifteen mercenary soldiers lay dead on the road. Rae bent down and used the shirt of one man to clean his weapons. As he stood, Rose was there with her left arm stretched out toward him. In her hand were his two knives. They were clean.

"Rose get and cleaned these for friend Rae. Rose cleaned them like I see you do."

As Rae reached out looking at her second pair of hands - there was no trace of blood. Taking the two knives, he tilted his head to the left.

"Thank you. I did not think your people fought and killed?"

"We do not kill like humans do, but we will protect ourselves and those around us from harm."

"I have a question. Why did you not hear or smell them?"

"Rose did not smell them because of the smell from the fields. Too much smell. Rose did not think enemy was this way. Rose will be more parade next time."

"You mean prepared. And thank you again for helping in the fight. Where is Alex? Did he run away?'

"Rose put him over there. When Nakobee dropped him he went to sleep."

Nakobee walked up next to Rae, smiling.

"You did well. You did not go into the rage and you handled yourself like you were in training. Your movements were smooth. Sword Master Zale would be proud of you. Where is the kid?"

"Rose took him over to there. He must have passed out when you dropped him."

Rose scurried over to where she put Alex. Alex was just opening his eyes when Rose bent down to pick him up.

"Not worry, I carry you. We go faster."

Alex glanced over at Rae, then he saw Nakobee smile at him as he came walking near.

"We need to move fast and we don't have time to wait for you."

Rose picked Alex up in her four arms and turned to face Rae and Nakobee as they came over.

"The door is only short way."

Rose moved off. Nakobee watched as Rose moved away.

"They are very strong. I would not think them very strong with those skinny arms."

"Yes, they are. Did you get to see her fighting? She took the head off one man and with those second hands cut through three others. No wonder the soldiers are scared of them. They must have seen or heard of the way they fight. Remember when we were leaving? The soldiers were attacked. I don't think I would want to fight them."

They did not speak as they walked to catch up to Rose. Down the road close to the mountain Rose stepped between two large boulders onto a small path. The path weaved along the mountain between rocks and bushes beside the mountain. They walked a mile before Rose moved toward a small clump of bushes. Stepping behind them, she pointed at the rocks and turned her back so Alex could not see Nakobee and Rae.

Nakobee moved up and saw a discolored rock with swirly lines. He pushed it and a boulder moved into the mountain. Nakobee entered followed by Rose carrying Alex. Rae checked their perimeter, then entered and closed the door.

"Not far be home in two of your hours."

Rose started walking. Nakobee and Rae walked side by side.

"Hey, how are you guys seeing? It is too dark in here. I can't see anything - we need a torch."

"Don't worry your eyes will get used to the natural light in here. Besides, Rose knows where we are going and she can see."

"Brother coming."

A few minutes' later coming toward them, were two large green lights floating in the air. When they got close they saw Buddy. In two of his hands were sticks coated with the green phosphorous.

"Buddy brought these for you."

Nakobee reached out and took them.

"Thanks, I was starting to think my eyes were not going to adjust."

He handed one of the sticks to Rae. There was a short blast of squeaking between Buddy and Rose. Buddy reached out and took Alex from his sister. She moved back three feet behind them as Buddy now carrying Alex moved on. They stopped once to rest. Nakobee passed his canteen around so everyone could get a drink.

As Rose handed it back to him, she stopped and tilted her head. Rae and Nakobee stood and drew their swords.

"Enemy coming from behind and up ahead are four tunnels, there are more coming. They smell different."

Buddy picked up Alex.

"We can make it to tunnels and take one that has no enemies."

"Lead the way. Rose, you get up here behind your brother. Nakobee and I will guard the back."

There was a long blast of squeaking from her, then Buddy.

"I need not to be protected. Did I not do well in our fighting?'

Rae smiled at her then at Buddy as he moved back toward her.

"Yes, Rose, you did very well. You saved me by killing that soldier and then helping me with the other soldiers. That is why I wanted you near your brother. If the enemy comes before we make it to the turn, you will have to protect him."

Buddy looked over at Rae his head moving back and forth. Buddy faced Rose and another blast of squeaking between them, Buddy turned with Rose right behind him. As she walked passed Rae, she looked at him.

"I protect brother and young human."

As they moved forward Nakobee stepped beside Rae.

"I do not think the females are allowed to fight. Did you see Buddy's reaction to the news that his sister had fought and killed humans?"

"Yes. It will be interesting if we encounter more. I do not think she will just stand around."

They began walking. As they came near the junction they heard talking.

"I don't care who this person is. We do not need a mercenary in charge. We can take back our own home."

They voices stopped talking as Buddy then the others came into the junction. There came sounds of swords being drawn as the men moved around so they could fight. There was squeaking coming from Buddy and the two bugs that were with the men.

Rose moved out in front of Buddy and her second pair of hands began clicking. The soldiers stopped and backed up as the two bugs that were with them moved in front and beside Rose.

Rae and Nakobee walked out next to Rose.

"It would seem these men are Lord Marcel's men. Hello there. Let me introduce myself and my friend. We are the mercenaries you were talking about. My name is Rae and the big guy is Nakobee. Just too clear things up for you, mercenaries fight and are motivated by profit. We are here helping Lord Marcel for free. So you should not label us mercenaries. We are more like friends or neighbors who came to help. As for doing it without our help, you don't look like you did very well before we came. You have been out for over six months and during that time what have you done? We have been here less than a week and we removed the enemy's leader and freed all your people from the prisons and are in the process of taking back your home."

Nakobee took hold of Rae's shoulder and lightly pulled him back.

"We do not need to make them mad at us."

Rae turned around and faced Nakobee. He saw the look and realized he had become angry and was venting. Rae turned and looked at the one man that had not moved back.

"You must be in charge. Please forgive my outburst. I am having a bad week."

"I am Lieutenant Pike. We received word that Lord Marcel had returned and he brought with him mercenaries. We were misinformed. I thank you for the help. As for not doing anything, I was laid up for most of the time and my men kept us hidden and only fought when necessary. We tried...."

"Enemy very close - they are running this way. You do not have time to get away. Fight is what you will have to do now."

Buddy, still holding Alex, moved off down the right tunnel, his sister and the other two bugs followed behind him.

Rae drew his sword at the same time as Nakobee and Lieutenant Pike and his men. Lieutenant Pike was about to speak when Rae spoke.

"If I might make a suggestion, if you and some of your men go back down that tunnel, the rest of us can draw them after us. When they get in far enough you can attack from behind and we will have them boxed in."

Lieutenant Pike looked at Rae for only a moment then he pointed at a man.

"Take fifteen men and go with them. The rest of you back down the tunnel and do it quietly and quickly."

Before Lieutenant Pike left he looked back at Rae.

"That is a very good plan. One I would not have thought of."

Rae and Nakobee moved off after the men as Lieutenant Pike ran down tunnel.

"Nakobee, for this to work we will have to stay here so they will see us."

"Bait. I have been bait before. It can be fun."

"You men move down the tunnel and wait for us."

Rae moved over to stand by the wall. Nakobee stood across from him. The soldiers moved off down the tunnel. It was not long before the enemy came running into the junction. Rae yelled out.

"Hurry! They are right behind us. Get everyone moving."

A spear flew by, two more hit the wall near him. Then they were around a slight bend in the tunnel. Rae and Nakobee stopped when they saw the fifteen soldiers lined against the wall waiting. The enemy came around the bend, and the hiding men attacked and the fight started. It was not long before they heard screaming from behind the enemy. The fight was over fast. There were only twenty enemy soldiers and when they discovered they were trapped they dropped their weapons, placed their hands behind their heads, and dropped to the ground on their knees. Lieutenant Pike's men moved in and after securing the weapons tied the soldiers up.

"It was not as much fun as I remember. We did not have to fight."

"Yes, I sort of like this kind of fighting." Rose came walking up and stood next to them.

"We can continue now, and we have a place to keep the enemy soldiers so they will not be able to escape."

"Ok, let's go tell the Lieutenant."

Rae and Rose moved off working their way through the men. Lieutenant Pike was standing in the back talking to a mercenary.

"We don't care that you were only doing it for the money. You have killed a lot of people and you will be tried for crimes against the kingdom, and I hope you all hang."

"Lieutenant Pike. Rose says she has a place to keep the prisoners. If you get your men ready she or one of her people will lead them there."

"Rose? Who is Rose?"

"I Rose, daughter of King. Friend Rae gave me human name. These two will lead your men and the enemy to a safe place."

As she spoke two bugs came up alongside her; they stopped and waited.

"Rose, daughter of King, I am honored to meet you. Sergeant, take some men and follow those two. Stay with the prisoners until I send for you."

"Yes, sir"

The Sergeant snapped a salute and began yelling out orders. Within seconds the prisoners were moving - fifteen men guarding twelve prisoners and two bugs leading the way.

"I am impressed with your men. They fight very well."

"Just because we do not have wars doesn't mean I let my men relax. They practice every day for four hours. We even stage little wars out on the mountain. I believe it keeps the men fit and on their toes."

"I would say what you are doing works. We should get going."

Rae turned and followed Rose. Two hours later they walked into the cavern where Marcel and his people were. The soldiers were greeted by the people. There were hugs, back slapping, and lots of talking.

Buddy handed Alex to Rose; there was some squeaking then Buddy walked away.

"What was that about?"

Brother needs to talk with father."

Rae and Nakobee followed Rose as she carried Alex through the people toward the far wall. When they reached it, Rose stopped a couple of feet from two humans who were standing in front a small cave.

"This young human hurt. Requires your assistance."

The men moved forward and took the young man from Rose. They looked at him and saw the clothes he wore, then looked at Rose then Rae as he stepped closer.

"He is a mercenary?"

"He was, now he is not. He would like to help you get your homes back. So please help him."

"What should we do with the swords?"

"After you remove them you can give them to your soldiers. They will need them."

The two men carried the wounded young man inside the cave.

"Let's go find Marcel."

Rae, Nakobee, and Rose turned and headed back into the crowd to find Marcel. After a few minutes they found him sitting at a long table. He was with his council talking with Buddy and Rose's father.

When the father saw them he stood and went straight to Rose. There was a lot of squeaking, hands, and arms waving. Rose did not move she just stood there her head bent down. She talked but did not move. Buddy stood off to the side and he only talked when his father pointed at him. Rae and Nakobee kept walking to the table. They looked at the bugs and then at Marcel.

"I take it he heard about her fighting."

"The whole mountain has heard about it. Their women do not fight or hunt, let alone kill. The females take care of the home and the young ones. King is telling her that her brother should have helped you and she should have not interfered. The females are very few and are guarded as a prized possession. Since she is to marry and move away and start her own clan he is worried the son of the neighboring tribe will not want her after what she has done."

Rae stood there looking at Rose and her father. Rae was not sure but it seemed obvious he was giving her a very stern talking.

"Well then, he would be a fool. I saw her fight and I would have her stand and fight with me anytime. She is fast and any man or bug should be proud to have her as a mate"

Rae suddenly noticed everyone was staring at him and went quiet. Nakobee and Marcel were grinning.

"I will tell King what you have said. It might help. Of course, the fact that you were the one that named her will be a bonus. Come sit and tell us what you have planned."

They sat at the table, Rae's hand moved up covering the amulet, and the recording stopped.

"Then it is settled, Commander Pike will take his men and begin attacking the mercenaries outside. You and Captain Jones, along with his men, will continue sweeping the tunnels and going after the priests and their men. I know you have accomplished a lot since coming here, but do you really think we can end this in two weeks?"

"Yes. Once the mercenaries find out they are not going to get paid, they will leave. It should not be that hard to convince them. I have talked a couple of times now with Alex. He told me the men he was with were complaining for the last couple of months because they had not received any money. Some were even talking about leaving. None have because they are afraid of what will happen to them. Once we remove the fear of the priests and convince them they will never get paid they will leave."

"Commander Pike, prepare your men and leave as soon as you can. Captain Jones, you will get your men ready. Rae, when you leave King has said Buddy will be traveling with you as a guide. He is hoping you will increase his son's knowledge. He is very happy with what you have done with him over the last few weeks."

"Buddy has been a great help. He has shown me almost all of the tunnels. He has said they go a lot deeper into the mountain and down further but he claims they are off limits because of the danger and the ancient history of something bad that happened there."

"I have heard of the history of the people who lived below. They were here a long time before my father came here. From what we have discovered they were experimenting on different things. Humans, animals, and anything they could get. My father believes that is where the Trackels came from. My father and some of his friends ventured down there a couple of times when they first came here to live. They found a lot of rooms that were destroyed - they thought from fire. He said the stuff that was there was very advanced. He said more advanced than the equipment our forefathers had when they came here in their ships that traveled between the stars."

"You believe that your people came to this world in a ship that travels between the stars?"

Alora was sitting across the table from him and leaned forward.

"Our ancestors lived on a world far from here. They built ships that could travel between the stars. Our history says that there were five ships that traveled together. During the trip they were caught in what they called a worm hole. Don't ask me how a worm could make a hole in space. Anyway, our records state the five ships were caught and the ship our ancestors were on dropped out above this world. Their ship was no longer working so they landed here. Well, not here on this continent - they landed on one far from here. They were there a long time and had created a large and powerful kingdom. Then a war among the people here on this world and our ancestors happened and our people lost. Those who survived were scattered around the world. So yes, we do believe that our people traveled in ships among the stars. And from what your friend Jon says, so did yours."

Nakobee sat there with his hand over his face. Rae looked around the table. Everyone was staring at him.

"That was all I wanted to know. I did not doubt you - I was just asking for clarification. Lord Marcel, if you will excuse us, Nakobee and I will get things ready."

Rae and Nakobee stood, turned, and walked away.

"They are a very passionate people and hold very firm to their beliefs. Why do you keep pressing the point about them coming here on a ship that travels between the stars? You have been in the Thorn ships. You have seen the planets from above."

"I am asking all these questions because if what they say is true, then they could very well be the lost people from our world. I always kidded Jon about his beliefs and his reading of the ancient records and about our people coming to our world on what they called space ships. I have seen pictures of them and read the records. This could be a very important event if their claim is true."

"You have seen pictures? How? I thought Jon said only some of the books were available in your library?"

"When I was young I got to visit my grandfather. I had access to all the records of the royal family."

"And how did you do that? Did your family work for the royal family?"

"No, they did not work for them."

"Then how could you have gained access to such records? I think if the royal family on your world was trying to keep it all a secret it would have been very hard for the common people to see and read such information."

Rae looked up at Nakobee.

"Yes, it would have been very hard indeed, utterly impossible for any common person to see and read what I have. Now let's go get our stuff packed and get these people back in their homes so we can leave."

Nakobee stood there his face wrinkled in thought; he was thinking about Rae's words. Then his eyes opened as realization came to him. He looked at Rae who turned and walked away. Nakobee smiled, squared his shoulders, then followed.

Getting their backpacks, they went looking for Captain Jones. They found him and twenty of his men with Buddy at the opening of the tunnel leading to the castle.

"We are ready. Buddy says his people have informed him that the priest's soldiers are still searching the tunnels around the castle. We are going to move out with Buddy and a few of his people we are going to trap them. We have already captured over fifty of them, counting the mercenaries. Your plan seems to be working."

"Yes. It would seem it is. Let's go. We have a lot of places to search.

Chapter Six

They began where they left off the day before - in the tunnels above the prison cells. Captain Jones split his men into four teams: each team had six people. They separated when they reached the secret door opening into the tunnels inside the castle. Rae, Nakobee, and Buddy, along with Captain Jones and two of his men, moved to the left after entering. The others went to the right to split off at the junctions further down.

The tunnel they were searching had rooms every ten feet and each room was used for different things as stated by the signs on the doors. Most were for storage. They found the stock pile of food and other belongings were still in the rooms. Captain Jones moved his men up the stairs leading to the next level. Buddy was in the lead because of his ability to smell and hear far better than humans. At the top of the stairs Buddy stopped - one of his arms moved out and pointed at Nakobee, then Rae, and waved them forward. Nakobee moved over to the other side of the stairs, his sword drawn and ready. Rae moved up behind Buddy.

"What is wrong? Are there people out there?"

"People not in hallway - down there in one of those rooms there is pain and death. I smell and feel it."

Rae turned back and waved for Captain Jones. He and his men moved up.

"What is wrong? Did he find something?"

"Buddy says there are no soldiers. He feels and smells death coming from one of the rooms down there. What were these rooms used for?"

"The rooms on this floor are used for studies and research. I was hoping they, like the others, were still intact."

"What kind of research was being done in them?"

"I don't know. I am a soldier. When I was young I had a class down here. We cut up small animals to see their insides - how their bodies are like our own. I was not very good at it. Later I was told it was a way for the teachers to find out who would be good at practicing medicine. Those that would become doctors or have anything to do with science or medicine would come down here."

"Ok. We will go door to door and check each room out. If we find anyone, we can make the decision about what to do with them."

Rae moved around to Buddy.

"Move out, let me know if you feel anything behind any of the doors."

Buddy walked to the first door leaned toward it and shook his head no. Nakobee opened the door and the two soldiers entered and began searching it. When they came out they both shook their heads no. Rae, Nakobee, and Buddy were already coming out of the door across from them. They all moved to the next set of doors. They repeated this for the next eight doors, then Buddy stopped at a door his body shook. He moved back and pointed. Rae stepped to the door placing his ear against it. He reached for the door handled and twisted and pushed it open. The door swung inward. Rae went in and moved to the right. Nakobee came in and stepped to the left side. The two soldiers came straight in as Captain Jones yelled out as he entered.

"Do not try anything - we will not harm you if you do not resist."

Three priests were standing around a table. On the floor at their feet were what looked like broken egg shells. One of the priests turned and tried to hurl a knife at them. It dropped from his hand as a knife from Nakobee hit him in the chest knocking him back against the table and then to the floor. The other two dropped what they had in their hands and raised them.

Captain Jones and his men with their swords drawn walked forward.

"Ok, move over there against the wall and put your hands on top of your heads."

Captain Jones and his men followed the prisoners as Rae and Nakobee walked to the table. Rae was looking around the room. There were various sizes of dead dragons all around the room. Some were whole, others looked as if they were used in some sort of experiment.

"Do you see this? These are dragon eggs. Some are from really big dragons. But most are from those little ones like Shaméd has."

Nakobee walked around the table. Rae stood there looking on. There was an egg in a large bowl. Some of its shell was missing. There was movement. Rae could see the animal moving inside. Reaching over, he picked up the egg and slowly removed the shell. When it was off, he laid the creature down on the table. Then he picked up cloth and began to clean it. It began moving and making little squeaking sounds. When it was clean, Rae stepped back - it was a little dragon. It tried to stand but it kept falling. Nakobee was standing next to him.

"It won't live. Look at the wings. They are not complete. We should kill it."

"We are not going to kill it. It has a right to live. We will take it outside the mountain and set it free."

"It will die out there all alone."

"Then it will die. But we will not just kill it."

The little dragon struggled to its feet and was walking around. It poked at the eggs still on the table then it came back and began to eat its own shell.

After it had eaten all of its shell it moved toward Rae where it sat looking up at him. Rae reached over picked it up and placed it inside his satchel. He walked over to the two priests standing against the wall. Their hands were now tied behind their backs.

"What were you doing here?"

They stood there without speaking. Neither of them looked at him. Rae took out his knife and faster than anyone could see sliced the ear off the priest in front of him. The man screamed and dropped to the floor. One of the soldiers came over and placed a rag on the wound. The other priest tried to move away, his eyes wide open, fear showed on his face. Rae's knife pressed against the man's throat as he leaned closer.

"I will ask one more time. What were you doing here?"

The priest was shaking. His body, as well as his voice, betrayed just how scared he really was.

"We were trying to find a dragon body for our god, Krakdrol, to posses."

"Your god is gone. We sent him away with some friends. He should be dead by now. So why were you continuing? You had to have known he was gone."

"Master Voren told us to continue our work. He said that he would find and return our god."

"Well, he won't be returning and you people make me sick."

Before Nakobee or anyone could stop him Rae slid his knife across the priest's throat. Rae stepped back as the priest's eyes grew even bigger. He tried to yell but only gurgled as he just slid down the wall to the floor. Nakobee grabbed Rae.

"What are you doing? There was no reason to kill him."

"You know I do not like taking prisoners."

"I know you don't, but you gave them to Captain Jones."

"I did not like what they were doing here, and for what they were doing, they deserved to die. I am done for the day. I am going outside to release this little dragon."

Rae walked toward the door. No one tried to stop him. Buddy watched everything from the doorway where he had stopped. He moved back into the hallway as Rae approached. Rae walked passed and Buddy followed. It did not take long to reach one of the secret doors to the outside. Rae found a nice place with grass and a hole behind a large boulder. He reached into his satchel and pulled out the little dragon. It was sleeping, but its eyes opened then closed, as Rae placed it within the hole. Standing up, Rae headed back to the secret door with Buddy still following.

Rae's hand came up and covered the amulet.

Buddy was walking next to Rae and Nakobee was in front. The tunnel they were in opened up to a junction. As they entered, they met up with Captain Jones and twenty of his men.

"Commander Pike sent word that all the mercenaries have left. Your plan worked. Once they found out they were not ever going to get paid and the priests could not attack them, they left during the night. The only ones left are the priests and about one hundred of their soldiers. We could move in and take them with very little trouble."

"I agree you could handle them. The priests are what worry me. They still can do a lot of damage with their magic. I do not want you or your men to die because we got ahead of ourselves. Give me one more day. I am going to see if I can remove that threat. When I do, you and your men can go after the priests' soldiers."

"What are you going to do?"

Rae took a drink from his flask. He put it away and looked at Captain Jones.

"You do not need to know the details of what I am going to do. Just trust me that I will take care of the priests. We are going to be gone until tomorrow so go ahead and have your men keep patrolling the tunnels. I will send word when I am ready."

Rae started walking toward the tunnel opposite the one he came from. Buddy was right beside him. Nakobee was walking passed Captain Jones when he raised his hand.

"Is he always so sure of himself?"

"This is what Rae does best. He has been doing this longer than I have been alive. And he is very good at it. If Rae says it is almost over then you can believe him. In the last six weeks you have only lost two men. How many has the enemy lost?"

Nakobee walked away. Within minutes he caught up to Rae and Buddy.

"Rae, when are we going to rest? We have been awake for the last fifteen hours. I know you are in a hurry to leave but it won't do us any good if we are too tired to go."

"We are going to our room to rest now. Buddy said he would keep watch and let us sleep for a few hours. Then I want to go to the meeting room. If they are on schedule, the priests will be there in eight hours. We should be able to take them all out then. Once that is done, Commander Pike and Captain Jones can do their thing and take back their home. Then we can be on our way."

They walked the rest of the way to the room Rae had chosen as his. It was on the other side of the castle and so far none of the priests or their men had come there since the fighting started. Opening the secret door, they entered the hallway and walked down to the room. Rae checked the door to make sure his traps were still there. They were so he disabled them and opened the door. Once inside, he locked the door and reset the traps.

"Wake us in six hours, Buddy. That will give us plenty of time to reach the meeting room."

"Buddy will wake you in six hours. Buddy will read the books you gave me."

Nakobee stretched out on the bed near the far wall and Rae walked over to the other room and stretched out on the bed in there. He fell asleep as soon as his head hit the pillow. The next thing he knew there was something moving between his legs. His hand wrapped around the knife under his pillow. He slowly opened his eyes, knife in hand, he looked down toward his legs. There was movement under the sheet. Just as he was about to rip the sheet off the movement disappeared and there was snapping sound next to his head. Jumping back and off the bed, he looked at his pillow. There on his bed was a little dragon. It was sitting there staring at him. Buddy came scurrying into the room a book in each hand.

"Buddy felt you move. Something bother you? Oh, it is the little dragon you saved. It must like you to have come back to you.'

Rae stood and pointed at the little dragon on the bed. It was making circles in front of the pillow then it lay down and closed it eyes.

"That is the same dragon I took outside? How can you tell?"

"Buddy can smell it and feel it. It calls to you. Buddy thinks it is what they say bondage to you."

"You mean bonded? Bondage is something completely different. How did it get in here? The doors are locked and it sure did not fly up here and come through the window."

"Buddy felt the air move twice. Buddy thinks it just came here by pooping."

"You mean popping. It popped in as if it transported here. I heard that dragons can do that. But I want to know how it found me."

"Does not matter. If it has bondaged, I mean bonded, with you it will be able to find you anywhere."

"Great. That is just what I need - a little dragon following me around. How long did I sleep?"

"Buddy was just getting ready to wake you. It has been six hours. You ready to go kill the priests?"

Rae looked at Buddy.

"What we are about to do is necessary. Those priests will never leave on their own. Given half a chance they will kill us all."

"Buddy know what you say is true. Buddy can feel the bad in them. It just does not feel right to kill them."

"You will not kill them. Nakobee and I will do the killing. Come on, we can leave and let the little one sleep."

Rae and Buddy walked out of the room. Nakobee was sitting on the side of his bed putting his boots on.

"What happened in there?"

"That little dragon came back. It is sleeping in bed. Rae says to leave it there."

"Never mind about the little dragon. It should not be too hard to take out the priests once they get into the room. I will drop the poison in the room and it will take affect almost immediately."

"It will cause them pain?"

"No, Buddy, it will not cause them pain - at least not a lot. They will get sleepy then they will pass out. The stuff lasts for about an hour. So we will not be able to enter right away. If anyone enters that room during that time they stand a good chance of dying as well."

"We have watched them for five days and they start their meeting two hours after sunup. Then they end it three hours later. Your plan will work. I will work my way into the hallway and take out the guard. We will then bolt the door shut from outside. No one will be able to enter or exit."

"Yes, that is the plan and it should work. I just have a strange feeling something is wrong. I had a dream, and it was very weird. I don't remember it all it except it left me feeling like things are going to change a lot faster after today."

"Buddy thinks your dream means we will win today and the people will be able to go back to their homes and we all live in peace again."

"I really do like you, Buddy. You have the best attitude I have ever seen. Come on, let's get going."

Nakobee finished putting his weapons on at the same time as Rae. Rae disabled the traps around the door. Opening it, Buddy scurried into the hallway. Rae shook his head and followed him. Nakobee locked the door after exiting and was about to set the traps.

"Don't bother with them. If things work out, we will be in control by noon today."

Buddy led the way with Rae and Nakobee close behind.

Entering the secret passageways they worked their way to the meeting room. Nakobee stopped at the secret door across from the room. Rae and Buddy moved on, and within a few minutes they stood in front of the door. Rae was about to open it when Buddy tapped him on the shoulder. Buddy shook his head no and pointed at a ledge about ten feet up the wall. Then he pointed at the steps cut into the wall for climbing up. They both climbed up to the ledge. It was five feet long and two feet wide. There were two seats carved into the wall. Once they were sitting, Buddy pointed at a blue colored rock. Rae reached up and carefully pulled on it. It came loose leaving a small hole. Rae started to move closer but Buddy stopped him. He reached up and pulled down what looked like glass in front of the hole. Everything in the room below from corner to corner was magnified through the glass. They sat there looking into what Marcel called his boardroom. It was where he and the council members would meet to discuss the events that were happening. Rae understood why Buddy stopped him from opening the door. The priests had arrived early. The head priest and his top five priests were sitting around the table. There were ten men dressed in black and red. They were the high priest's personal body guards. They stood along the wall. One priest was talking.

"Master Voren, our men have searched all the tunnels. There is no trace of the body of the half-elf called Loorn."

"Do not use that name when speaking about our God Krakdrol. The vessel he is in does not matter. You will always call him Lord Krakdrol. As for searching all the tunnels, I do not believe it. Have more men go below and search. Take those scum mercenaries and have them help. They have done nothing since they arrived but eat and drink."

"Master Voren that is another thing I want to bring up. They are asking for their pay. And since we have as yet found the vault for this kingdom we have very little money with which to pay them. Some of them have already left, what are we to do if the rest decide to leave?"

Master Voren slammed his fist down on the table and stood. His old body shook as he yelled, "Leave? They will not leave! You will take some of the young priests and make an example of any that try to leave. Burn them all, if you must. But they will not leave here alive. Now I want to know..."

There was a bright flash of light behind him. Everyone in the room flinched as they cowered and covered their eyes. As the light dimmed there stood what could only be a demon. The demon was large - he had to be at least ten feet tall. The horns on his head scraped the ceiling as he moved. He moved around looking at the men in the room. When he took a step closer to Master Voren its tail dug grooves as it raked back and forth. When it spoke its voice bellowed out,

"My Master Gormorrah is not pleased with the gift he gave you so many years ago. He told you that one day a half-elf would come and it would hold the power of the black dragon called Krakdrol. Did my Lord Gormorrah not promise you power beyond your imagination? And were you and your people not protected from your enemies? Did you not prosper?"

Master Voren had fallen back into his seat when the demon arrived and now he stood on his shaking legs and faced the demon.

"Yes, everything you say is true. When your Lord Gormorrah came to me over a thousand years ago I was young. I took the orb and used it to advance myself and those around me. There was great evil that happened to those that did not do my bidding. As for what has happened, tell your Lord I have it under control. We will find the ones that have taken our Lord Krakdrol. We will fulfill our promise to him and we will become powerful and we will rule all the lands on this world."

Smoke billowed out from the demon's nose as it roared,

"Enough! I was sent here because you have failed. The one called Krakdrol is no longer. His brother and those that follow him have destroyed its life force."

Master Voren was shaking so hard he fell into his seat as he spoke,

"How could anyone destroy a god?"

"You old fool. Krakdrol was not a god. It was a dragon. One of the first dragons ever created. Lord Gormorrah worked on him for centuries twisting him to our way of thinking. When his body was killed it was us who placed his life force into the orb to be passed from world to world causing pain, suffering, and death."

Master Voren hands covered his face, dropping them he looked up at the demon.

"Why would you do such a thing?"

"You pathetic little creatures are all the same. Thinking you're better than others just because you have a soul."

If it were possible the demon's voice roared louder.

"WE should have been the chosen. WE were created before any of the others and long before *your* kind. As for why we do what we do, it is because we can. Because of your failure you are all to die."

Everyone but Master Voren ran for the door when they heard his words. Master Voren just leaned back in his chair. No one made it to the door. Flames shot from the mouth of the demon engulfing the entire room. Rae and Buddy jumped back. Rae would have fallen off the ledge if not for Buddy who reached out to grab him. When they looked again the room was filled with smoke. As it cleared they saw nothing but ashes. Nothing was left in the room. Even the metal had melted.

"Well, that was sort of what I dreamed last night. I just did not see the demon, only the fire. As soon as the others find out that they have no leaders they will leave.

Let's head back and tell Captain Jones so he can send word to Marcel and the council."

Rae stood and started down. Buddy grabbed his hand.

"We should pray for them."

Rae looked up at Buddy.

"Pray for them? Are you kidding? Those people in there do not deserve our prayers. They were willing to kill all of your kind and anyone that did not follow them. They were evil men that got what they deserved."

"No one is truly evil. Those men in there were only misguided. They were tricked into their beliefs because of the evil demons. Demons are always trying to trick and corrupt everything. Do you not fight the demons that try and take over your own body?"

Buddy let go of Rae's hand. Rae continued climbing down. Once down, he waited. Buddy reached the ground and stood facing Rae.

"I, like everyone, have my own inner-demons. I do not believe things like that in there could ever make me do something I did not want to do."

"You do not hear voices in your head telling you things you know are wrong?"

"Of course, I hear voices. It is my own mind. I talk to myself all the time. It is the only way to figure out things I am thinking about. It is not some other person trying to influence me. Now stop worrying about those dead men in there and let's get going."

"Did you not tell me the one you call Shaméd can talk to you in your head? And did you not tell me that others you know can to do the same thing? Why do you have so much trouble believing there are real demons that can do it and are out there doing it to everyone?"

Rae took a deep breath, then let it out slowly.

"Because if I believed there were demons out there trying to make me bad, then I would have to believe in

God. The faith on my world is the belief in "The Three in One." It is the Father, Son, and Spirit. Here Marcel's people say trinity. Alora calls them the same only instead of spirit they say ghost. To me it is all the same. I have been on many worlds. Each has its own god or gods. Some are good, but most are bad. I have come to my own conclusion that people make up these gods to control others."

"You do not really believe that. I can see how you treat others. You are a good human. You have taught me many things and they are all good."

"Buddy, if you knew half of what I have done you would not want to be my friend. I have killed people out of anger and for money. Sure, I have tried to do good whenever I can, but I do not believe I am a very good person. If there is a god then he, she, or it will not want me. Do not speak anymore about this please."

Rae turned and started walking down the tunnel. For the last few weeks his eyes had become so accustomed to the soft green light he no longer carried them on a stick like the others. It did not take them long to reach Nakobee. When they did they stopped and Nakobee stood there with a strange look on his face.

"What is wrong?"

"I don't know if you saw or heard what happened in there but what I saw was the door burst into flames and the guard standing in front of it did the same. Then a very large demon came out and shot flames down the hallway then disappeared."

"We saw the same thing happen inside. The demon or whatever it was killed everyone. We still have a lot of work to do, but we should be able to leave in a week maybe less. Come on, we have to go inform Marcel about what happened.

Chapter Seven

They reached the cavern where Marcel and the others met every day. Rae walked straight toward the table where Marcel was sitting. Before he got there Alora came walking up beside him.

"I would like to talk to you when you have time. Do you have time now?"

"No, I don't. Something important has happened and I need to tell your father and the others."

"Then I will come along. If it is that important I should hear it as well."

"Yes, I suppose you should."

Alora kept pace with Rae, Buddy dropped back to walk with Nakobee. As they drew near the table Marcel saw them and stood.

"Rae, Alora, I am glad you are both here. I would like you to hear what I have just told the council. Come both of you sit next to me."

Marcel waved at some men and they brought two chairs over. He pointed to the one on his left and motioned to Alora who looked at her father then took the seat.

"Rae, please sit here on my right. Now let me tell you the good news."

"Lord Marcel, before you speak I have something I need to say. It is very important. It is about the priests and I think everyone will want to hear it."

Marcel looked at Rae, then waving his hands, he sat.

"I suppose I can wait a few more minutes. Go ahead and tell us your news."

Rae looked at each face, then the saw the people come gathering around them.

"What I am going to tell you will affect the outcome of the battle we were going to have tomorrow. A beast came to the meeting room during the priest's meeting. After it raged at them for some time it shot flames out of its mouth and burned everything in the room. The priests are all dead. I believe we should attack now that they have no leaders. They may even know by now their leaders are dead. We stand a very good chance in taking back your home with very little fighting. They only have about a hundred men left. Your men can surround them."

"The room was destroyed? The pictures, furniture, everything burned?"

Rae stopped talking and looked down at Marcel. He saw the look of a man that just lost his sole possessions.

"Yes. The room was completely destroyed. Even the door to the room burned. Is there something I should know? Was there something in the room? Why are you so upset? I thought you would be happy to hear that they are all dead?"

"My boy, I am very happy to hear they are all dead. I am just not happy all the things in the room were destroyed. There were family heirlooms in that room - pictures of my ancestors going back six generations. That table was a gift from the king my Grandfather served under. No, I am sorry they are gone, but you are right, this is good news, almost as good as what I have to tell you. Now sit down, I want everyone to hear what I have to say. Come, all of you, come closer so you can hear my words and spread them to those not here."

Humans and Trackels gathered close to hear what Marcel was going to say. Marcel stood up.

"I have talked with the council and they have agreed with my wishes. I am naming Rae as my legal heir to the throne. I hope with the marriage to my daughter, Alora, that the two of them will protect all of you better than I ever could. I know a lot of you have come to know Rae and his companion, Nakobee. I believe most of you will agree he is a good a man and will be a great benefit to our kingdom. Now don't worry, I am not dying, - I am just naming Rae as heir. In two years I will step down and let him and my daughter take over. Rae, is there anything you would like to say about this great news?"

Marcel turned and smiled down at Rae. Rae sat there, a blank expression on his face. He saw Nakobee move. When he looked at him, Nakobee's brow was wrinkled, and he slowly moved his head back and forth. Rae slowly stood. He looked at Marcel, then at the council members sitting at the table. He looked at the people and the Trackels standing there waiting for him to speak.

"Lord Marcel, I am deeply honored you think so highly of me that you would name me heir. I really don't know what to say to all of this. I am not sure Lady Alora would take me for her husband since I have not asked her. I must inform you at this time I am not free to except your offer. I was left here to help you by Lord Shaméd. He gave me six months to accomplish this. Once I have helped you, I am to return to him. I have two months to reach the city called Na-Car. I can talk with Lord Shaméd about your offer at that time. Maybe he will let me out of my contract. But until he does, I am afraid I will have to continue with his wishes. Now about the death of the priests, if you will give the order, I will have your men begin reclaiming your home."

Marcel looked at Alora, then at Rae.

"Yes, I forgot why you were here. Please go take control of my men and chase out the last of those evil men and their mercenaries. We can talk more about my proposal later when this is all done."

Bowing, Rae turned and headed out of the cavern with Nakobee and Buddy close behind. As he walked, he felt something on his shoulder. Some of the people around him jumped back, some screamed, others made a loud gasping sound.

"Look little dragon is here. It sits very well on your shoulder."

Rae moved his head a little so he could see the dragon. It was sitting on his left shoulder with its tail wrapped around his neck.

Before he reached the tunnel Alora had caught up to him.

"What do you mean I would not marry you? And why do you have a dragon on your shoulder?"

Rae stopped and looked at her. The crowd was moving away but was still watching them.

"This is dragon friend Rae saved a few days ago. He..."

"Lady Alora is not interested in the dragon. She is mad because I turned down the marriage proposal."

"What makes you think I am not interested in the dragon? I think it is very pretty. Have you given it a name? Is it a male or female?"

"No, I have not given it a name. I do not know if it is male or female. I won't be keeping it. It just thinks it needs to be with me for some reason. I am sure once it finds others of its kind it will leave. Now if you will excuse us we have to get your men ready to fight. Nakobee and I think within a day you will be back in your own room and sleeping in your own bed."

"Do you know anything about dragons? I don't think so from the look on your face. They do not just hang around people. They choose someone and they stay with them for life. So I think you need to get used to having it with you a long time. And thank you for thinking about me and where I sleep. Please go on about your business. When you have time I will talk to you about what my father and the council are going to tell you. Oh wait, my father has already informed you."

"Lady Alora, I am sorry if you have taken offence to my words back there. It is not that I do not find you attractive, I... "

"So you do think I am attractive? Then does that mean you might even consider marriage with me?"

"I, well, I, what I mean to say is..."

Nakobee stepped in front of Rae and looked down at Alora.

"What Rae is trying to say is right now all we can think about is the upcoming fight. Men like us try not to plan too far ahead. We never know how long we will live, if we might be killed today or tomorrow. Rae was just caught off guard by your father's proposal. He, as well as I, did not know the feelings you and your father have for him. If you would give him some time, I am sure he will be able to explain it all to you. Maybe when you and your people are back in your homes the two of you can go somewhere alone and talk."

Alora stood there looking at Nakobee. She glanced over at Rae, who just stood there not saying a word. She saw the little dragon sitting on his shoulder twisting its head back and forth from her to Rae. Taking a step back, Alora gave a slight bow of her head.

"I understand. I forgot the two of you are professional soldiers and as such will stick to your job until it is complete. Rae, I will wait for you to come and talk to me about us. Little one please take care of yourself. I know you will look out for him. I want you both to be careful."

Alora turned and walked away. The people close saw her and turned and moved away fast. Rae looked up at Nakobee.

"When we get done I will go someplace alone with her and talk? What are you crazy? Alora and her father want me to stay here and marry her. You and I both know I cannot stay."

"There is no reason you cannot stay here. Lord Shaméd and the council back home would not keep you from starting your own life. You have been away from your world how many years? Three, four hundred? They will not interfere with your happiness."

"My happiness! I don't want to stay here. I like my life. Yes, it is sort of lonely at times, but I am free and I get to go and do whatever I want. Well almost. Sometimes Lord Nogar and the council tell me where to go and what do, but that is different. Why am I standing here having this conversation? We have a job to do. I will talk to you later about this. And did you hear her talk to this little dragon? She acts like it can understand her. She asked it to look out for me. What is this little guy going to do?"

Shaking his head, Rae turned and walked away. He did not see Nakobee smiling. Buddy was about to speak, but Nakobee put his finger up to his lips and shook his head no, as he walked passed. Buddy shrugged his shoulders and followed Nakobee and Rae down the tunnel.

Within two hours Captain Jones and Commander Pike had their men ready to attack. They each had a job to do. Commander Pike was taking the majority of their men and going after the few mercenaries that were left. Captain Jones would take thirty men and move into the castle to start fighting the priests and their soldiers. Rae, Buddy, and Nakobee would go with Captain Jones.

Captain Jones had his men spread out along the hallway as they exited the secret passageway a hundred feet from the great room. As Rae, Nakobee, and Buddy entered and the door shut behind them a small group of soldiers and two priests came out of the great room. The soldiers standing near the wall moved forward attacking the enemy. When the fighting started Buddy started to move forward but Nakobee placed his arm out in front of him.

"You will wait here. We do not want anything to happen to you."

"Buddy not get hurt. Buddy a better fighter than sister."

"I am sure you are a great fighter. But you will stay here. Remember you and your people do not believe in killing. So we do not want you put into a position where you might have to kill."

Buddy moved back as Nakobee ran down the hallway after Rae.

The fighting was almost over before it began. The priest's soldiers were all dead before Rae or Nakobee reached them. The two priests, seeing their men getting slaughtered, turned back into the great room. As they ran across the room to the other door, Rae came in and tossed a knife. It stuck between the shoulder blades of a priest who crashed forward into the other one. They both went hurtling down to the floor. The priest rolled over and as he sat up his hands were moving in a circle and he was chanting words. A ball of light began to grow between his hands. Soon it was a small ball of fire. When Rae was ten feet away the priest tossed it at him. Rae dove to the left and rolled away. The ball of fire exploded against the wall. The priest stood and ran out the door down the hallway, yelling.

"Guards, guards, we are under attack."

Rae stood and was about to give chase when Nakobee grabbed his arm.

"We do not need to chase him. He will return with others. We should move on and meet them head on."

Captain Jones entered the room with his men.

"I am leaving five men here. They will stack the dead against the wall and wait for our return."

Rae and Nakobee stepped aside as he marched passed with fifteen men. The rest stayed behind.

"It looks like the captain is going to take back this place without our help."

"Let's go the other way. If we split up we may make better time."

Rae moved back into the hallway, Buddy was still waiting where they left him. As they walked passed Buddy he turned his head.

"Friend Rae, your shirt has been burnt. Was there a fire?"

Nakobee tapped Buddy on the shoulder. And they both followed Rae.

"One of the priests tried to cook Rae. He tossed a fireball at him. Rae jumped out of the way but not fast enough."

"Is he ok?"

"Yes, he is. I won't say the same for the people we meet next."

A few minutes later, after turning left at a crossway, they met ten of the priest's soldiers coming out of a room and swords and shields clashed almost instantly.

Rae blocked blow after blow as the soldiers pressed at them. He tried several times to get a hit, but it was not easy as the hallway was narrow, only two people wide. Nakobee used his spear reaching around Rae, and jabbing at them. Slowly they were pushed back into the junction. Once there, Rae and Nakobee moved into the center of the room, Buddy with them. As the other soldiers moved in the fight worsened. A sword sliced across Rae's left arm, and another man came at him from behind. Before Buddy or Rae could do anything, Rae was standing two feet to the right. He drove his sword into the side of the soldier then with a swift backswing he took out another soldier. Buddy twisted his head at how fast Rae moved, and a soldier came charging at Buddy. Without looking Buddy stretched his bottom right arm out and sliced across the man's chest. The soldier dropped his sword grabbing at the wound and moved away.

The soldiers began moving with Rae and Nakobee into a more open area. When the last soldier dropped, Rae used a dead soldier's garment to clean off his sword. Putting it away, he stood there looking around.

"Buddy, are you ok?"

Buddy looked at Rae twisted his head to the right then to the left.

"Buddy ok, why should Buddy not be ok?"

"I just thought you might feel bad about killing those two men?"

"Buddy not kill two men, Buddy only kill one."

Nakobee stepped closer.

"No you killed two. After you took out the one you stood there and your second pair of arms came out and you moved forward and took out another soldier. Don't you remember?"

Buddy now twisted his head back and forth so fast they thought it would fall off. He stopped and looked from Rae to Nakobee."

"Buddy not remembers doing this."

"That is ok, once the fighting starts most people block out what happens. It is a good thing if you don't remember. This way you will not feel any grief. Come on, let's keep going."

Five hours later they were back in the tunnels on their way back. Buddy left them half way, saying it was time for him to go pray. Rae and Nakobee kept going until they reached their sleeping area, they cleaned up, and Nakobee stretched out to get some rest. Rae changed his shirt and found his needle and some thread. He went out of the room and sat against the wall to fix his shirt. He was almost done when Alora walked up.

"Are you ready to talk to me?"

Rae finished and put the needle and thread away. Looking up at Alora he slowly stood.

"Let's go for a walk."

They walked side by side not talking until they reached a secret door. Rae pushed the button and the door swung open. He waved Alora forward then followed her out. They both stepped out on the side of the mountain. They stood there looking over the fields. The sun was setting and they could see men working in the fields below.

"It amazes me that those men can keep on working when there is fighting going on around them."

"They are a protected people. The fairies will not let anything happen to them."

"Yes, these mysterious fairies. I would like to see them up close one day."

"If you stay here and marry me you will meet them. They, along with all the people, will come to our wedding."

Rae sat on a rock and looked at Alora.

"I cannot marry you. I have an obligation to Shaméd. I still have to return to him."

"Yes. I heard what you and Nakobee said and I can wait for you to go see him and return."

"I have a question for you? Why would you want to marry me? You have only known me a couple of months. You do not know me, who I am, or what I am. You know nothing about me. So why would you want to marry me?"

Alora stared at him.

"I know who you are; your friends told me."

"They told you I was a thief and an assassin. I know you weren't that impressed."

"I did not know you then."

"You still do not know me. Nothing has changed - I am still a thief and assassin. I am killing for your father, and your people. That is what I am and that is what I will always be."

"Why do you find the thought of marrying me so bad? Am I ugly or just not your type?"

Taking a deep breath and letting it out slowly, Rae looked around, then stood to face her.

"I do not think you are ugly. In fact, I think you are very attractive. As for my type, I do not know what my type is. I have been doing what I do for a very long time. Longer than you would believe. Since we first met, you have argued with me and treated me like dirt."

"I treated you that way at first because I did not know what you wanted and I thought you were like all the other men I have met since leaving this place. After watching you and being with you these last few weeks I have come to know you better. You are a good man - a little strange at times - but a good man. I think I fell in love with you the first time I saw you. By the second week we were here, I knew I was in love with you. I do not know what you did but I felt a great pride the day you stood there and told my father and the others that the man Rose is going to marry would be an idiot if he did not marry her. I do not think my father would have said that. You always speak highly of those you like. I would like to know more about you."

Rae sat and faced the fields.

"I ran away from home when I was fifteen years old. I met Shaméd when I was hired to help him during a migration. At that time I thought Shaméd was about my same age, maybe a few years older. I found out later he is many years older. I have been away from my people for a long time. They have all grown old and died. I see by your face you do not understand. The people on the world where Shaméd took me do not age in a normal way. Their bodies grow old a lot slower. If you took the date I was born and the date right now on my world, you would find that almost four hundred years have passed. I have been on many worlds and traveled to so many places, I have forgotten most of them. I do not know if I could ever stop doing what I do. I do know that most of the time I like what I do. You will have to give me time. Wait until you and the others are back into your homes, give me time to return to Shaméd. I will talk to him - after that I can give you an answer."

"I can wait. Just do not let me wait four hundred years. You might not like what you find when you return."

Rae looked at Alora, who had a big grin on her face.

"Yes, I would imagine if I did wait that long you would be very angry."

Chapter Eight

Shaméd pressed a button making the recorded images blur as he scanned ahead. He stopped when he saw Buddy standing over Rae.

"Buddy not understand why you stay outside. You save my people from being hunted down and killed. You helped humans take back their homes. We are all safe now. The human King is sending soldiers to take the priests and their soldiers away. You will be leaving soon?"

Rae was sitting under a tree, the same tree where he had first met the farmers. The little dragon was curled up on the ground beside him.

"I like the outside and I stay outside because I have been inside the mountain for almost three months. Yes, I will be leaving in a few days. Where is your sister? I have not seen her in over a month."

"Sister Rose is in preparation to go marry. But the one she was to marry will no longer marry her. Father says she is no longer Trackel. He says humans have capered her. He say you were the one who do this. So Father tell her she is to stay inside until he finds another mate."

"You mean corrupted. I think you should take me to this one that will not marry your sister. I can change his mind."

Buddy started making clicking sounds and his body was shaking.

"Buddy was told by Father not to let you near him. He thinks you not normal he says you are very strange human and you might hurt the one that will not marry Rose."

"Well, your father is right. I just might hurt him. The man is not in his right mind. He should be happy to marry your sister. She is very smart and a fast learner, just like you."

"Serelodolfer is not a man he is a Trackel."

"Man, Trackel, it does not matter, he is a fool. You go back inside with Nakobee. I will be here if anyone needs me."

"Buddy go and be back when sun goes down. Buddy not like the sun. It hurts Buddy's eyes."

Buddy turned and scurried away toward the mountain, his four legs moving so fast they did not leave prints in the dirt.

Rae leaned back and closed his eyes. After weeks of not sleeping more than a few hours he dozed off. He woke when he felt something moving on his left hand. He did not move. Slowly he opened his eyes and looked down.

There was what looked like a little person on his hand and there were tiny wings on its back. It was walking up his arm. When the little man reached his shoulder it took out a sword and poked him in on the chin.

"Ouch! Why did you do that?"

"You are thinking of never coming back. You should remember the people here. They do not have long to live."

"Are you what they call a fairy?"

"My people have lived on many worlds and been known by many names. You need to come with me to meet our Queen. She wants to meet the one that has helped the humans."

The little man jumped and his wings carried him up and he flew back and forth in the air waiting.

The little dragon raised its head, looked around stood, stretched, walked around in a circle, and laid back down. Rae watched it then slowly stood.

"Lead the way."

The fairy flew slowly down the road. Rae followed. They were almost to the main road to the outside when the fairy turned toward the mountain. He flew across a small stream of flowing lava. A group of humans were sitting around a fire singing. The fairy flew around, weaving in and out among the humans. His movements were to the sound of the song then he shot up and headed for a large boulder disappearing behind it. The song filled the air...

As winter rains and snows recede
And spring draws closer still;
Flitting fairies spread their wings
To sing and drink and dance at will.

And all the while
They dip and whirl;
As twittering they go
Sending bees and ladybugs
And tiny leaves to twirl.

They only seek the nectar's honey;
To taste the blossom's wine.
They dance upon the bottle's top;
Sipping from the vine.

And all the while
They dip and whirl;
As twittering they go

Sending bees and ladybugs
And tiny leaves to twirl.

Of blossoms, twigs, and seeds,
Their abode is built of silk and glue
Of sunshine, breezes, cattails
Of cobwebs, toadstools, and dew...

And all the while
They dip and whirl;
As twittering they go

Rae jumped over the stream of lava as the people just sat there singing. There was meat roasting over the fire and what looked like a keg of some sort was on a rock. They were filling their cups and drinking. They smiled and waved as Rae walked by and stepped behind a large boulder.

There was a tunnel and Rae entered. It was narrow with small patches of the green fungus on the walls giving off just enough light for him to see. The light grew brighter as Rae walked further into the tunnel. As he went around a bend he entered a large cavern. The walls were covered with the green fungus making the chamber glow green. Rae saw small fires burning on the ground and in small outcrops in the walls. There were thousands, if not millions, of the little fairies! Rae noticed not all had wings. Some were walking around on the ground and climbing up ladders and steps carved into the walls. Rae stopped at the entrance of a smaller cavern, as he stood there he thought how amusing all of this was

"Come inside. Her Majesty Queen Baelia awaits you."

The fairies on the ground parted clearing an opening for him to walk through. The two turned and flew in front of him. One carried a spear the other carried a bow and had a quiver of arrows on his back. As he walked, he noticed most, if not all, had some type of weapon. He started to rethink his amusement. When he reached the other side of the cavern he stopped in front of a shelf. He noticed there were five shelves built into the wall. There was a fire burning on the top one and it was level with his face. There were several fairies standing around one who was sitting in a chair. The chair looked like gold and it was inlaid with gems. The woman sitting there was dressed in fine clothing and wore a crown with gems. Rae bowed his head toward her.

"Your Majesty, I am honored and I thank you for the privilege to be allowed to meet with you. How can this lowly human be of service to you?"

Rae stood straight and looked at the queen. She stood and a female moved forward to sweep her dress back. The Queen walked gracefully to the edge. Four of her men followed. When she stopped, they moved out along either side of her.

"You are indeed a well-mannered human. Most that have come before me have never bowed, let alone given such a formal greeting. I am even more impressed with you."

"Your Majesty, you do not need to be impressed with me. I am of no importance. I am just a hired man sent here by his Lord to help the people reclaim their home."

The Queen laughed and waived her hand.

"You do not have to pretend with me. I know full well who and what you are. I know you are from another world. I also know you saved the life of a dragon and that the dragon has bonded with you. You are a lucky human for that to happen."

"May I ask how the Queen has acquired this information?"

The Queen walked a few steps to the left before stopping and looking at him.

"I have acquired this information from the one you saved. She and I talk a lot about you. She is very impressed with you."

"She? And who might I ask is this she that I saved?"

"Your dragon, you silly man. She is the one I have been talking with. She has read your mind and knows all about you: what you have done, where you come from, and who you are. She knows about this king of the dragons called Nogar and the one you call Lord Shaméd. She told me you are a human with potential and should be watched after. I do not know how she would know this, but I have learned never to doubt a dragon no matter how small or large they are, or even how young and confusing. Dragons have the ability to inherit their knowledge from their parent. So I have had my people watch you and they have given me good reports about you. Of course, the most positive ones were from my warriors so I have taken them in stride. Over all I am impressed with what you have done."

"I am pleased you are impressed."

"Do not mock me human. I said I was impressed with what you have done. I am not happy that you are going to leave the humans here to die"

"Why do you say they will die? What do you know?"

"I know many things and what I know about them dying I cannot tell you or any human. What I can say is you have it in your power to save them."

"I have done all I can. I have helped them reclaim their home. They are happy and their King is sending men to take the prisoners. So how can I save them?"

"You can take them to your world."

Rae looked down at her and then around the cavern trying to see if there was a way he could run without fighting them. There was no way out.

"I cannot take them to my world. To go there they have to get permission from the council and Lord Nogar."

"I do not mean that world. I mean *your* world, the one *you* came from. I believe it is the one these humans were meant to be on. They came here in ships that flew between the stars. Your people did the same. They could be the ones that were lost. You could find out when you return to your world and if they are, you can come and take them home."

"I still don't know if I could do that. To take them there they would have to travel through the mirror and that would require the council's approval. I..."

"You could have the blue people send a ship for them."

Rae stopped talking and stood there looking down at the Queen. His mind spun with what she knew and how she treated it like nothing out of the ordinary.

<"How could she know about the Thorns and their ships? Oh yeah, the little dragon and its mind reading trick. I am going to have a talk with it when I get back.">

"One does not just walk up and ask the Thorns to use or borrow their ships. They are very protective of them. Very few people have even been on them, let alone travel in them. I have seen them but never been in one. I would not know who to ask."

"You could ask the one called U-rick."

"How do... Never mind. You got it from the little dragon reading my mind. I did not know it could do that. If I had, I would have taken precautions. Ok. I do not know what I can or cannot do but I give you my word that if I find out the humans here on this world are the lost ones

94

from my world, I will do what I can to get them moved to my world. I do not know how but..."

"That is all I ask of you. You have given your word and I except it. Please except this as a thank you for the help you have given us."

Queen Baelia held out her hand and a young woman came forward and handed her a small cloth. The Queen held her hand up toward Rae. Slowly he placed his hand near and a little over the edge of where she stood. The Queen walked forward and dropped the cloth over his finger, when it touched his flesh it began to grow. Within seconds it was a long piece of cloth about eighteen inches long. The Queen stepped back and looked at Rae.

"It is very soft. I do not believe I have ever felt anything like it."

"I can understand why. It is material known only to the fairy folk. You should wear it around your neck like a scarf. It will keep you warm."

The Queen stood there smiling.

"Warm? That might be nice if I was cold. How about if I just put it in my pocket?"

"No, you must wear it. If not around your neck then anywhere as long as it touches your flesh."

"I will wear it around my neck. Now if your Majesty is done with me I should be leaving. I do not want to take up anymore of your time."

"Yes, you may leave. One more thing, the human King's men will be here tomorrow. You should leave once they have taken the prisoners and left. It will be easier on Alora."

"How do you know about Alora? Sorry I forgot, mind reading dragon telling you all about me. Thank you for the gift."

Rae gave a slight bow and then wrapped the cloth around his neck. The Queen clapped her hands and the fairies began disappearing. Within seconds the cave was empty except for him, the Queen, and the four guards and her lady-in-waiting.

"I will be waiting to hear from you. Have a safe journey."

The Queen turned and the young woman picked up the train of her dress and followed her. The guards, with spears in hand, were a few steps behind. Rae stood there a few seconds longer.

"I have met the little people and they have given me a task. Jym will laugh when I tell him this story. They may not be his little people, but they are little people."

Rae turned and walked back down the tunnel. When he reached the exit, the humans were gone and the fire was out. The sun was rising over the edge of the mountain. Standing there, Rae looked around and saw people working in the fields.

"How long was I in there? I really don't like this magic stuff."

Rae headed to the tree he had claimed as his. When he was a few feet away he heard cheers. Turning, he saw a group of soldiers on the road heading toward the castle. The farmers came to the roadside to cheer for them.

<"The King's men are here, might as well head in. Marcel might want me there. They look very clean for having traveled so far. The way they are riding and marching down the road they act like they are in a parade.">

Rae walked over to where the little dragon was laying. It was still curled up under the tree. When Rae stopped it looked up at him, slowly it stood, stretched, and yawned, then walked to Rae's feet and sat looking up. Rae reached down, picked it up, and held it up so he could look into it eyes.

"So you can read minds and talk to the fairies. That is nice to know. You, my little friend, need to stay out of my head. What is in my head is only for me to know. So stop telling fairies what you see there."

It made some sounds like little bells. Rae placed the dragon in his satchel and headed for the tunnel that would take him to the castle. As he neared the door, it opened. Nakobee and Buddy came out. Buddy walked straight to him.

"You not here last night, little dragon was sleeping by tree. It was not worried so I waited, then little dragon went hunting."

"It went hunting? How do you know it went hunting?"

"It came back with its kill and ate it next to me. It was very disrupting. It did not smell good. It did not seem worried you were not there so I went back inside. Where were you?"

"I met with Queen Baelia, the queen of the fairies. We should go inside. The King's soldiers are here. Marcel might want us there."

Rae walked through the door with Nakobee and Buddy following. It did not take them long to reach the secret door that opened behind a tapestry in the hallway. Once in the hallway they went around one corner and down the hallway before they reached the doors to the king's meeting room.

Chapter Nine

Rae, Nakobee, and Buddy entered the chamber by one of the side doors. It was the third time Rae had been there. The room was massive; it was fifty feet wide, the ceiling was twenty-five feet high, and it was a hundred steps from the two large doors to the steps leading to the throne. The room was an ancient cavern and it was not cold. They were told it stayed warm like all the rooms in the mountain because of the lava that flowed inside the mountain.

All along the walls were huge tapestries. They were woven pictures telling many stories. About how the people came to this world, how once on a different continent they were a very powerful nation. The war, many years in the past, killed many of them and caused them to flee for their lives. It told how this group of humans escaped and came here to live. The tapestries were not only very beautiful, but were very intriguing.

Rae and the others walked over to a few men who were standing off to the side waiting.

Marcel was sitting on his throne dressed in his finest robes, a small crown laden with a small fortune in gems sat on his head. The council was sitting in their chairs two steps below, three on one side and two on the other. They had not replaced the council member who was killed by the priest.

Marcel's men were lined up along the walls. They all had weapons drawn and stood at attention. The big doors opened and a group of men dressed in fine military clothes entered and marched straight to Marcel.

"Welcome, Commander Demister. It is good to see the King's men. I trust your journey here was not too bothersome. Did you have a nice trip? I heard you stopped by the river yesterday afternoon to rest and clean up. How was the water? I suppose you were not in a hurry to get here. I see that you are all clean and refreshed."

One of the men stepped forward, took off his helmet, and without even a hint of a bow started speaking.

"Duke Marcel, the King sends his greetings and that he is sorry it took so long for us to come to your rescue. He hopes..."

"He hopes nothing." Marcel's voice was venomous. "He was hoping we were all dead and he could take over this land. Well, he will never have it. As you can see we did not need your King's help. We are good citizens and have captured his enemies for him. You can stay the night and in the morning you, your men, and the stinking prisoners will leave. I see by your faces you are upset with me. Is it by chance that you were promised this land as yours if by some small chance of fate I was dead? Do not even try and deny it. I do not care to hear it. You and your men are excused. You will be shown where you will stay. Food will be brought to your men. You and a few of your officers may attend the banquet tonight. It is in honor of your arrival and taking the prisoners away. One more thing: For your men's sake, inform them not to leave the compound. We would not want anything to happen to them. My men are still rounding up a few stragglers. You are dismissed."

The man stood there, his jaw working. He started to speak but Captain Jones walked up to him.

"If you would please follow me, I will take you and your men to your quarters. You will be very comfortable. You will be staying in the compound at the base of the castle."

The man put his helmet on, turned, and followed Captain Jones. His men marched out right behind him.

Rae, Nakobee, and Buddy walked over to stand in front of Marcel. When the soldiers were gone and the doors shut the cheers rang out from the council and the soldiers along the walls. Marcel slapped his hands on the arms of his throne and stood taking the four steps down to stand on the floor near Rae and the others.

"I have wanted to say that for so long. How I despise that man. I should have known the King would send him and his goons."

Rae looked at the council members then back at Marcel.

"Marcel, have I missed something? I was under the impression you were looking forward to the arrival of these men?"

"Oh, I was. We have wanted to show these buffoons we did not need them for a long time."

"I hate to say it, but you did need them. If Shaméd had not left me here to help do you think you and your men could have retaken you homes?"

Marcel looked at Rae. Everyone stopped talking and looked at them. Commander Pike walked over to Rae.

"I do not think you should be talking that way to Duke Marcel. We could have taken our home back without your help. After all, we did most of the fighting."

"Yes, I suppose you could have taken it back on your own. It would have taken you two to maybe five years. Your people were hiding. You did nothing. If it had not been for Buddy's people you would still be trying."

Commander Pike was about to respond but Marcel spoke.

"Commander Pike apologize to Rae. He is, or I hope will be, the new Duke, and your new leader of this land. Rae, we did not mean anything bad. It is just we have had a lot of bad dealings with that man and his king. Three times Commander Demister has tried to have me removed. He owns the land to the west of here - all the way to the ocean. This place and fifty thousand acres of land around this mountain belongs to us. It is what separates him from the main kingdom. His father and mine were bitter enemies. My mother was supposed to be married to his father. My mother was the daughter of a duke in the land north of here. The king at that time told her she would marry Duke Demister. My mother did not love him. She didn't even like him. She was in love with my father. She ran away, came here, and married my father. Now you know some of our past. That is enough of this talking of ancient history. Let's get things ready for the party tonight in honor of all we have done."

Marcel walked toward the side door on the opposite side of the room from where Rae had entered. It opened up to a hallway that would take Marcel to his chambers. Commander Pike turned, snapped his fingers and his soldiers snapped to attention. After the council walked out of the chamber, they followed. Rae, Nakobee, and Buddy stood there alone in the room.

"This place is crazy. Come on; let's go to our own rooms. I need to rest. I have been up all night and suddenly I am very tired."

Rae went to his room. His hand covered the amulet and everything went blank.

They were sitting in the banquet room. This room was twice as large as the King's meeting room. It was where all the people of the land could come together for large meetings and celebrations. From what Rae and Nakobee had heard there were many occasions where the room was used.

The news of the fight between Commander Demister's men, Captain Jones and ten of his men, came during the party. Commander Demister and six of his men were sitting at a table eating. They were six tables away from Duke Marcel and the council members. The door opened and a man hurried over to Marcel and whispered in his ear. Marcel stood, looked over at Rae, who was sitting at his table next to Alora. Nakobee sat on her other side. A servant hit a chime and the room went quiet.

"Commander Demister, it seems some of your men did not want to stay inside the compound. There has been a commotion between my men and yours. If you would be so kind as to come with me, we can get things straightened out. Rae, would you and Nakobee please accompany me?"

Rae and Nakobee stood and followed Marcel. Alora stood with Rae and was about to follow when Duke Marcel stopped her.

"No, my dear, you must stay here and entertain our guests. We will not be long."

Alora started to speak, but instead she curtsied and sat back down.

Commander Demister and his men stood and followed Duke Marcel out of the room. In the hallway Commander Demister walked up beside Duke Marcel.

"Can you tell me what happened?"

"I would if I knew. I was told that some of my men found some of your men in the tunnels. When they were told to leave, there was a fight. We can find out together what happened and why your men were down in the tunnels. Unless you know why your men were sneaking about?"

"I assure you if my men were sneaking in the tunnels they were doing so without my knowledge or permission."

"I am glad to hear that. By the way, you have not been formerly introduced to my friends here. That rather large man is Nakobee. This is Rae, he is engaged to my daughter."

Commander Demister barely looked at Nakobee but openly glared at Rae before turning away. No one talked again until they reached the courtyard.

Entering the courtyard, the breeze from the night air caught them by surprise. It was warm. Fifteen of Commander Demister's men were on the far side of the yard sitting on the ground next to the wall. Twenty feet away along the left wall were ten of Duke Marcel's men. They were also sitting on the ground. Captain Jones, with twenty of his soldiers stood in the middle of the yard, facing both groups of men with their weapons drawn. Captain Jones put his sword away and saluted as Duke Marcel walked up.

Duke Marcel and his group stopped a few feet away.

"Captain Jones, I will hear from you first. Commander Demister we will hear from your men afterward."

Commander Demister moved alongside of Marcel.

"I would like to go and talk with my men."

"That will not happen. You and those with you will stay here with us. We will all hear the stories together and at the same time. It will make sure there are no misunderstandings. Now, Captain Jones, please explain what happened."

"Sir, my men were on patrol in the tunnels south of here. They encountered Commander Demister's men and ordered them to return to their barracks. Words exchanged and the fight started. From what I can gather, Sergeant Tucker threw the first punch. Word was sent to me that there was a fight. I, along with these men, came and after some persuasion, stopped the fight."

"Did they tell you why they were in the tunnels? Or why they would not return?"

"No sir. After we arrived and stopped the fight they all went mute."

Duke Marcel looked over at the Commander.

"Commander Demister, you say you do not know why your men were out of the buildings and sneaking down in tunnels."

"I give you my word I do not know why they left the building. Those men are new to my company. They joined two months ago."

"I did not think you were the type to bring new recruits with you on a mission like this."

"I would not have. These men were sent to me from King Becker. He said they were a gift to my family from his. They are soldiers with special training."

"What type of training? Spying?"

"I was told they were highly trained professionals. They were to train my men in hand-to-hand and war tactics."

"Well, it seems they are not so good at their job. Fifteen of them against ten of my men? Maybe they would have stood a better chance if only five of my men had caught them."

"I am impressed with your men. I have seen those men fight and none of my men can stand against them."

Duke Marcel smiled. Turning he looked at Nakobee.

"Nakobee, it seems all that training you gave my men was indeed more valuable than I thought. Commander Demister, Nakobee here is probably the best fighter in the world. He has spent the last three months teaching my men how to fight without weapons. He and Rae have also taught them some tricks with the sword. My men have learned ways to kill and fight with their weapons that would scare you. I know, because it did me when I saw them learning. Ok. Let's go talk to your, or I should say, King Becker's men?"

Duke Marcel's group turned and walked to the King's men. They stopped ten feet away. Commander Demister glared at them.

"Lieutenant, come here and explain what you were doing disobeying my orders."

A big man stood and staggered over. He stopped three feet in front of them. He was bleeding from several cuts, his uniform looked like he had been in a war, not a brawl. The man looked at the Commander then the others. When he saw Duke Marcel, recognition flashed in his eyes. He began to straighten up his tattered uniform. Brushing his hair back out of his face, he slapped his chest, then he bent down to straighten and dust off his left pant leg, then his right. He shot up, lunging at Duke Marcel, a knife in his hand. He never made it.

Rae saw the man's eyes, the pretention of cleaning his uniform, the hand pulling something from his boot. As the man came up, Rae stepped in front of Marcel. Nakobee reacted to Rae's movement, grabbed Marcel, and picked him up. He turned his back to the assailant and moved away.

Rae's left hand reached out, wrapping around the Lieutenant's wrist. He twisted and pulled the knife and the man to the right. Rae's right leg shot out, his foot connected to the Lieutenant's knee. The man yelped in pain from the kick. He went silent with shock when Rae drove his own knife deep into his chest. He fell to the ground dead.

The soldiers jumped up and started to rush forward. They stopped when Captain Jones and his men ran up. Those that did not stop in time ran into the soldier's swords.

"Do not move. All of you back against the wall now, or die like your leader?"

The men moved back. Captain Jones' men stood there. Captain Jones turned and looked back at Duke Marcel. Nakobee was beside him, about five feet from the others. Rae wiped his blade off and put it away then stood over the dead man.

"Once again you have disobeyed orders."

Rae looked at Captain Jones as he came closer.

"I do not understand what you mean. I have not disobeyed any orders."

"Were you not in the banquet hall eating?"

"Yes, we all were there."

"Then you disobeyed orders. You were the one that made the rule."

"What rule would that be?"

"Rule number three. It is the one where only guards are allowed to have weapons in the presence of the Duke.

No one who enters the banquet hall, the throne room, or any room where the Duke is, can carry or have a weapon."

"Of course I know that rule. Like you said, I was the one that made the rules. So again how did I disobey it?"

"You are carrying a weapon. You used it to kill that man. Therefore you disobeyed the rule."

"Now there you are mistaken. The rule clearly states that only the guards can carry a weapon. Did I not just guard the Duke? Since I did, then it must mean I was on guard duty. See? No rules were broken."

Captain Jones smiled and shook his head.

"You are complex. You give us these rules to live and die by. Rules that you said would make us all safer and more disciplined. Yet, you keep twisting them to fit whatever you are doing."

"Twisting is such a twisted word. I like to think I am teaching you how to interpret the rules."

Commander Demister stood there as the event played out. As Rae and Captain Jones were talking, he finally realized what had happened. He saw Duke Marcel a few feet away, the dark man standing next to him. His own men had moved away from him during the incident. He was the only one still in the same location.

"What is going on? How did you do that? I want to know what is going on. Why did the Lieutenant just try to kill me?"

Rae and Captain Jones both turned to look at the Commander. They walked over to him.

"He was not trying to kill you. He was trying to kill Duke Marcel. It would seem since you said you know nothing about this, your King Becker was trying to remove what he considers an obstacle. If the Duke was killed you would be given this land. The King would then be able to take more of its resources. You, Commander have been played. You should take a deeper look at all King Becker has given you. You might find someone waiting in the wings to take *your* place."

Rae turned away and faced Captain Jones.

"You should make sure those men don't have any weapons. Do a strip search, then lock them up."

Rae faced the Commander again.

"It would seem you will have more prisoners than anticipated. You should be safe, though. The men you left at your camp by the river are all men loyal to you and your family right?"

Commander Demister stood there. His men slowly moved closer as Duke Marcel and Nakobee walked over.

"I am sure the men he brought with him are loyal. Commander, you may go with Captain Jones and his men. You might be able to get some information out of them. As for me, I do not care. They are now your problem. Shall we go back to the party?"

Duke Marcel started walking away, Nakobee by his side. Rae nodded good-bye to Captain Jones and followed. Commander Demister looked at his three men, made a grunting sound and turned to face Captain Jones.

"I would very much like the chance to interrogate these men. We will come with you."

Captain Jones called out to his men.

"Ok, men let's search these prisoners. You men start stripping your clothes off."

Duke Marcel entered the castle. When they were out of site he fell against the wall. Nakobee grabbed him.

"Are you all right?"

Marcel was visibly shaken.

"No, I am not. I am shaking and scared out of my mind. I almost died out there. If it had not been for you and Rae, I could very well be the one lying out there spilling my blood."

"You did not show any fear out there. You handled yourself very bravely."

"I was too scared and too proud to show what was going on inside. Again, thank you both for what you did. Give me a minute to calm down, and then we can get back to the party. I know I need a drink. Rae, how did you know what that man was going to do?"

They were both looking at him. He shrugged.

"I saw his eyes when he looked at you. Then I heard in my mind, "He is going to kill Marcus." I started forward and when I saw the knife I just reacted."

"Well, I for one am glad you hear voices. Ok, I am ready. Let's return to the party."

Marcus walked ahead. Entering the banquet hall, they saw the party still going on. Some of the people looked up and cheered at them as they passed. Five hours later Rae and Nakobee left the party heading for their room to get some much needed sleep.

Chapter Ten

In the morning Commander Demister and his men left, taking all the prisoners with them. Rae woke to the sound of bells and chirping - it was the little dragon. She was sitting on the bed with her head leaning on Rae's. Her mouth was next to Rae's right ear - the sounds were coming from her.

Once again his sleep had been filled with strange dreams. There were flashes of pictures in his mind of soldiers lining up on the road. He and a group of others were walking between them.

Opening his eyes, he looked at the little dragon. He patted her head, picked her up, and rolled his legs off the side of the bed.

"Ok, I am up. Were you in my mind again? I told you to stop it."

"Brrell chip brral sissh brre ell."

"I do not understand what you are saying. Wait until we meet up with Shaméd. You can talk to him and his dragon. Maybe you can even talk with Nogar. Come on, let's go eat and make plans for leaving here."

Rae reached over and picked up his amulet and placed it around his neck. After getting dressed he went into the other room where Nakobee was exercising.

"You really know how to make me feel lazy. Are you ready to eat? Bella is."

Nakobee stopped. He sat on the floor. He saw Rae holding the little dragon close to his body curled up in his left arm.

"You have named the little one Bella? That is good. I am sure she was not happy with the other names you were calling her."

"Bella? Oh yeah, Bella. I guess that is her name. It fits. She is always making those little bell sounds."

"I am ready. Are we leaving today? Or do you wish to say a little longer?"

"We can leave tomorrow. Commander Demister and his men are leaving today. We can pack and get ready and leave at first light tomorrow."

"I will tell Buddy. He has been worrying we would sneak away and not tell him."

"Why would he think that?"

"Because when Marcel informed us he was going to give us a going away party, you mentioned it. You said we should just sneak away at least a half dozen times."

"I only said that because we do not need a party. Maybe leaving tonight would be a good idea. We can ride a few hours then rest when the sun comes up and take our time going back. We still have two months before we have to be at Na-Car."

"We have to get there by ship. I have checked the maps. It will take us three weeks to walk to Coastal City. It will be two, maybe less if we ride. From there we book passage on a ship. I was told by the bookkeeper in the library there is no ship that goes straight to Na-Car. We will have to catch another one. He said we will have about three or four weeks of traveling by ship."

"When did you find this out? And why did you not tell me earlier? We will definitely have to leave tomorrow if we are going to make it on time. Three maybe four weeks on board a ship? I dislike traveling by ship - too confining. I like to be able to move around."

"You will be able to move around on a ship. We will make sure it is a large one so you can walk around the deck. Besides you will be busy training. You have been slacking off the last two weeks. You need to keep your sword arm in shape."

"In shape? Nakobee, did Shaméd tell you to torture me? You have been on me to work on my sword and fighting skills ever since we came here. You know we are no longer at school. We can relax and take it easy."

"In our profession we can never relax. You know very well you have to be ready for anything, at anytime. You taught me that. Remember on my homeworld? You did not relax and it saved our lives."

"I did not relax because I do not ever relax in a new place. As for saving our lives, I was just out wandering around in the middle of night."

"Yes, and you saw the enemy slithering up the mountain toward us. If you had not sounded the alarm we might have lost a lot of men. Instead, they lost. Now let's go eat. My stomach is making noise. It sounds almost like Jon's."

Rae started laughing. As he opened the door Buddy came walking in.

"Thank you for opening the door. How did you know I was there? You have told me I am too quiet. Was I noisier today?"

Buddy stood in the doorway looking at Rae, then over at Nakobee.

"I did not know you were there. We were just leaving to go eat. Come with us and you can tell us why you are here."

Buddy turned around and stepped back in the hallway and Rae followed. Nakobee shut the door and caught up to them. Buddy started talking.

"I am here to inform you that my sister is going to marry. The one that turned her down has changed his mind. He sent presents and a messenger to my father asking for her to be his."

"That is very good news. Nakobee and I both are very happy for her and your family."

"It is good news. Did you go talk with him? My father thinks you did. We do not know how you could have found out who or where he was but he still thinks you..."

"I had nothing to do with his changing his mind. I do not know who or where he lives."

"Breeree sissheing berre it rose."

Bella's head was up, she was looking at Rae.

"We are going to get food. Relax we will be there soon. If you are that hungry why not do your disappearing thing and meet us there."

"sihsshi breeee eerd"

"I still do not understand. We need to walk faster I think she is hungry."

"She is not hungry. She is saying something about Rose."

"Ok, now you are going to tell me you understand dragon speech."

Buddy jerked his head around a few times before looking at Rae.

"Only a little, she has been coming to me and making those noises. She brought a little fairy person with her a few times. Some of her noises are words that I understand from you. I think she is saying she went and talked to the one that asked to marry Rose."

"Breeee treep shreurr"

<A picture of one of Buddy's people sitting on a rock next to a fairy appeared in Rae's mind. The picture disappeared.>

"I think you are right. Bella here must have read my mind and knew I was not happy about the bu… I mean the one who refused to marry Rose. She must have gotten one of the fairies to go with her to convince him to change his mind."

"Now that is fascinating. You have your own little persuader. Just think how handy she will be."

Rae shot a dirty look at Nakobee.

"I do not need a persuader. I can do my own persuading."

"I am just saying it could be handy."

Buddy watched as the two walked down the hallways laughing. When they reached the food hall, the room was almost empty. After getting their food they found a table near the wall.

Alora came walking in as they sat. She grabbed a plate of food and came over. She sat across from Rae.

"I know you will be leaving tomorrow. I have made arrangements for three horses for you. When you get to Coastal City give this note to the proprietor of the stables. He will take care of them until they can be returned."

"Which stables?"

"There is only one. It is called the "hole. It is outside the city near the main gate. You won't miss it."

"That is very nice of you, but you do not need to give us horses - we can walk. We would just need some supplies."

Nakobee took another bite of his food after speaking. Rae looked at him then Alora.

"Of course, we will be happy to borrow them."

112

"It is not borrowing. They are three of your horses. The others will be here if and when you ever need them."

It got quiet. Nakobee kept eating, but Buddy sat at the end of the table watching Rae and Alora. Bella was on the table eating.

"Is there anger between you two? Your bodies seem to be going tight like when Rae is getting ready to fight."

Rae took a drink before looking at Buddy.

"We are not angry. Thank you again for arranging for the animals, Alora. I was going to ask you and Marcel if we could borrow some. According to Nakobee the trip by land was going to take three or four weeks and just as long by ship. We have eight weeks to reach Na-Car to meet with Shaméd."

"Then I did you a favor. Father still wants to give you a party. I told him you were leaving in the morning. He is making arrangements for the party tonight. Of course, you will both attend. It would be very rude if you did not."

Rae smiled and pushed his plate away.

"Of course we will attend. We both think giving us a party is unnecessary, but if it is what Marcel wants then we will let him."

"It is what the people want. You helped us get our home back. We lost over half of our people before Shaméd and you came here. It was a blessing from the Holy Three that you stayed. You and Lord Shaméd helped my father turn his life around. Do you know he has not been drunk since we returned? He has a drink but he sips at it. I have even seen him refuse ale. I watched Lord Shaméd put a powder in my father's drink during our first day together. He said it was to help him get sober. I believe it did more than that. He is more like he was when I was a little girl, full of life and energy. But, I have taken up too much of your time, and I have things to do. I will see you tonight at the party."

Alora stood picked up her half empty plate and cup and walked away.

"You know you are really thick. That girl loves you. I do not know why, but I see it in her eyes. You should stay here, marry her, and start a family. Shaméd would understand."

Rae emptied his drink and picked up the last of the meat on his plate, wrapped it in bread, and looked at Nakobee.

"I have already told you I do not want to get married. Shaméd did not tell me to stay and help these people then marry Alora. He said help them then meet him at Na-Car. That is what I am going to do."

"You have feelings for Alora. After we meet up with Shaméd, we both can talk with him."

Nakobee finished his food and sat there. Rae took a bite of the wrapped food in his hand. Buddy's head was twitching back and forth. Bella swallowed down the last of the meat on her plate. She sat up and looked at Rae.

<Pictures of men and women in a large room, soldiers standing along walls, and then he saw himself sitting on a large throne.> Rae shook his head and dropped his food.

"Ok, let's stop talking about me getting married. I want to get packed so we can leave as soon as we can."

Nakobee reached over, picked up Rae's empty plate, and stacked them onto his.

"We are already packed - we never unpacked. Why don't the three, I mean the four of us, go to the bathhouse and relax in the hot water. It will help. I give you my word I will not talk to you anymore about you getting married. At least until we reach Shaméd."

"Good, and relaxing in the hot baths sounds like a very good idea."

Rae stood and looked at Buddy.

"Buddy, you coming with us?"

"I do not understand the need for you humans to get in water heated by the fire in the mountains. Cleaning your body I understand, but getting in hot water. It is like watching you cook your food. It is very disturbing. I must leave. I myself have things to do - to make arrangements for my sister marriage. I will of course be here tonight to say my farewells to the three of you."

"Three? Oh yeah, Bella. Ok, we will see you later."

Buddy stood, unfolding his body, turned and left the room. Rae picked up Bella and placed her inside his satchel. Nakobee returned their plates to be cleaned. Captain Jones passed them in the hallway on their way to the bathhouse.

"You both are going to be at the party tonight, right? I know how much you wanted to leave. It will do the people good to show you how much they appreciate what you both have done."

"Yes, we will be there."

"That is good. I have something for you both. I have to go but I will see you both tonight."

Captain Jones walked away. Rae and Nakobee continued.

"That man is very honorable. He should be the commander, not that Pike person."

"Someday Captain Jones will get what he deserves. He treats his men well and they all respect him."

Entering the bathhouse, they walked over and took two large bath towels, then walked over to a bench. Rae removed his amulet and laid it on the bench with his shirt.

The picture and sound fades.

The scenery blurs, fading from black to a clear picture of the hallway. Rae and Nakobee were entering the banquet room. It was full of people - food and drink was everywhere. There were sections set apart for each class. The farmers were along one wall, they took up four tables.

Next to them were ranchers who also had four tables. On the other side of the hall were the mining and smith's guild. All the guilds were here. Each guild had four tables to show they were all equal.

"Looks like the party has already started. You would think they would have waited for the guests of honor."

"I am glad they did not. These people like to party and after all they went through the last year, I they deserve it."

Rae and Nakobee headed for the table where Duke Marcel and Alora where sitting. As they passed people, they were told how much they were appreciated and would be missed. When they walked up to the table, Duke Marcel stood.

"Welcome to your party. I know you both will be leaving in the morning and knowing you, Rae, you will not stay to the end. Everything is ready for the both of you. You should not want for food or drink on your trip. Of course, drink has never been your problem. I would very much like to have one of those flasks you and Lord Shaméd carry."

"When we get back, I will ask Lord Shaméd if we can make one a gift to you. They are a controlled item and I would give you mine but it would only stay with you for a couple of days before returning to our world."

"Yes, that is another thing I find fascinating. You told us if you lose your equipment it will return to your home in forty-eight hours. That is very powerful magic."

"I call it science. I have always felt magic is just a word people use to describe something they do not understand. On Nogar's world there are wonders that would amaze you. Most, if not all, can be explained through science."

"Rae, you sit here to my right next to the Commander."

Rae sat and reached over to get the tankard and took a drink. It was wine. These people made the best wine; not too sweet and not too dry. It was almost like the fruit drink Shaméd liked. Nakobee pulled out the chair next to Alora.

"You amaze me by your words. Talking about science like it is an every day occurrence. I pictured you as the type to play up magic, something to make yourself seem more powerful and aloof."

Rae looked at Commander Pike. Setting the tankard down, Rae answered.

"What you think of me is unimportant. I have nothing to prove to you, or to anyone. To me you are no more important than the man who cleans out the stables. Well, that was poor comparison. I believe the stable man is more important."

Commander Pike jumped up knocking his chair over. His hand went to his side where his sword should have been. Standing there, he realized everyone was staring at him. The people at the table nearby had heard the words between them. Everyone knew the Commander did not like Rae or Nakobee. Most, if not all, knew the Commander had his eye on Alora for his wife.

"Since you are leaving, and for all the help you have given to our people, I will not take offence to your words and challenge you. I understand you are just a commoner and not used to being around those who are your superiors."

Rae started laughing. Nakobee shifted in his chair so he would be in a better position to grab Rae if he decided to react. The room slowly became quite. Whispers were traveling throughout the crowd about what was happening.

Rae slowly got his laughter under control. Taking a long drink, he sat the tankard down and stood. He looked over at Nakobee.

"It is ok."

Rae looked at Alora; he saw the fear in her eyes. Marcel sat there looking very noble. They had talked about Commander Pike and his arrogant behavior. Marcel would have never promoted him to Commander if there had been any other to take his place.

Placing his hand on Alora's shoulder, Rae looked at Commander Pike. The Commander was trying not to show fear. It was not working.

"You do not know my family or anything about me. You only know, or at least I hope your little brain knows, if we were to fight you would die. You are one of the most arrogant, self-centered, pompous men I have ever met. You are in your position because of your family. You should sit back and think about what you have, and what all of these people have made here in this land. Alora and Duke Marcel are very lucky to have such people. I have never met such wonderful people as you have here. They are happy despite the great loss of family and friends. These people love life and each other. They have built a family that encompasses everyone, human and nonhuman. If I thought it would benefit these people, you would have been dead long ago. My hope for you and everyone here is one day you will grow up and see what you have here."

Rae looked about at the room, then over at Marcel.

"I am sorry if I have spoken out of place and if I have ruined the party."

Marcel stood. He was smiling as he faced the crowd and threw his arms out.

"People, now is as good of time as any to make the announcement. I was going to make it later but it seems more appropriate to make it now. I have made my choice on who will marry my daughter, Alora. I have told the council my choice and they all have agreed. When the time comes, Alora and Rae will be wed. Rae will become the next duke of our land. I hope you all will give him the same love and respect you have given me. Alora, Rae would either of you like to take this time to say anything to the people?"

Rae slowly removed his hand from Alora. He knew Marcel wanted him to marry Alora; they had all talked about it. He was hoping that Alora had spoken with him and explained that he could not stay here and marry her.

Alora saw that Rae was not going to speak, so she stood.

"Father, Rae, and I have talked and we both agree he must leave. He has to return to Lord Shaméd. Once that is done, he has given me his word that he will return and if he can marry me, he will. If for some reason he cannot, then he will explain to all of us why."

Marcel looked at Rae then Alora.

"Oh. I was not aware of this decision. I knew they were returning to Lord Shaméd."

Turning Marcel faced the crowd.

"That still does not change my mind. I have given Rae my blessing to marry my daughter. When he returns it will be a happy occasion. Now let's all celebrate what we have and hope and pray for a safe and fast return for both Rae and Nakobee."

Cheers rang out, the music started up and people began to dance and sing. Rae held Alora's chair so she could sit, then he sat. Nakobee stood there. Commander Pike looked around. He looked at Captain Jones and his men. There were ten men - three officers beside Captain Jones and seven enlisted. None of them looked at Commander Pike. He pulled on his coat and walked away, leaving the room.

"Well, I told everyone I would wait for you. You will not keep me waiting for very long will you?"

Rae looked at Alora, his hand covered the amulet the picture and sound went blank.

Shaméd removed the amulet and handed it back to Rae, and placed the box back in his satchel.

"That was very interesting. Now will you tell me how you were able to stop the transmission of the amulet?"

Rae looked at Shaméd.

"You really do not know how?"

"I would not ask if I did."

"You have not ever looked into my mind to see how I do it?"

"Contrary to what you might think, I do not like to look into or read other people's minds. Some minds can be very disturbing. It has taken me many years to learn how to shut most, if not all, the voices out of my head. So, I do not willingly just look into other minds. So to answer your question, no I have not."

"Oh, I was sure you knew how I did it since you took the training long before me."

"What training?"

"All the training. You must just not have caught the understanding! I find it hard to believe. You know about the Thorns' material. Like how no one is ever to have any of it. I did not understand why until I heard in one of the classes that it stopped all radiation and it was totally impregnable to any known sound, heat, or energy. That is why they use it for underwater exploration and out in space. It is the perfect material. It is light, strong, and protects the wearer in any environment. Anyway, I found a small piece one day and I wrapped the amulet in it. Five hours later I removed it. Then, I talked with Jon. I had him show me the ten hour mission I was on. He checked and it showed the first three hours, then it went blank, and then it started again, only showing the last two hours of my mission. He kept going over to see what was wrong. He blamed the amulet. I never told him."

Shaméd sat there looking at Rae and Nakobee.

"Ok. That is how you stopped yours. How did you stop Nakobee's?"

"For someone as smart as you are, I thought you would have figured that out. You gave him a shirt."

"Yes. To protect him when he is off-world."

"The shirt has an opening in front exposing the amulet."

Shaméd looked at Nakobee, the shirt was blue, and yes there was a v shaped cut in front where it exposed the amulet burned into Nakobee's chest.

"You had him put the shirt on backwards. That is how you blocked his signal. That is fascinating. When we get back we will inform the Thorns about this."

"Are you crazy? They will take back our shirts. They have to know it blocks the signals. Why else would they not let everyone have them? Let's just not tell anyone, it can be our secret."

Shaméd grinned.

"You have kept your secret for this long. I suppose we can keep it longer. Now, about your mission, I am glad it all worked out. You will be happy to know Loorn is free of the evil power. He is recuperating, and he has been united with his family. We have a lot to do here on this world and I need to talk with you about your homeworld."

"Yes. My homeworld. What about it? Has the council changed their minds about helping them? If they have not, then I need to return and try to figure out how I can help."

Chapter Eleven

"I am glad you feel that way about returning to your world. That makes what I have to tell you a little easier. The King on your world is dying; there is no legal heir. There is a power struggle going on to see who will take over. On your behalf, Nogar has gone before the council.

They made a decision dealing with your world. They have decided you will become the next king.

Before you say anything, you know very well you have a legitimate claim to the throne. I think we can make you king with vary little trouble. I see the look in your eyes and the answer is no. I did not tell anyone about your secret. I was not even told of this decision until just before I came here. It seems someone much bigger than I found out a long time ago. They thought it best for you and your world. Your training was changed a few weeks after your arrival. This someone wanted to make sure you would be ready for this day."

Rae sat there looking at Shaméd. He caught Nakobee move out of the corner of his eye. Rae looked at him, Nakobee leaned back grinning.

"It would seem you are destined to be placed into a position of power, if not a duke then king. Your days of roaming from place to place appear to be over. With any luck you will get married, have half dozen children, and watch them grow and then get to play with your grandchildren."

Rae's eyes narrowed - he was about to reply when there was movement on the bed. Shaméd turned to see what it was. Rae looked back at Shaméd, as did Nakobee.

The blanket moved more again, Shaméd saw what could only be a baby dragnet crawling out from under it. Across each shoulder were long bumps; there were no wings. It was about twelve inches long from its nose to the tip of its tail. It looked up at Shaméd tilting its head. Shaméd heard a blast of words; she looked over at Rae before walking to the end of the bed. She sat there on it haunches looking around, then curled up and closed it eyes.

"I assume this is the little dragon you saved?"

Shaméd stood there looking at the two of them. Nakobee leaned back and pointed at Rae. Rae moved his chair to face Shaméd and the bed.

"Yes I suppose she belongs to me. I have not been able to get rid of it, I mean her."

"You have had her for over six months and this is as big as she has gotten? Have you fed her? Does she have a name? And have you been able to communicate with her?"

"At first she answered to here kitty and here stupid, but she reacts faster when I call her Bella. As for communicating with her, I sometimes see images. A few times, I thought I heard a voice, but could not make out the words. I started calling her Bella because I heard bells whenever I thought of her. I do not believe she is mentally all there. She does the strangest things, and as you can see, she is deformed. She cannot fly, and as for walking, she can barely do that. I have tried to leave her in the woods twice and both times, she found me. If I do not pick her up, she will blink onto my shoulder or into my satchel and ride there. Since she returned to me that first night, I have not been without her for more than a few hours. She only weights a couple of pounds. I do not think she will ever get any bigger. As for eating, when she is hungry she will eat. I have seen her attack and kill an animal twice her size, and she ate all of it. When I am eating and she wants some of it she sits there looking at me until I give in and give her something. Consequently, I thought I would bring her to you and Nogar to see if you can help me with her. I think it is the least you can do after you trapped me back in time to help people I did not know."

"That was a decision I had to make and believe me it was not easy. I told you there were two ways to restore Marcel to his home. You were the best choice. If they had waited for their king, the priests and soldiers would have regrouped, and it would have taken years of fighting to drive them out. You did it in a couple of months. It is something you and Nakobee should be very proud of."

"Yes, that part was easy, the hard part was convincing Duke Marcel and Alora that I was no longer needed and could leave. She and her father had other plans. I stayed until the King's army showed. I made sure all the prisoners were turned over to them and the day after they left, Nakobee and I left to come here.

Having Bella here hanging onto my neck was another thing that made it hard to convince them I was not predestined to be their ruler. They were convinced, since I had a dragonet, I was some powerful being, and I would be able to lead them, and keep them safe. When we arrived at Coastal city, we took the first ship we could. It took us to some place I don't remember the name, we were only there a day, and we caught another ship here.

Nakobee was putting the cards away, when Rae stopped talking. He looked up at Shaméd.

"Shaméd, you should have seen him. Even I was beginning to think there was something different about Rae. During the battles he was amazing. I have never seen him fight so well. I know he is good, and in his rage mode there is almost no stopping him. I know the Thorn shirt he wears protected him. I just have trouble believing the spears and the arrows kept missing you, Rae. The men attacking you from behind just happened to trip and miss you - no one is that lucky. Yes, we rode away, however we left in the middle of the night so no one would know."

"That was because at our going away party Marcel named me his heir and gave his blessing to marry Alora. We both knew I could not stay there. As for those other things I told you, I was just lucky, they missed me." Rae turned and looked at Shaméd. "Now I make it here and you show up telling me I have to return to my world to become king. You have been making my life interesting ever since we met. Why do I have to be king?"

"I will take you back to the world room and show you. However, I need your help here before you go home. I need you to lead the combined armies of the kingdoms here to fight the one that is coming to enslave them."

"What is it with you and helping all these people? Did they ask for your help? Why have you not helped the people on my world? They are in need of help. How are you getting away with all of this? All the training I have gone though, the number one rule drilled into us, I remember very well. The council has forbidden any form of intrusion or intervention to the worlds where we travel. Moreover, they have always forbidden any help or advancement to my world. So here you are helping this world and you now want me to go with you to help. Why, what happened?"

"I cannot speak for the council. I have always believed we were wrong in not helping the worlds we go to. I just found out that you have a much bigger friend that has been helping your world and you. He has been doing it for many years. Additionally, I can tell you when word of it gets out there will not be one person on the council who will not back you and your claim. We can go over all this later, but for now we need to leave and meet with others on the plans of the upcoming war. Will you stay and help?"

Rae sat there looking at Shaméd. He was about to answer when he felt weight on his shoulder. Bella was sitting there, her neck was curved around so her face was in front of his. She looked him in the eyes. He tried to move her but stopped when he heard words in his head.

< *"You must help Shaméd, then you can go home and help the people there or they will die. They need you. Trust this man and the one who has been helping you. I feel it is what you must do."* >

Lowering her head, she dropped to his lap, closed her eyes, and went to sleep. Rae sat there looking at her. Shaméd spoke before Rae had a chance.

"She talked to you - I heard her. How could she know these things?"

"I heard her, too. I don't know why, but I will agree to work with you. Nakobee, it looks like we are staying longer. You, of course, were going to stay anyway. So before we get started I have some more questions. Why did we have to go back in time and why did you keep us in the dark about what we were really doing?"

"I told you in the room before we left that I had traveled to this world and looked into its future. I saw many different timelines, each one as bad as the first. Going back in time and taking Krakdrol was the best choice. If we had not taken him when we did, he would have become too strong for me to fight without killing Loorn. Now is the time Krakdrol would have met with Gormorrah. The two of them together would have been nigh unstoppable. It would have taken the combined force of the whole council to stop them.

In one timeline, we were trapped here and a lot of people died. Gormorrah and Krakdrol left this world and began attacking other worlds. That was when I returned and decided to make my own plan. I had to stop them."

Rae moved his chair back, scooped Bella into his hand and stood.

"Thanks, I just wanted to know what and why I was doing all of this. Fighting evil in one form or another is what we do. Fighting it on a planet-wide scale sounds like fun."

Rae walked over to his bed to place Bella there. Nakobee followed and they began gathering their things. When they were all packed the three walked out of the room. Shaméd went over in his mind what Rae and Nakobee had said. The part about spears and arrows missing Rae during the battles was interesting. It had to be because of Bella, she must have been protecting him. It would be interesting to find out more.

< "Benn, are you there?" >

< "Yes, I am here. Did you need something?" >

< "Yes, can you please find Demahs? I believe he is still with Nogar. Find out if he can come here?" >

< "I will send a message and let you know. ">
< "Thank you ">

They stepped out of the building onto the walkway. Shaméd led them down several streets. The city was busy. Vendors were calling out trying to get people to stop and buy their products. These people were going on with their lives, none of them knew in a few months all of this would change forever. They walked up to the door of a tavern. Shaméd opened it and they walked in. The place was packed. It was dimly lit, smoke and the smell of sweat and booze was thick in the air.

"We will be meeting some people here and getting an update on the preparations for the war."

Shaméd talked as they walked in and went to the back of the room. They sat at a large table facing the door. It gave them a complete view of the room. A serving girl came over.

"What can I get for you?"

Shaméd looked at her.

"Some of that blue wine. The both of you should try it, it is very good."

"That will be fine,"

Nakobee nodded. Rae had taken the seat next to the wall. He sat there looking around the room one more time before answering.

"Sure, I will try this blue wine."

The girl left and Shaméd looked at Rae.

"Is there something wrong?"

"I am not certain. I just got a strange feeling when we entered. I think someone is watching us."

"I think it would be strange if no one was watching us. Everyone turned and looked at us when we entered, and most are still looking."

Nakobee looked around the tavern. When he looked at those who were staring, they turned away.

"That is not what I meant - I *feel*."

Rae stopped talking. His eyes glazed over and Shaméd felt the power. The air in front of the table blurred, then cleared. A man appeared there. The hood of his cloak was down around his shoulders and he smiled. His eyes were forever shut from the scar across his face; he had a walking stick in his left hand.

"Good day. May I join you?"

Without waiting, Boone grabbed a chair and sat.

Rae, knife in hand, sat there pointing it at the old man who had appeared before them. He felt in his mind that everything was ok and this was a friend. Bella, her head out of Rae's satchel, looked at Rae before looking up at Boone.

"Oh, I see you have a baby dragonet. It looks deformed. There must have been an accident during its birth. That is very interesting. You did not have this youngling with you during the war. She is very interesting indeed. Did you know she is a time dragon? Yes, little one I am a time dragon also. He cannot hear you? That is a shame. We will have to do something about that."

Boone sat there rambling on, his arms and his hands clasped together, he looked from Rae to Bella as he talked. Shaméd looked around then cleared his thoughts.

"When you say that you see, you are speaking metaphorically correct?"

Turning to face Shaméd, Boone smiled.

"Am I? Yes, of course. I sometimes see with my mind and forget it is not with my eyes. She looks and feels older but she is very small. How long has she been with you?"

Rae looked from the old man to Nakobee then Shaméd. They were both just sitting there. Rae put his knife away and looked back at Shaméd.

"Can I bother to ask a question? Who is this person? And why should I answer his questions?"

"Sorry, let me introduce you. His name is Boone. He is a dragon and a friend. Boone is here to give us an update on what is happening with the preparations. That is why you are here correct?"

"Of course. I have the documents explaining our progress. Dwarfs have everything ready. The fortress is completed. The tunnels under it have openings to look out over the ravine. As for the land bridge, the tunnels are ready. You can collapse it opening the water way again. All you have to do is explain to everyone this young man will be placed in charge of the combined army and we will be ready to defeat the Nanzorban army."

"How did you know I was going to place Rae in charge?"

Shaméd sat there. No one spoke as the serving girl walked up to the table with a pitcher and four mugs.

"I saw your friend here show up, so I brought him a mug."

After speaking, she placed the mugs and pitcher on the table then she turned and left.

Boone reached over, took the pitcher of wine, sniffed it, and filled one of the mugs. Rae sat there looking at him. He could tell the man was blind, there were no eyes, only the large scar across his face, and empty eye sockets.

"How do you do that?"

Boone turned his head to face Rae as he kept pouring.

"Do what? Oh, I see, you want to know how I knew where the mugs and wine were. My boy, when you are as old as I, you learn to use all your other senses. About knowing how I knew you were going to be in charge of the army, I knew because I traveled into the future and saw you there. You do very well, I might say. I, of course, cannot tell you how well, or what you do, but surmise that you win and do it very well."

Shaméd filled the other three cups.

"That is good to hear. Can you say the same for my mission?"

"All I can say about your mission is you find the items you are seeking. I tried to see what happened while you are inside the ruins, but I could not. For some reason when I tried to travel there, I was blocked. I have faith you will succeed. Your time training you recently received from Red, King of the dragons should make you almost unstoppable. He was a very impressive dragon in his day, and we all loved him very much. Now, here are the documents. Most are updates on the uprising in the Nanzorban kingdom. There seems to be a Duke there who is willing to help overthrow the King and set all the slaves and people there free. Mordock wants you to meet with him, in the next few days."

Boone tilted his head, turned to look at Rae.

"What? Oh yes, I can help you a little. However, you should speak with Shaméd. He has a dragonet now off world learning how to be…"

Shaméd looked at Boone as he spoke. There was a blur and Demahs appeared. He flew over and landed on the empty chair next to Shaméd. The patrons in the tavern saw the dragonet appear out of thin air, most gasped out loud. The barmaid squealed and dropped her tray as Demahs flew by. Shards of ceramics flew across the floor. Others dropped their drinks, got up, and ran out.

"Demahs you have grown a lot since last I saw you. At this rate you will be as big as Nogar in a few years."

< "I cannot be as large as Nogar, but he says I will be twice this size in two more years. Why did you not come get me when you woke? I could have helped you when you went to rescue Loorn."

< "Because you were in training and I could not tell Nogar what I was doing. He might have tried to stop me. Now I need your help in talking with the dragonet Rae has acquired. For some reason, I cannot completely hear or

communicate to her. Can you talk with her and find out what happened and why she has chosen Rae?">

<"She has been talking to me since I showed up. I have told her who I am and who you are. It is a little difficult to understand her. Some of her words are all mixed up. I will take her away and find out everything I can.">

Demahs and Bella disappeared. Rae looked at Shaméd."

"I heard her say goodbye. That was very interesting. Where are they going?"

Shaméd sipped his drink.

"He is taking her away so they can talk. They will be back soon. Now about the information we have. How about you and Nakobee take it and look it over, and I can go meet this person that Mordock wants me to see."

"That will be fine but how do we get to this fortress? Do we contact the world room? Or do we have to take the long way? And most important, when are you going to inform the people here that you plan on placing me in charge?"

"I can take you to the fortress now and after meeting with Mordock I can meet with the Rulers and inform them."

"You do not have to take them. I am going there. I can take them back with me."

Boone emptied the pitcher of wine and after drinking the last drop from his cup, sat it down, and stood.

"In fact, if you are done and you two are ready, we can leave now."

"How are you going to take us?"

Smiling, Boone looked over at Rae.

"Just take hold of my arm and we will sort of transport there, much like Shaméd was going to do. I have been doing this for many years so you do not have to worry. Besides this will give me time to figure out why you cannot hear the little one."

Rae looked at Boone, not sure what to make of him. Even if what Shaméd said was true and he was a dragon, the old man was very strange.

"I was under the impression most people who have dragonets do not hear them talk."

Shaméd said as he and the others stood. Boone looked over at him his empty eyes staring.

"Most people do not want to hear them. Your friend here wants to, but for some reason is having trouble. It is probably a minor thing and I can fix it very easily. Come, let's go. The men will be stopping for their lunch break and you can take a tour of the place they built."

Rae and Nakobee stood and stepped up close to Boone. Nakobee took hold of Boone's left sleeve; Rae took hold of the right. Before they could say or do anything, they disappeared. Shaméd's face had a smirky little grin on it. He took out a silver coin and sat it on the table.

< "Benn, do you have the location of Mordock? I need to meet with him.">

< "I have his location. Take two steps forward.">

Shaméd took the steps and appeared in the world room. He looked over at Benn who turned to him.

"Ok, step back through."

Shaméd turned and stepped back through the mirror. Mordock was sitting at a table with two men. When Shaméd appeared the two men drew knives. Mordock sat there with his back to Shaméd. Mordock's greeting took both men off guard.

"Good day, Lord Shaméd. Please come sit and meet these gentlemen. This is Duke Nactoon who has a very large estate in the south with over five thousand slaves. This is his cousin, Nortoon, who has the land west of him. He has over three thousand slaves.

"We do not have slaves. We have workers. All of our people who live on and work our land are free."

"Yes, that is what I was going to say. Lord Shaméd, these are two of the men who were marked for assassination. However, after finding out what the Duke and his family have been doing the last hundred years, I thought we should meet. We did, and I became convinced that they should meet with you. They are a little hesitant in working with us. Maybe you could convince them that working with us would be in their best interest."

Mordock sat there. He still did not turn to face Shaméd. He kept his eyes on the two men. Shaméd walked over and stood next to Mordock. Shaméd looked at the two men. Both were in their late fifties. They were big, but not fat. They looked healthy and fit. Their bodies did however show their age. He touched their minds. He found they were building a resistance against their King. He also felt the caution from them. They were not sure, if they should trust Mordock and him. He saw in their minds that others had trusted outsiders, and were betrayed, caught, and killed.

"Gentleman, let me first put you at ease. We are not here to take over your country, or betray you to your King. We are here to make sure your country and the other counties of this world can live and work in peace. If you would permit me, I can prove it to you. We are not from your government. If you will each place your hands flat on the table, I will show you."

<*"Benn, can you inform Nogar that I will be bringing guests to his balcony?">*

<*"Benn is gone. How do you plan to bring guest to Nogar's balcony?">*

<*"Reklan, good to hear your voice. I will have to show you when I get there. Please inform Nogar I will be there in a minute.">*

Shaméd looked around everyone placed their hands flat on the table. Shaméd placed his left hand flat on the table, raising his right hand and using one finger he tapped the crystals on the gauntlet of his left arm. The table and surrounding area began to glow. When the glow was completely around them and the table, it began to shrink back in around them. As the light touched them, they began to shrink. Duke Nactoon tried to move - fear showed in his eyes. When the glow was no more than a speck, there was a small flash and it disappeared. On the balcony, a speck of light appeared. It slowly grew brighter and larger, moving chairs and other items back. It stopped growing, the light dimmed and there sat Shaméd and the others. The two men now able to move, jumped up as they saw the sky and a tall man standing in the doorway. Nogar stood there looking at them.

"Greetings, Shaméd. Reklan told me you were bringing guests. Please come inside. You can introduce your friends to me as we have some refreshments."

Nogar stepped back inside. The two men stood there watching him leave. They looked at Shaméd.

"Where are we? How did we get here?"

Duke Nactoon's voice trembled as he spoke. His cousin moved closer, both were scared witless.

"Like I said, you have nothing to fear. This is my homeworld. We are a long way away from your world. As a matter of fact, you cannot even see it when you look into our night sky. Now, please come inside. We can explain it all better there. We do not have much time to get things going. Your king has already sent his army to invade the other nations."

Shaméd walked inside leaving the two there with Mordock.

"I told you he is a very powerful wizard. You will have nothing to fear from him or his people. Come, the food and drink have always been good."

Mordock stood and pointed to the door, the two men went in with Mordock right behind them.

The next few hours the two men listened and asked questions. Nogar and Shaméd answered them all. They ate and saw things that would have driven most people crazy. In the end they pledged to follow Shaméd. They would do whatever it took to overthrow their king. They agreed and were willing to let the other nations live in peace. They wanted to rebuild their country and join the other nations in a united front to help build and unite the world. They signed the treaty papers Shaméd had drawn up. The treaty stated what they would do in the fight and in over-throwing their king and where they stood after the upcoming war.

Nogar stood and looked at each one.

"Now you must leave. I have work to do and so do all of you. Shaméd, I will see you later. Gentlemen, it was a pleasure to meet you. Mordock, you take care and keep your head down."

Nogar walked out of the room. Shaméd and Mordock led the two men back outside to the table.

"If you would all sit, we will return to your home."

They sat. Shaméd repeated the process he had done to get them there. As the light dimmed around them, there was movement behind Duke Nactoon. Mordock drew his sword, pushed out of his chair and rolled away. Coming up with his back near a wall, he stood looking at five men standing in the doorway. They stood their staring. Duke Nactoon called out, stopping Mordock.

"It is ok - these are my men. They must have come in to check on me to see why I had not come out. Please, everyone relax."

Duke Nactoon stood between Mordock and his men, everyone relaxed. Duke Nactoon's men stepped in and closed the door. Shaméd was the only one who didn't move. Mordock sheathed his sword, went, and stood next to Shaméd. Shaméd's head tilted a little as he looked around the room. He held up his hand.

"Do not move, Duke Nactoon. I am afraid there is a spy among your men. He has orders to kill you today."

"That is impossible. I trust these men with my life as well as my family. I have known them all their lives. Why would you possibly say such a thing?"

The men stopped walking. Everyone stood there looking at each other. A man standing closest to Duke Nactoon began shifting his eyes; sweat beaded up on his face. Before Shaméd could say anything the man collapsed down to the floor, he began crying and begged forgiveness from the Duke.

"Please, I was ordered to kill you. They have my children and wife. The soldiers are waiting for my return and I was so scared, I knew I would never be able to go through with it. Please you must help my family. The soldiers are in the forest out passed the barn with my family."

They stood there as the man fell on his face and laid there crying. The Duke looked at him. The other four drew their swords and stepped back. Shaméd walked over and knelt down to him, placing a hand on the man's back he spoke.

"Stay here. We will go get your family. Trust me and protect the Duke with your life. Duke, you must gather your people together. This man may not be the only one compromised. We won't know until they are all together how many spies there are. Start giving orders. Your part of the war has just begun. Mordock and I will go get his family."

Shaméd stood as he spoke and walked over to Mordock. With his right hand, Shaméd tapped three of the crystals on the gantlet of his left arm. The crystals began to glow, the glow spread out covering both of them. Mordock and Shaméd disappeared. They reappeared outside in the woods. They heard talking off in the distance. Looking through the trees, they saw a group of men sitting on logs, drinking. Shaméd held his right hand up - he opened and closed it twice letting Mordock know there were ten men.

He pointed to the right and held up one finger. Mordock slowly moved between the trees heading toward the man that stood with his back to the camp. Mordock sidled up behind him using his knife to slit his throat. As Mordock moved away Shaméd walked boldly into the soldier's camp.

"Good day. May I ask why you are holding this woman and her children against their will?"

The men jumped up swords and spears at the ready. They stood there looking at Shaméd as he boldly walked toward them.

Shaméd turned heading straight to the woman and children. One of the men yelled at the others then Shaméd.

"How did he get by the guards? Do not let him get close to the prisoners. You, stop moving. What are you doing here? If you do not stop we will be forced to kill you. You two, if he takes one more step kill the prisoners."

Shaméd stopped, turned, and faced the one who spoke.

"I have stopped. Now answer my question. I want to know why you are holding this woman and her children against their will. If you are waiting to hear from her husband, you can stop waiting. He has not killed the Duke. The Duke is alive and the man is safe. If all of you lay down your weapons and surrender, you will be treated fairly. If you do not, then you will all die."

Shaméd stood there waiting. The soldiers looked at each other. Two men worked their way around him getting closer to the woman. A few started laughing when they realized he was alone. One of the men walked up to Shaméd holding his sword out front. He stopped when it was a few inches from Shaméd's chest.

Shaméd looked at the man. He slowly raised his hand and touched the tip of the sword. As soon as his finger touched it, the sword glowed red. The man yelled as the weapon heated up and twisted as it began to melt. It happened very swiftly. He dropped the weapon and jumped back holding his hand. The leader seeing what happened, squared his shoulders, sheathed his sword, and moved closer.

"Who are you?'

"I am Lord Shaméd and I order you to release the woman and her children. I cannot let any of you leave here to return to your leaders. As I said before, surrender and you will not be harmed. If you do not, then I will have to kill all of you. What will it be? Death? Or life? You have two seconds to make up your mind."

Shaméd snapped his fingers and the ropes holding the woman and children disappeared. They slowly stood and moved closer to Shaméd. The two soldiers standing near them moved back, with fear on their faces.

Shaméd looked at the woman. He smiled and touched her shoulder.

"Take your children and go. Return to the main house. Your husband is there waiting. They will not harm you."

The leader yelled, drew his sword and one of his men tossed his spear. It flew toward the woman; it twisted in the air and headed straight to a soldier off to the right. The man never had time to react - the spear slammed deep into his chest.

The soldier stood there, looked at the spear, surprise on his face. He gurgled and fell back into a tree then slid down to the ground dead.

The man who tossed the spear looked at his fallen comrade not believing what just happened. The others dropped their weapons. Three ran off to the right into the woods where they met arrows. They all dropped dead.

Mordock stepped out into view. The soldier who had talked with Shaméd looked at Mordock and back at Shaméd.

"No one told us there was a wizard. We surrender. You gave us your word that you would not kill us."

"No one will harm you as long as you do not try anything. Start walking to the Duke's home. When we get there, you will need to offer your life to him. He will place you into a holding cell and later you will be given your freedom."

Without talking, the soldiers dropped the rest of their weapons, placed their hands on their heads, and began walking. Mordock put his bow away and drew his sword and followed. Shaméd saw the woman and her children disappear into the woods. They started running when the fight started. He knew they would not stop running until they were home.

Shaméd could hear their thoughts. They were afraid, especially the soldiers. He started walking.

As they entered the clearing to the yard of Duke Nactoon's estates, men came running out with spears and swords. The captives surrendered to the soldiers, their hands were tied behind their backs, and led to a building and locked inside. Duke Nactoon came walking forward; there was a large crowd of people standing around watching. Shaméd saw the woman and her children. They were standing next to her husband, the children hiding behind them.

Duke Nactoon stopped in front of Shaméd and Mordock.

"I will not ask how you two could capture these six soldiers of the King. I believe you could do just about anything. My men will make sure they stay locked up and I have people leaving today to spread the word that the time of rebellion is at hand. We will wait for your signal before attacking. I hope it will not be too long."

"There were eleven men. Mordock killed four, and they killed one of their own. The bodies are back in the woods. You might want to send men out there to bury them. As for the signal, I believe it will be within the week. We still have to do some things. Mordock or one of his men will let you know. Now if you will excuse us, we must leave. I have to go meet some more people."

"Of course. I will wait for the signal."

Shaméd gave a slight bow, in his mind he called out to Reklan.

< *"Reklan, if you would get the IDG ready for us, we need to go meet with the others."* >

< *"I have it ready. The others are talking about the plans and Rae is off to the side reading the reports and waiting for you."* >

The Duke stepped away. Mordock walked up beside Shaméd. They both took three steps and disappeared.

Shaméd and Mordock appeared in the world room. Reklan had aligned the mirror so it showed the door to the room where Rae and the others were. The room was at the Raven Bridge inside the new fortress. Shaméd and Mordock walked over and stepped through the mirror.

Chapter Twelve

Stepping into the hallway, they stopped outside the doorway. The room was full of people: King Kalona, his niece, Princess Lila, General Tull, and his son, and Captain Na-Took from the kingdom Kaloon. Rae and Nakobee were standing next to Kinn talking. Next to them were Prince Já-pheth and three of the men from his council. There were several Elves and Dwarves and one very large man sitting on the floor with his back to the wall. Shaméd and Mordock stepped into the room and everyone turned to face them. Those that knew Shaméd called out greetings. Nakobee called out to Mordock. The others stood there looking at Shaméd and Mordock. King Kalona waved at Shaméd.

"Lord Shaméd, we are glad you have returned. With the help of our new friends, we have completed the defense system you left for us. We were just going over some last minute decisions. Please come close to the table so we can get you caught up."

Shaméd walked forward. People moved out of the way. Mordock stayed near the door. Shaméd stopped next to the table, King Kalona began introducing the people in the room.

"This is Lord Taloree. He is the Elf King's eldest son, and he has brought with him three thousand elf warriors. This is Lord Digdeepest, nephew of the Dwarf King. He has brought one thousand dwarf warriors. His men were the ones that dug the tunnels under the land bridge. They designed and built the fortress we are in. It overlooks the gorge. There are even tunnels under and around it. You know the others except the man sitting back there. He is Cuchulainn. He is a Titian. His king sent him to help in the war. They have had some dealing with Nanzorba and none of it good. Lord Taloree and Lord Digdeepest went to the King of the Titians to ask if they would help in the war. The King agreed and sent his nephew."

King Kalona leaned closer to Shaméd.

"I asked why only him, he said one Titian is worth a thousand warriors."

Shaméd looked at each one as King Kalona introduced them. When King Kalona introduced Cuchulainn, the Titian leaned forward and their eyes locked. Shaméd felt the mental touch of a greeting.

"It is good to meet all of you. I see Rae and Nakobee arrived safely. Where is Boone?"

"Boone said he had some business to take care of and would be back here in three days."

141

Rae walked through the crowd to stand next to Shaméd. Bella stuck her head out of Rae's satchel; she looked at Shaméd and chirped.

"Hello, Bella did you and Demahs have a good time?"

His head filled with pictures and other thoughts, most understandable.

"Yes, we should talk later when Demahs comes back, until then I have to talk with these people."

Bella disappeared back inside the satchel. Shaméd turned and looked at everyone. Everyone had stopped talking and stood there looking at him as if he had gone insane.

"You can communicate with that?"

Lord Taloree took a step closer to Shaméd as he spoke.

"I cannot understand "her" completely, but yes, I can hear her. I can also talk with my own dragnet. Is there a problem?"

"No. I was just wondering why anyone would want to communicate with such creatures."

"Do you have a problem with dragonets or dragons, in general?"

"I have found that dragons are a nuisance and they kill without purpose. They have caused more destruction in our homeland than any other creature. We discourage them from coming there."

Everyone except the Elves and Dwarfs slowly backed away. Kinn felt the anger from Shaméd. He moved to stand next to him. Rae looked at Shaméd. Shaméd's eyes had grown steely with anger. Rae moved forward a smile on his face, stepping between Shaméd and Lord Taloree. With his back to Shaméd, he stopped a foot from the Lord. Rae looked up into his eyes.

"You must have done something very bad to the dragons to make them plague you. Or maybe you are dealing with some that are renegades. Before you speak, you must be informed Lord Shaméd was saved from certain death by the King of all dragons. He was taken back to the King of all dragons' home. There he was adopted, and raised by dragons as well as elves and dwarfs. They live on a world where everyone lives in peace and harmony.

Lord Nogar is the King of dragons. He is a very special being. He believes everyone, no matter how pointed their ears, how tall, or short they are should be considered equal. I know this, because I come from a world he has been helping for many years. As for your trouble with these dragons, have you tried to talk with them? If not, I believe Lord Shaméd can help remedy your problem in a very short time. That is, if you would like his help. Do you?"

Lord Taloree stood there wanting to turn his head away, but dared not. This human, was standing in front of him and staring straight up at him as if he was an equal. He stood straighter, and without looking away, answered.

"If Lord Shaméd thinks he can fix the trouble we have with these dragons I would welcome it. I know my father would. As for you, what gives you, a mere human the right to address me in such a tone?"

Rae was about to speak but Shaméd's anger had dissipated. Reaching out, he touched Rae's arm. Without looking, Rae stepped back as Shaméd looked at Lord Taloree. Shaméd raised his voice so they all could hear him.

"Rae has the right to speak to you, or anyone in this room in any manner he feels necessary. I have given him complete power and authority over the combined armies. Before you say anything, I do this because he was on his way home to be crowned king. I asked for his help. He graciously said yes. Rae will not only be crowned king of his people but of the complete planet. Being the king of his own world places him in a unique position. He would never try to stay here or sabotage any of you. His only goal is to make sure all of you survive and live in peace. If you have any doubts, I can give you the names of people he has helped here on this world. Help that if not for his training, and his wisdom, would have cost many lives. Rae has more training in fighting and war maneuvers and diplomacy than any of you here. That includes you Lord Taloree. You may be an Elf, but you have only lived a thousand years. You have had only the basic training in combat. We come from a world that knows no time restrictions. Rae has been in training for the last four hundred of his world's years. If you need or want proof, I will be glad to show you. That goes for anyone here."

When Shaméd started talking Rae worked his way back to stand next to Nakobee and Kinn. Nakobee had also moved closer to stand behind Shaméd and Rae when the incident started.

King Kalona called out after a cool silence settled over the room.

"Lord Shaméd, I for one will trust anyone you want to put in charge. I have been to your world. I have met Lord Nogar, the King of all dragons. I will trust him, you, or anyone you say."

"That goes for my people too."

Prince Japheth said as he pushed closer to stand next to King Kalona. Lord Taloree was standing there looking around. Lord Digdeepest walked up to him, and gave him a big grin as he patted Lord Taloree's arms.

"I think your big mouth got you in trouble again. It is a good thing your father is not here, he might slap those pointy little ears and send you to bed. Why not apologize, and let us get on with the war. We were sent here to fight our enemy. Not argue and fight each other over who is in charge."

Lord Taloree looked down at Lord Digdeepest. Taking a deep breath he let it out slowly. He looked at Shaméd who stood eye to eye with him.

"My teacher, Lord Digdeepest, is very wise, and once again I heed his wisdom. Please forgive me and my words. I have never been outside my own realm. I am not use to dealing with others - only my people and Dwarfs. You are correct in stating my age and training. I am not sure how, you would know this, but is does not matter. Lord Kinn has told me that you are a trusted friend, and that he has known you for many years. I must believe this to be true, because elves do not lie. Lord Kinn said words of such magnitude and praise about you; I thought you were an elf. I and my people will do whatever you ask."

Shaméd looked around the room. The Titian had stood up or stood as much as his tall body could. After Lord Taloree stopped talking, he grinned and returned to his seat on the floor.

"I am sorry for not telling everyone at the beginning I was going to place Rae in charge. Now if you will all excuse me, I have a meeting I must attend. Rae will stay here. You can tell him what is completed and what more needs to be done. I will return as soon as I can. Lord Taloree, I will check into the dragon problem you are having. I believe I, or someone I know can help."

Shaméd turned and left the room, walking down the hallway. He entered the first empty room, touching the crystals on the gauntlet and disappeared.

Rae worked his way to the door trying to catch Shaméd. Rae saw Shaméd entered the room, when he got there and opened the door, Shaméd was gone. Rae called out to Reklan.

< *"Reklan, is Shaméd there?"* >

< *"No. he did not return here. The MA-TED says he went straight to Nogar. I will let him know you want him when he is done."* >

< *"That won't be necessary. I can talk to him when he returns."* >

Rae turned around, started to leave, and almost bumped into Nakobee and Mordock who were standing there in the doorway waiting.

"What are you two doing here?"

"We are making sure you are safe. You are in charge, so we must protect you. Besides, if the King of a world should die when I was his protector, it would look very bad on my record."

Nakobee stood there staring at Rae.

Mordock looked at Nakobee.

"Bad for your record?"

"Ok, it would look bad for both our records."

They stood there looking at each other. Nakobee's cool blues eyes were staring at Mordock with no expression on their faces to show if they were kidding. Rae raised his hand in a stop signal, shook his head and he pushed between them. When he stepped into the hallway, they both started laughing. Rae turned back glaring at them. When he saw their faces he started laughing, too.

"Do not tell Jon or Jym. The longer it takes for them to learn about me, the better. They will never let me live this down. Come on; let's go see if we can save these people.'

As Mordock followed he tried to figure out how Rae, a thief and an assassin could be brought here and placed in charge of four country's armies. Then later he was going to go home to be crowned king of a world. These people were indeed strange.

Shaméd appeared in the hallway a few feet from Nogar's room. He walked to the large double doors and knocked. The door on the right slowly opened, he walked in and headed straight to the balcony where Nogar was sitting. Taking the seat across the small table, Shaméd looked at Nogar.

"I almost lost my temper. I was talking with Lord Taloree and every word he said was making me angry. If not for Rae stepping forward I believe I would have killed him. I don't understand why I was so upset."

Nogar took a sip from his cup before answering.

"I believe it may have been because of your contact with my uncle, Krakdrol the dark dragon. His presence and his words have always driven those around him to anger and evil. You had to contain him inside Loorn's body for hours. That alone would have driven most people insane. You are very lucky you trained for so long with my father. You need to get some rest. You have been awake for over thirty hours. Go to your room and sleep. I will send word to you when you are needed."

"How is Loorn? What did you do with Krakdrol after you removed him?"

"My uncle will never bother anyone, again. We placed him in an orb and dropped it into a sun. He is now completely gone. As for Loorn, his body handled it very well. Two days after we removed Krakdrol he woke. He is in a room and is doing fine. Moiran is there with him. You should stop there and see them."

"I will do that. Thank you for talking with me."

"I have always enjoyed our talks. I want you to know I would have gone with you. You did not have to rescue Loorn alone."

"I was not alone, and I was not sure what you would say or do if I had told you. I was only going there to save Loorn. I really did not care about your uncle."

"I assure you, I would not have stopped you. You did something we have tried to do for many years. We could not find my Uncle. No one knew he was on that planet. The last location we had was in a completely different galaxy. We do not know how he was able to move from world to world, but now we do not need to know. He is gone and we will never have to worry about him again. Go see you friend then get some rest."

Shaméd stood gave a slight bow to Nogar and left, going straight to Loorn's room. Knocking on the door, he waited a second then opened it and entered. Moiran was sitting next to the bed. They both looked at Shaméd as he walked in. Moiran stood and walked over to Shaméd giving him a hug. Shaméd was not sure how to react, so he just let her hug him. She stopped and looked up into his eyes.

"Thank you. I was told he was here yesterday. They said you and some others went to save him. How did you know he was alive?"

Moiran let go and they both walked over to stand next to the bed. Shaméd looked at Loorn who was staring up at him. He looked the same except for the white streak in his hair. Loorn motioned to Shaméd.

"I knew you were a powerful wizard, but I had no idea you were this powerful. Thank you for what you did. I was going crazy with that other entity in my head. You have no idea how much hate that person has. It hated everything living. All of my hate and anger was nothing compared to its hate. After what I have gone through, I have no more hate. I now see how it can turn your mind and body inside out and make you crazy. As for Moiran's question, I would like to know how you found me. And who was that inside my head?"

Moiran sat in the chair by the bed, Shaméd shrugged his shoulders.

"The world found you, or I should say, Rednog. That is the name of the world. Before you ask, the world here is a living entity and it talks through the MA-TED. When we first met, I slipped a placer in your drink. It helped me locate you if the need ever arose. As you can see, it did. Rednog monitored you for a few days, trying to find out how you came back. When he discovered you had two minds, he informed me. He told me who had taken over your body and that you were alive. He showed me how I could rescue you, so I did. I made the mistake of not checking you completely when you were brought to me. If I had, I might have been able to save you. When I found out you were alive, I made the decision I was not going to lose you again. You are needed here."

Moiran leaned on the bed and took Loorn's hand. Shaméd looked at her. She was smiling. He thought about her babies, she would have had them by now.

"I take it you have told him he is a father of twins."

They looked at each other, then smiled at him.

"I had triplets. Doctor T told me a week before I delivered. I have met many trolls and I can say this, none have ever been like him. He is very gentle and very good. Since I have been here I have met many other races. They are all wonderful. This is indeed a very special place. Thank you for bringing me and my children here."

"You are welcome. You are my friends and I would help you whenever you need it. You had three children. Are they boys or girls?"

"We have two boys and one girl. You should stop by the house to see them."

Shaméd smiled and stepped back.

"I will try to do that very soon. Now if you will excuse me, I have to go get some rest."

"How is the war coming?" Moiran asked

"It is going very well. The people have come together and built a strong alliance. They do not have the manpower to face the Nanzorban army alone and straight on. But with all the preparations, they stand a very good chance in winning."

"Can you not just stop the army yourself?"

Moiran sat there looking at him. Shaméd looked at each of them.

"I cannot. The council will not allow it. A long time ago, long before I arrived here, on a world not much different than yours they agreed to help a group of people who were enslaved. The council sent an army to fight for the people. They won their freedom. Later they found out it was wrong, the people they left in charge were worse than the ones they replaced. The council now says people do not appreciate what they have if it is just given to them. People have to fight and work for what they want. However, do not worry. I can tell you this; I have given the people on your world everything they need to win. The people are standing together and their defense is such that no army can get passed. They may be out numbered, but they will win, trust me. Now, good day and I will see you both, later."

Shaméd turned and left the room walking straight to his room. He undressed, climbed into bed, and slept. He was wakened by the MA-TED.

"Shaméd you are needed. Word has come about the Nanzorban army."

Shaméd rolled over, and sat on the edge of his bed.

"How long have I been asleep?"

"Ten hours. I informed everyone you were indisposed so you could sleep"

Thank you. I will get ready and go to the world room. Please inform everyone I will be there soon."

Shaméd went to take a shower, dressed, and headed to the world room. He arrived one hour after waking up.

Walking in, he saw Benn standing by the MA-TED. "Hello, Benn."

Shaméd headed straight for the IDG. The image showed a room with Rae and others standing around looking at maps and talking.

Chapter Thirteen

Earlier, Sara reported that twenty-five thousand enemy soldiers split off from the main group eight days ago. It would take four days of traveling through the forest and five days to cross the swamps. They were heading for the land bridge by the sea. With no road it would take ten days of hard marching to reach the bridge.

Rae, Shaméd, and the others knew this. They continued with their own plans. They had to make sure they were ready when the main group showed up at the ravine.

Eight days later, Sara returned from scouting. The group of soldiers was only a few miles from the bridge. Shaméd asked Sara to go scout out the main army. Then he told Rae and the others to stay at the suspension bridge and fortress.

Shaméd transported to the land bridge. He arrived and met with the men waiting for him. There were ten Elf and ten Dwarf warriors, along with a hundred humans. Two days ago, the trap was finished. All the men who help prepare it were now back at the ravine. These warriors were here to help Shaméd. They would not need to do much fighting; they were here to guard the bridge or in the worse case, clean up the aftermath.

The humans moved off to hide in the woods. Only the elves and dwarfs were going to stand with Shaméd. The dwarfs stood there holding axe, or hammer, towering over and behind them stood the Elves with their bows. Shaméd stood a couple hundred feet out on the bridge. They did not have long to wait for the invading army.

Thirty minutes after Shaméd arrived, the enemy scouts showed up. Seeing Shaméd and the others, they stood there and laughed. All but two ran back to the main group. Fifteen minutes later, the main group showed up. A tall man walked out onto the bridge. Shaméd started forward, they met at the halfway point. The man began talking when they were within five feet.

"I am Sub General Portus. You and your men will surrender at once and let me pass."

Shaméd looked at him not responding to his words.

"Good day to you. I have the task of giving you three choices on behalf of the combined kingdoms of this land. The first is that you return to your land and never return. The second is if you continue in your quest, you all will die. The third choice is for you and your men to surrender. Here are the requirements for surrendering."

Shaméd let go of his staff. It floated there in the air. He reached into his satchel and pulled out a rolled paper which he handed to the General. The General took it and opened it. After reading the document, the General stood there looking at Shaméd. Still holding the paper, he crushed it with his hands and tossed it to the ground. He looked passed Shaméd at the twenty men on the other end. He started laughing. His soldiers behind him started laughing. Then he stopped and with a very serious look and tone stared at Shaméd.

"Boy, you must be kidding. You think because you have a stick that can float in the air my men and I will be afraid of you. There is no way I, or any of my men, would ever surrender to you or any living creature. We would rather die, and it won't be by your hands and it won't be today."

Turning around he began walking back, and as he did he raised his hand and dropped it; a flight of arrows came up and out heading toward Shaméd. Shaméd stood there watching the man walk away. As the arrows climbed higher, he took hold of the staff and slowly turned his back. As he started walking back to his side of the bridge, the ten elves raised their bows and shot their arrows. As the arrows coming toward them curved and began their descent, they burst into flames, their ashes falling down on the ground almost in the exact spot the General and Shaméd had been standing. When Shaméd reached the other side, he stopped, turned, and faced back at the soldiers. The ten arrows his men fired each hit a man. As they fell to the ground, Shaméd called out.

"Surrender now and you will live. Continue with this foolishness and it is very likely all of you will die before the hour is gone."

The General did not say a word. He raised then dropped his arm and the invading army began marching, ten men side by side their spears out front. As they came, their archers shot another volley of arrows. These arrows ignited and they burned up just as the first. Two more volleys met the same fate. When they were three quarters of the way across the invading army was now completely on the land bridge. The sky went black with arrows from the invading army. As the arrows began to fall, they slowly curved up arching back in mid air. All of them headed up and back toward the invading army. There were screams as the arrows fell and began hitting their own men. Shaméd and his men just stood there.

They heard the screaming from the soldiers as the arrows hit. Then they heard the command to charge. That was when Shaméd raised his hand and dropped it. The elves behind him shot their arrows. They went flying up into the air. As they went higher, each arrow spit, becoming two, then those two split becoming four, soon there were a thousand arrows raining down on the invaders. Shaméd raised his hand again and as it dropped, the Dwarfs slammed their hammers and axe heads on the ground, and then they and the elves turned and fled, running as fast as they could. Shaméd slowly rose into the air. The ground began to rumble then shake, within seconds the ground began cracking. The side facing inland split and opened. The land bridge began crumbling and disappearing into the canyon below. The split began to grow, within seconds the land bridge collapsed. The ocean came pouring in tearing apart what was left of the bridge, sweeping the remaining soldiers away. It was all over in less than two minutes, the invading army was destroyed.

Shaméd floated in the air watching the destruction with remorse. He closed his eyes and blocked out all the screaming from his head. He did not like what was happening but he knew it had to happen. He opened his eyes and saw the leader as the ground fell away from under his feet and the water swept him away to certain death. Shaméd raised his hand as the Sub General fell. The man's helmet came off his head and floated up and over to toward Shaméd. Taking it in his hands he turned around and slowly floated back to his men. Reaching them, he landed and began walking toward the group of elves, dwarves, and humans who were waiting for him. They stood there and saw the destruction caused by the underground work they did. The land bridge crumbling, the sea pouring in, that was the plan. The sight of the entire army falling to their deaths, that was something they would never forget. There was no sign of any soldiers. One of the Elves stepped closer to Shaméd.

"Lord Shaméd, you seem upset in the victory. May I ask why?"

Shaméd looked at the man and the others, and then he looked back at the rushing water.

"Those men were only doing what they were told to do by evil rulers. Most beings want to live in peace. Even if it is easier to destroy than to build, most beings want to build and create. It is always sad to have to kill for no reason, and this was for no reason. I could have done it differently, but I had no choice. They had to die so others could live.

Take your men and search the river banks for survivors. Bring them and all the equipment you find back to Na-Car. Place any equipment you find in the warehouse and any survivors you find, doctor their injuries, and put them in the stockade at the fort. Keep alert and do not mistreat any of them. I'm leaving. The main army will soon arrive at the ravine."

Without another word, Shaméd touched the crystals on his left arm and disappeared.

The man turned around and began yelling out orders. Within seconds humans, Dwarfs and elves all began the trek down to the new river. Once there they would spread out to start searching for survivors.

Chapter Fourteen

Shaméd appeared at the door of his tent. It was on the other side of the bridge fifteen feet away and to the left side of the road. Since the landscape was flat and open there was no way the invading army could not see it.

Opening the door he walked in. Inside sitting at two tables were Rae, Jym, Nakobee, Mordock, Kinn, and Prince Já-pheth. Rae stood when Shaméd entered.

"Shaméd, the ships have arrived. They are anchored on the other side of the fortress. The men are waiting for the word to come over."

Shaméd stopped at the end of the table.

"Have them come over and set up two tents. The only ones that will stay over here are Cuchulainn, Smash, and ten men with rifles. Make sure they have enough shot and powder for a thousand shots each. They will need food and water to last four days. Those men have to be volunteers. They will stay and sleep here on this side. In the morning, we face the Nanzorban army and all its power. Now if you will excuse me I need to rest. I could feel something watching me. As I blocked out what was happening to the Nanzorban army, someone or something was searching and probing my mind. Tomorrow will be an even more interesting day."

Mordock stood as he spoke.

"Philip has already said if Smash is to come over here then he will, too. They have been through a lot this last year. Philip has grown very fond and protective of Smash. I don't think it has anything to do with the fact Smash is the son of the Ogres. I believe he really likes him. So he said he is not going to let him fight without him."

Shaméd looked around at them.

"Smash is a prince among the ogres? I was wondering what he was hiding. I tried to probe his mind in the swamp but couldn't get a clear reading. Tell Philip he can come, but remind him it will be very dangerous and to stay low."

The others stood without speaking. Prince Ja'-pheth gave a slight bow as they left. Shaméd waved his hand. The tables, chairs, and other items in the room began to glow. They floated up and began shrinking as they moved to the walls of the tent. When they reached the side they fused with them becoming like pictures on the inside of the tent. A picture of a bed came away from the wall, floating out, growing until it was complete, and sitting on the ground. Shaméd walked over, placed his pack and other items on the chair that had come to rest by the bed. There was a blurring and Demahs appeared. Flying over, he landed on the ground by the bed. As Shaméd took off his boots, Demahs sat watching.

"Hello, Demahs. How are you? Have you completed your training with Nogar?"

< *"Yes. He said there is no need for me to come back. I have told him I will work with Bellatona to try to get her mind as close to normal as possible. As you requested, I went to the island of the Elves and Dwarves. I found the dragons that live there. They told me the people that lived there thousands of years ago killed many of them. They also tracked down and killed as many of the dragons as they could find."* >

"Were they Elves that did this?"

< *"These dragons do not know the difference between Elves, Dwarfs, or other two-legged creatures. They are very primitive. They have no magic in them. The*

156

pictures I received from their minds looked to me like they were deformed men. They were tall and very evil looking. They had disappeared for many years. Then the two-legged people returned and buildings began showing up across the land. The fighting began again a few years later when the new people killed a dragon that attacked one of their villages.">

"What you have described sounds like the original fight was between demons and the dragons. The people that live on the island now have only been fighting because they were attacked. Let me rest for an hour or two. We need to go there and talk with the leaders of the dragons and the dragonets."

< "I will sleep also. It is very difficult to train a female and one who hasn't all of her senses is even harder. The leader of the dragons requested that you come to see him. He wants the promise of a two legged creature before they will stop fighting.">

"I will go there soon. As for Bellatona, she cannot help the way she is. If she had been allowed to hatch normally, she would not need your help. You also said she was inside her egg as her siblings were taken out one at a time and slowly destroyed. Think how you would be if you had to witness that. I know I would have not been normal after that. It was a good thing Rae came when he did and saved her."

< "I am not sure. She has attached herself to him unlike any other dragon has ever done. She is of the mindset that as long as he is alive so is she. When he dies she will die. That is why she protected him. Dragonets do not think this way. We choose only those that might help us grow. If they do not, we move on. If and when our human dies, we leave and search for another. There is no history of any dragonet doing what she is doing.">

"Then she is indeed special. Continue helping her. I think she will be a great asset to Rae when he returns to his world. I can't wait to see the people's reactions when they see him with her."

Laying down, Shaméd closed his eyes.

Rae and the others walked back across the bridge. Orders were issued for tents and men. It was not easy to pick ten men - all of them wanted to go. Finally, ten were chosen. They, along with Cuchulainn, Smash, Philip, Jym, and a group of dwarves came over to help.

Off to the left of Shaméd's, tent they found an incline in the land. They began digging a trench for them to hide and fight from. The work went fast with Smash and Cuchulainn doing most of the digging. The men carried rocks and filled bags with dirt, stacking them, and making holes so they could see. They built walls up and around both sides of the trench to help protect them when the fighting started.

They built it using Jym's instructions and drawings. Cuchulainn dug at one end a deeper hole so he and Smash could stand and be out of harm's way. Smash and Cuchulainn found large boulders and placed them on the side of the trench.

Jym was there because Rae called Reklan the day Shaméd told him he would be in charge and asked for him. Nogar approved the request and Jym came that day right after Shaméd gave his speech and left. Jym worked with the Dwarves as they finished the fortress and the surrounding buildings.

Rae stood on the roof of the building to the side. He watched as Jym and the others built their trench. It would be their home and only defense for the upcoming fight. He hoped it would be enough to protect them. They dug a trench to the bridge so if they had to retreat they could do so undercover. They would of course be exposed as they ran across the bridge. Rae looked out over the fortress and all the preparations these people had accomplished in the last year. He stared off across the land in the direction where the enemy would be coming. Closing his eyes, he went over everything.

<This side of the ravine was twenty feet higher. They would be looking down at the enemy. The bridge was built here because it was the narrowest space. The bridge was twenty feet wide and over a hundred feet long, crossing the ninety-foot gap. It was a marvel and a great accomplishment to the people who built it a thousand years ago. But it was the easiest way for the invaders to come. They could trek two hundred miles along the ravine and river, where the sides gradually sloped down to fifty feet above the old lake. Then they could climb down and walk across the old lakebed. Or they could continue to walk around the old lake, crossing hundreds of miles of sand dunes before reaching the beginning of the forest. They would have to travel all the way back to reach the cities. Of course they could do what they had done and split off a group and send them traveling through the forests that led into the marsh lands. They would travel two to three hundred miles to the land bridge that was no longer there.

Nanzorba was the largest nation on this continent. Its people were not a sea faring race. They had ships but they were sailed by the people they had conquered – none were war ships. They were sending ships with men but they would not arrive for a few more days. No, if they wanted to get where they wanted to go, this was the easiest way. He had heard about the men they had sent by ship. Those ships and men never returned.

The fortress he stood on was built solid. The dwarfs dug tunnels into the ground going out to the cliff side. They made over twenty rooms below ground. There were four large openings along the side of the ravine. Each one had a small ballistic, or what I would call a canon. These people on this world did not know about the exploding powder until last year. When Shaméd found the old weapons it brought back the knowledge they had lost. The dwarves rebuilt the weapons making many changes. These cannons now used the powder giving them more distance and more power to cause greater damage.

There were one hundred Dwarves, each armed with rifles hidden in rooms built in the cliff. One hundred elves and five hundred humans with bows would be on the top of the buildings to shoot. One hundred elves and four hundred humans with rifles would be behind the walls built all along the edge of the ravine. All the dirt from the digging of the tunnels was used to help build the building and walls. One hundred humans would be in the cliff shooting the canons across the ravine. Altogether, the combined forces of the defenders were twenty five thousand men. Less than 1400 of them were here. The rest were back inland and at the coastal cities to help defend them when the enemy's ships reach land. Heather had informed them that five large ships were heading toward Na-Car, and two were heading to reinforce the soldiers trapped on the coast in a small village. Shaméd had trapped the first wave of soldiers there last year. Heather and Sara were going to wait until the ships were two miles out before they would attack. They would burn and sink them. Their own soldiers would deal with any survivors that came ashore. The two ships sailing to the trapped soldiers, they would ignore. Once they arrived, they would discover there was no place for them to go but back home.

Rae knew they were outnumbered and it might be a long battle, but they would win. Everything was in their favor.>

Rae took one last look and went below.

They saw the dust from the advancing army one day before they saw them. Sara left early in the morning to fly out over them. It was now past noon and she was coming back. As she glided down toward Shaméd's tent almost everyone came out to watch.

Lieutenant Jorge stood off to the side. He was watching for a different reason. His thoughts were on her, not the upcoming war. His mind drifted in thought about her.

<Over the past year, the two had become very close friends. He wanted to be more than just friends, but she said it could never be. Her mother would never allow it. She said if her mother got angry she might just eat him. Sara said something about the people of this world would never accept the two. She reminded him of the looks from the soldiers whenever they were together. He did not care what others thought. He was happy whenever she was around. If all they could be was friends, then friends they would be.>

Sara glided in close to the ground. When she was ten feet above the ground, the dragon leaned back with wings outspread, and became blurry. A shadowy outline of a dragon was hovering in the air, and then Sara's form floating in the middle as it descended down. A second later, her foot touched the ground and Sara walked over to Shaméd.

Lieutenant Jorge never got tired of watching her change forms. She almost never did it the same way. In his mind she was magnificent. He walked over with the others.

Sara turned to Shaméd.

"The army is spread out for miles. When they get here it will take all day for them to stop and make camp. I would estimate there are at least seventy-five thousand soldiers. There are over two hundred wagons, with ten siege weapons. They look like catapults. There are two large battering rams. At the very end there are about four or five hundred people walking. They could be slaves or just the normal riffraff that follow armies, trying to make money from service they can provide."

161

Shaméd smiled.

"That is good news. By tomorrow they should be in sight and we should be able to start this thing. Ok, everyone, go back to whatever you were doing. We have one more day."

Shaméd started to walk away. Sara coughed.

"It might be sooner than that. Their front riders were already heading back when I left. They have seen you, and the buildings. I think they are going back to report."

"It will not matter. No one will get here until tomorrow. Lieutenant Jorge, could you inform all the commanders to come and meet in my tent at sundown. I have some news."

Shaméd turned and entered his tent. The others began to walk away. Lieutenant Jorge looked at Sara.

"Do you want to go with me to inform Rae and the others of the meeting?"

Without speaking, she took his hand and they began to walk toward the bridge.

Philip stood there looking around. As everyone walked away he kicked Smash.

"Hey big guy pick me up and let's go back - I'm hungry."

"Ok, but Smash cannot stay. I am going to play catch with Cuchulainn."

Smash bent down, picked up Philip, and began walking. Philip was mumbling the whole way.

"Playing catch? Tossing a large rock at each other is not playing. You two could hurt someone if you miss. Yesterday you hurt your finger, so be careful. I cannot stand to hear you cry, and listening to that big creep Cuchulainn laughing at you as you cried made me want to sneak in and kill him in his sleep. Shaméd said I could not do it, so I will wait until he is no longer needed, then I will make him pay for laughing at you."

Smash grinned at Philip.

"You are a good friend. It was ok. He is not that bad. I like playing catch - it is fun."

Smash sat Philip down in front of the food tent, and turned and went looking for Cuchulainn. It was not difficult to find him because he was over by the ravine tossing rocks down at the trickle of water that had shown up last night.

Chapter Fifteen

An hour before sunset, Rae, Mordock, Jym, Nakobee met the other commanders as they came walking across the bridge. There were twenty as they gathered in front of Shaméd's tent; a couple of them were mumbling.

"How are all of us going to fit in there? Why did he not just come to us? The war room is three times the size of his tent."

Lord Taloree stood there pointing at the tent. Lord Digdeepest stood there looking up at him.

Rae watched as Nakobee opened the door and Jym and the others began walking in. Rae stopped at the door and nodded at Nakobee. Nakobee entered, Rae held the door open and looked at Lord Taloree and the others.

"You have forgotten something important. Lord Shaméd is a wizard. Not everything you see and hear is as it seems. Please enter and see for yourself."

Rae left them standing there as he entered the tent. They followed. As they entered, each one let out a small gasping sound. The room was huge inside. Shaméd stood there as they came in.

"It is good that all of you have come. Please sit and help yourself to food and drink. I will begin the meeting when you all are ready."

In a few minutes Shaméd pulled a map out of a folder. Holding it in the air, it began to grow. Within moments it was floating above the table. The map showed the land from coast to coast.

163

"Here is a map of the whole continent. Look here starting from the sea near Na-Car all the way down to the dry lake bed. If you look close you will see where the dry lakebed was is now showing water. That is because for the last two days, I along with others, searched and found where the water went. We found there were several reasons. Two dams were built sometime in the past. The one near Na-Car is gone and the one at the other end was removed this morning. The water that flooded the land around the ancient city is receding. The dirt mounds around the lakebed were in fact dirt from under it. I found the hole and began putting the dirt back causing the water to slowly refill the lake. It will take about three weeks, but already the water is flowing normally again, filling the lake and the river. The land will become fertile and people will again be able to live there. Since this land belongs to King Kalona, I am offering him the chance to expand his homeland by offering it to anyone who is willing to go there and live. This, of course, will make some of you nervous. I hope to remedy this. Prince Ja'-pheth, your kingdom can expand north. I am sending men there to clear out the plants and Klic-Klic. You will share the land with PKel's people who have said they only want some of the land - you may have the rest. The land on the other side of the great lake I would like to offer to the Elves and Dwarfs for their help. I have laid out my suggestions in these documents. Of course, I am not saying this is the only choice you have. I am saying I feel this is the best choice in making all involved happy. Now if you will go over them, we can talk about anything you feel should be changed."

They all opened the folders Nakobee was handing around the table. The documents stated that the land boarding north of Prince Já-pheth, would be given to him, this would give him an added land of ten hundred thousand acre's expanding his kingdom up to the small river and down to almost the end of the inland sea. This would double Prince Já-pheth holdings. The Dwarfs for their help would receive the chance to come and live in the mountains. They could pick out ten thousand acres for themselves, or a section of the mountain range that would be theirs. They could dig and use the minerals they find to help build their homes. For their help the elves would receive the land on the other side of the inland sea where the lost city was. The last item listed, had them talking the most. After a few minutes Shaméd stood.

"I can tell by the whispering and talking among you, that you have gotten to the last item. I have put that there because the people of Nanzorba are mostly slaves. They will be set free when this is over. Most will want to go back to their own homes. Many will have no home to go back to. Therefore, I have put here an option for them and you. It gives them the choice to come live in your land and be free. I have also given this choice to the soldiers of the Nanzorba. I will be dropping flyers to all of them giving them the chance to surrender. You will be giving them and many others the chance to live free and out from under the threat of death. I hope you will agree to what is there. I have given it a lot of thought and I have asked others wiser in the diplomatic field to go over what I wrote. Most have said I have been very fair and I hope you people will feel the same. So please help yourself to more food and drink. Think about all of this, and tomorrow let me know. I plan to drop the flyers before the army gets here. Now if you will please excuse me I have to leave. I have a meeting I need to attend on Lord Taloree's homeland. Rae will answer any of your questions."

"What meeting are you talking about?"

Lord Taloree and Lord Digdeepest both looked at Shaméd.

"I am meeting with the dragons on your island. They have agreed to stop fighting with you. Heather has found a place close to the dark wall. It is a very large island. Because it is so close to the wall there is only lower life living there. She and I will offer it to them. If they agree, you and your people will be free from them."

"If you can do this we agree with all you have stated here."

Lord Taloree and Lord Digdeepest both said at the same time.

Shaméd nodded at them then looked around, took two steps back and disappeared.

The questions began immediately, the next four hours they sat there talking. Finally, everyone agreed to the land deal to expand each of their kingdoms. The problem some were having was the idea of offering slaves and the soon ex-soldiers from the invading army, land, and money to surrender. This did not sound wise or safe.

"Why not make the offer. You can give them each a contract stating that at any time during their life, if they do anything against this country they will forfeit their land and life. You can also add that their families for two generations will be held to the same contract. With the threat of life on their family, most, if not all will stay true. Think about it. Tomorrow get back with me and let me know your decision. Each one of you must agree or Shaméd will not make the offer. Lord Shaméd made the offer to the soldiers on the land bridge and the commander answered for all of his men. They died for his decision. Lord Shaméd believes if given a choice most of the soldiers out there will surrender. You must remember many of those men are slaves and only do what they are forced to do. After reading all the reports on the country and its leaders, I believe, like Lord Shaméd. Given the chance, they will not fight. Go get some sleep and tomorrow at the morning staff meeting come prepared to give me your answer and to vote. Thank you and good night."

Rae stood there after speaking. Nakobee went and held the door open for the others to leave. Jym, Mordock,

Lieutenant Jorge, and Sara stayed sitting at the table. After everyone was gone, Nakobee came back and sat. They all looked at Rae. Jym spoke.

"This does not sound like you. You have always been of the opinion that you do not take prisoners or trust the enemy. Those must have been some very convincing reports you read to have changed your mind."

Sitting down, Rae took a drink. He looked around the table.

"I read all the reports that Mordock collected from his spies. I also read the ones from Reklan about the Nanzorban nation. If I had my way, I would destroy the government and place people there that would help rebuild it. Shaméd, of course, said I could not do this. So I will let the people on this world work together and rebuild it."

"What about the government makes you hate it."

Mordock lifted his cup to his lips. They were all now sitting at the table with a drink. It was their time to talk and relax. Rae motioned with his hand around to all of them.

"What I hate is that the rulers and the religious leaders forced their religion on everyone there. Letting them live, think, and do what they want infuriates me. I believe people should believe in any god they want and live anyway they want, as long as it does not harm others. When a religion begins to make people hate and despise others and forces them to hurt or kill others, then it and those that preach it should go away."

Mordock looked at Rae, he sat his cup down.

"You sound like the people you say you are against."

"It might sound that way, however I would not force, threaten, kill, or enslave anyone for not believing the way I do. These leaders have not only forced people, but they have killed people who do not do what they say. How could anyone believe in a god who would make you kill others? Forcing their people to live like animals just so a select group can do whatever they want? Trust me when I say this, we can talk a long time about how I feel about people and their gods. Maybe when this is all over we can sit and have that talk. I would love to know what god or entity your people believe in."

Mordock had picked up his cup and was drinking from it when Rae said the last words. He sat his cup down and looked at Rae.

"What do you mean? My people?"

Rae looked around at the others before looking back at Mordock.

"I mean you are a constructed being. There was no supreme being that created you and your people. Your creators were living beings who mixed human and other DNA together to make you."

Rae looked at Mordock. He was not sure, but it seemed the words he said were only making Mordock angrier. He hoped he could move fast enough if Mordock got too mad.

"I am sorry if I have offended you. I only say this because everyone in this room knows this. I for one would like to see your true form. I have seen what the MA-TED says you should look like based on your DNA. I have seen more beings from so many worlds I am amazed at the variety. I almost wish sometimes I was different."

Rae threw back his cup and looked around. Everyone was staring at him. He knew he had once again said more than he should have.

Jym slid his chair back. He was now clear of the table. Sara moved her chair at the same time. She looked at Jym and nodded her head. They were both ready to stop Mordock if he should attack Rae. Mordock slowly slid he chair back and stood. He did not look upset. He was very calm. He looked at Rae sitting there and he knew he did not mean anything bad.

"My ancestors were constructed. All of us after the first generation are born like any of you."

Mordock looked over at Sara.

"Except maybe you. I understand you are a clone of your mother. As for you, if you truly want to see what I look like, then I will show you. I must warn you most people who see my people's true form never want to see me or my people again."

Rae sat there trying to seem brave. In fact, he was very scared that when Mordock stood he was going to jump over the table and rip him apart. Listening to Mordock's words helped him relax; the butterflies in his stomach started to settle.

"I am not like others, and I do not think anyone here will think of you differently. You are a friend and friends except each other for who they are. Except maybe Jon, but you don't care what he thinks. You do not even like him."

Mordock started laughing. The other others looked at him trying to understand what was funny. Mordock reached for his cup, raised it like a salute toward Rae, and drank it down. Setting his cup down on the table, he stood there looking at them.

"Jon is a very different person. If you and the others can like him the way he is, then I will try to understand him."

Standing there, Mordock began to blur, but his clothes remained the same. The only change was his face. He was dark and hairy. His eyes went up and down when he blinked and there were inside lids that went left to right. His fingers were long, there were points sticking out above his knuckles that looked like spikes. Rae sat there looking at him, twisting his head to one side as if he was examining him. He looked over at Jym.

"I know why you do not like Jon. Jon almost looks like you when he has not shaved for a week. Mordock, you do not look all that different. Ok, you are a lot hairier and the eyes might take some time to get used to. I like the teeth, there very pointy. You vaguely resemble what the MA-TED thought you would. I however believe you look better. To me, you look human, or as close to whatever a human is supposed to look like. You need to go to one of the big parties on Nogar's world. You will see many different kinds of people there. One day you should come to my world. I would love to have you walk the streets with me."

"That is not funny Rae. You know very well the people there would think he was a werewolf from the ancient legends and run away."

Jym sat there frowning at Rae. Rae just sat there smiling.

"I know, and I would love it. The people there need to be shaken up and told about the rest of the universe. We need to regain the knowledge we had before. Well, this like many other things needs to wait. We all need to get some sleep. Tomorrow will be a very busy day. Those who are staying on this side, I bid you goodnight. Those who are going back over to the other side, we should leave. And thank you, Mordock, for trusting me, I mean us."

Mordock blurred again, returning to his other form. The others stood and left the tent.

Chapter Sixteen

Shaméd called Philip, Nakobee, Sara, and Mordock to his tent. They arrived just as the sun was rising.

When they walked up to the tent the door opened and they entered. They saw Kinn and another man sitting at the table with Shaméd.

"Welcome. Please help yourself to a drink and come sit."

After they each got a drink, they sat.

"I asked you to come here this morning because you will be going with me to the island. You all know Kinn. He will be in charge of another group. Mordock, Sara, Philip, this is Atrell. He will be with Kinn."

The three looked at Atrell. He sat there sipping his drink. He had shoulder length blond hair and green eyes. He was stocky but not fat. He carried a saber and a long knife. His clothes were brown leather, not dragon skin, but some type of animal. He looked younger than Shaméd - maybe in his early twenties. He carried himself with confidence. They greeted him and he nodded his head, but did not speak. Shaméd continued.

"We will meet on a raft about a mile from the island. We will row ashore then walk about two miles to the ruins. Once inside we will split up. When we find what we are looking for, we will transport it off world and leave as fast as we can. We should be gone from here no more than five hours. We cannot be inside the building any longer. If we are, we will be trapped. Look over the map of the building. You will see the red marks. They show the locations of demons. You can see they guard all the entrances. We are not sure why since only demons are on the island. There are never more than three by the entrances. We believe it is because when there are more, they begin fighting. That must be why they do not meet and walk the same pattern. It looks like there are only four ways in or out. We will enter here. It is close to the trees and should offer the best cover. We do not have a very good map of the inside, but we do have this. We have every reason to believe all the floors are similar to this one.

When the fighting starts, you four return here. We will leave for the island from inside the tent. Kinn and Atrell will leave in a few minutes on the Dragonfly. As I said, they will meet us there. Now, if there are no questions we have a long day ahead of us. Are there any questions?"

No one spoke, so they all stood and left. Shaméd began putting the furniture away. When he was done, he walked out.

As Shaméd stepped out of the tent, he saw Boone walking toward him. Shaméd stopped and waited for him. Boone walked up, took a deep breath and looked into the sky, then let it out.

"So, this is the big day. I saw everyone leaving. They will be the ones you will be taking with you to the island?"

Shaméd was impressed how Boone handled himself in human form. Being a dragon or human without eyes must be tough.

"I assume when you say you saw them, you meant you felt them. And yes, they are the ones coming with me. Before I forget, I have a question to ask. The other day you said something and it has been on my mind. Let me get it correctly - you said. "He was a very impressive dragon in his day, and we all loved him very much." Can you please elaborate on what you meant?"

"Certainly. You know I am a time dragon, and I am very old. No, not just very old - I am what you would call ancient. I was only three hundred years old when Red, as you call him was King and the war with his brother began. I was on his side and I was fighting a dragon here on this world. I was young and very inexperienced in fighting. I should never have tried to take on an older dragon alone. During the fight four more dragons attacked me. I was hurt and fell to the ground. As they came down to kill me, and they would have killed me, I shifted. I was hurt and blind, so I hid for a few years, not sure of where or when I was. I met Heather's mother. She helped me adjust to this world. I did not know until I met with Heathers mother, that I moved thousands of years into the future. Farther than any dragon should ever be able to. Since I had traveled so far into the future and had stayed hidden for so long, I could not return. I have spent my life traveling back and forth in time on this world looking and searching. When I saw you I started making plans so you would be able to find the items you needed. I had Lucy go to the bookstore and show you the books. I had Heather meet you and offer you help. Of course, she did not know why at the time. Now she does and is a little annoyed with me. She is a lot like her mother. When you see Red again inform him that Boonarae says hello, and it is about time he came back. Now you have a lot to do and I am in the way here. I, also, have some things I have to do to get ready. You are not the only one who is making plans."

"So it would seem. You have been busy, but do you not think it would have been easier to just come and introduce yourself to me. We could have reached this point sooner?"

"No. If I had introduced myself to you, you would have found the items on this world and left. The people here would still be in trouble. You had to have a reason to stay and help. Besides, it had to happen this way for more reasons than you know. You have found people here who will become very important. Now I must leave. Like I said, you have things to do and so do I. Take care. I will be watching you and will see you very soon."

Boone started walking, when he reached the edge of the ravine. He stepped over the edge dropping out of sight. A second later a large silver-blue dragon rose up and flew away. Shaméd heard the people call out and wave as the dragon circled the camp before leaving.

Shaméd saw Sara and Lieutenant Jorge standing on the bridge. They were in the middle and watched Boone go over the edge and change. When Boone disappeared, they walked toward Shaméd. When they were close, Sara called out.

"I see Boone came and said goodbye. Do you have the flyers you want me to drop?"

"Yes. They are in my satchel - all you have to do is fly over the soldiers and open it. They will fall out. I think if you make two passes that should be adequate. Everyone should get one and then you can return."

He handed her the satchel. Sara kissed Lieutenant Jorge on the cheek and ran over toward the ravine and dove off. A few seconds later reappearing in her dragon form, she came up twisting and twirling around in the air, and like Boone she circled the camp then the fortress before she headed off toward the incoming army.

"She is a very beautiful woman. You know if the two of you get together, she will outlive you. And if her mother finds out you have an interest in her, you might be her next meal."

"I know. Sara already explained it to me. We are only friends. We have not taken it further than that. She is fun to talk with. I enjoy her company. I do not understand why, but I can be myself around her. I do not have to impress her or be like someone I am not. Somehow, she can get me to talk about things I have never told anyone. She is an amazing creature and I mean that in a good way. Whether in dragon or human form, she is impressive."

"I am glad to hear you are happy. Now you must go back and stay with Rae. I will be meeting with the General in a few hours. When the fighting starts I will leave."

"Yes. I still do not know why you will not let me go with you."

Lieutenant Jorge stood there. He looked disappointed he was not going with Shaméd.

"Because it is too dangerous and the people I am taking have done this kind of thing before. Do not worry. You will prove yourself to the others. You have already proven yourself to me."

"Thank you, Lord Shaméd. The time I have spent in your service has been very interesting and educational. I would not have missed it for anything. Have a safe trip."

Lieutenant Jorge came to attention, saluted Shaméd, subsequently turned around, and walked away. Shaméd watched him leave. Lieutenant Jorge did not walk - he marched. He carried himself as a true soldier, head up, shoulders back, and chest out. He was proud of who and what he had accomplished. As he stepped onto the bridge several men called out and waved from the trench. He waved back as he walked across the bridge.

Shaméd looked toward the men that were staying on this side, everyone was in place. Smash and Cuchulainn were going to be tossing a large rock back and forth, playing catch as they had been for the last few days. They agreed the site of it would give the approaching army something to ponder. The others were all in the trenches. The two tents were a few feet behind them. Of course, no one had the slightest thought of entering them once the fighting began. Each man had three rifles and plenty of ammunition.

Shaméd started walking down the road away from the bridge and his tent. When he was a mile away from the bridge he stopped. Looking around he saw the landscape was the same for miles in all directions. It was low rolling hills, more grass land than anything. He reached into the bag he was carrying and pulled out a folded cloth, poles, and ropes. Laying it all out on the ground, he began setting up a large a canopy. He placed a table with four chairs under it. A large keg of ale sat at the end of the table; the table had an assortment of food. A white flag topped it all off, it was waving high over the canopy. Stepping under it, he poured a drink and sat to wait.

The Nanzorban army stopped moving as the scream of dragon was heard. All long the column people dove under wagons. The soldiers started moving around, some raised their shields, others theirs spears, and those with bows got them ready.

A light warm wind was blowing toward the ravine. Sara used it to her advantage. She flew high and when she reached the end of the enemy's line, she twisted in the air and came back. She was just out of bow range when she twisted her claw and the satchel opened and began dropping the leaflets. The wind caught the paper. It began floating down toward the army. When Sara reached the front of the line of soldiers, again, she twisted up and around and headed back to do it one more time. The soldiers saw the dragon was not attacking; it was only dropping papers. They relaxed and began to grab the leaflets. Those that could read told the others what they said.

Sara saw the soldiers stop marching. They were standing around reading the flyers. She few higher. When she reached an air current she spread her wings and using the current she did a few rolls and twists playing in the air. Then she twisted around and headed back to the ravine. The leaflets continued to fall around the soldiers.

Terms for Surrender:

Every soldier must surrender their weapons and return to their home.

Every soldier that agrees to this will be given enough food and water to make the journey home.

If for any reason a soldier believes his life, or that of his family, would be in danger for surrendering, then we offer the below conditions to them.

1. *Each soldier that lays down his weapons and pledges his loyalty to our Kingdom will receive three (3) gold coins and thirty (30) acres of land.*
2. *Each officer that lays down his weapons and pledges his loyalty to our Kingdom will receive ten (10) gold coins and one hundred (100) acres of land.*

3. *Each senior officer that lays down his weapons and pledges his loyalty to our Kingdom will receive twenty (20) gold coins and two hundred (200) acres of land.*

4. *If the commander of this group convinces his whole battalion to surrender and is the first to lay down his weapons and pledges his loyalty to our Kingdom, he will receive one hundred (100) gold coins and one thousand (1000) acres of land.*

You have one hour. If you do not accept this offer by that time it will be determined that you all wish to die. We will, with great regret, fulfill that wish.

This is a just and valid offer given by the emissary of the New United Kingdoms of Calamor.

Lord Shaméd

   The General sitting on his steed finished reading the leaflet he caught. Those nearby who read their own leaflet could see the anger on his face. Staring straight ahead and without looking at anyone, he began yelling out orders.

   "Rip those papers up. Any man caught with one will receive ten lashings. Lieutenant, pass the word around that I mean what I just said. I will not have my men getting any ideas that I do not give them. We will make camp here. You five come with me; the rest of you go, do what I said. I want all those flyers destroyed."

   The men saluted. Those on foot ran, the others turned their animals around and rode back toward the men. A few seconds later, you could hear officers yelling to their men to destroy all of the flyers and to make camp. A few of the soldiers folded the paper and put it in their pockets. The five men the General pointed at sat there on their animals, waiting.

He faced toward the bridge and the enemy, slowly ripping the paper in half. Then half again doing this until he could no longer rip them, holding his hand out, and dropped the paper to the ground. The ravine and the bridge were less than two miles away. He could just make out what looked like tents on this side of the bridge. Between him and the bridge, he saw a tent in the middle of the road. Then he saw the buildings on the other side - buildings that were not there last year. The information he had did not include this. If this was all new, what other information did he not have? Why were there tents? Also, how did they build those buildings so fast? He kicked his animal and began riding forward. His men followed. He would be at the tent in the middle of the road in less than ten minutes, then his questions would be answered or someone would be in a lot of pain.

Shaméd sat there facing the approaching army. Demahs lay curled up off to the side in the sand. The staff floated behind him. He watched Sara drop the flyers and the army stop. Now she was coming back. As she flew over him, she dropped his satchel. It fell in front of the canopy. Shaméd held his hand out. The satchel rose from the ground and floated over to him.

"Well, in a few minutes we will see if this General is any different."

Demahs raised his head, looked around, then he went back to sleep. Shaméd watched the army as they began to spread out making camp. Almost an hour after setting up the canopy, and fifteen minutes after the flyers were dropped, he saw the six riders coming toward him.

"And now it starts."

< *"You know the General will not come straight here."*>

"I know. He will send someone to see why I am here and what is going on. Let's hope he is smart enough to come and meet me when they get their answers."

The riders stopped almost half a mile away. One of the riders was the General - Shaméd could tell by the helmet. It was more flamboyant than the one he took from the leader on the land bridge there were more feathers and braids. Four riders came forward slowly. The one in front carried a spear with a white cloth at the top. When they were ten feet away, they stopped. The one with the spear and white flag kicked his animal closer.

"Greetings. We are here to find out why you are blocking the road and stopping us from crossing the bridge. We also want to know if you know anything about the fliers that were dropped over our army today."

Shaméd took a sip from his cup trying to act indifferent.

"Please come in out of the sun and sit. Help yourself to food and a drink. I will be more than happy to answer your questions."

The man who spoke stuck out his arm stopping the others when they began to move up.

"I am afraid we cannot accept your offer. If you would just please answer my questions we will leave."

"I will be happy to answer your questions."

The man looked at Shaméd his face twisted up in confusion.

"Well?"

"What were those questions, again?"

Shaméd took a sip from his cup and sat there staring at the four men. They looked at each other and whispered. The man turned back toward Shaméd.

"My General wants to know why you are blocking the road. So why are you? In addition, he wants to know if you had anything to do with the fliers. Did you? I would also like to ask, are you a wizard?"

179

Shaméd sat his cup down and stood. When he did, Demahs uncurled, stretched, and walked out from behind the chair. He stopped and looked up at the four men. They saw the movement and watched as the dragonet came out. They looked at the dragonet and then at Shaméd. The man holding the spear spoke.

"I think that answered your last question, Karl."

The man called Karl shot him a dirty look, then turned to face Shaméd.

"Will you answer my questions?"

"Of course. I am not blocking the road, only camped in the middle so you will not miss me. I had a friend drop the pamphlets over your army to give everyone a chance to read it and know what their choices were. I gave the same offer to Sub General Portus, who was sent to cross the land bridge. I am sorry to say, he did not let his men have a voice or choice. He spoke for all of his men and turned down the offer. Now I am sad to tell you they are all dead. I was hoping your men were smarter. Yes, I am a wizard. I am here to stop you from invading. Now did I satisfy you? Would you give a message to your General? Inform him I will be here waiting for him. I would like to meet with him in person, or if he does something stupid and tries to attack, I will leave and anyone who does not lay down their weapons and surrender will die. Since you do not want to come in and rest for a few minutes, I think you should go and report back to your General. One more thing, here is the helmet that belonged to Sub General Portus. It is all I could find of him when I was done."

Shaméd waved his hand and the helmet floated up off the ground from behind the table. The helmet floated over to the man. Slowly he reached out and grabbed it. The men looked at it and then back at Shaméd. Without speaking, they turned their animals around, kicked them, and began running. Shaméd could hear their words as well as their thoughts as they left. He spoke aloud to Reklan as he listened to them.

"They are afraid. They know their General will not surrender and two of those men would if given the chance. Reklan, try to get close to the General's tent to see what they talk about."

< "I will. Do you think he will believe the helmet belongs to his man?" >

"It won't matter. It will take days for a courier to go there and find out, unless one of his priests can do it. This time tomorrow the battle will start."

Shaméd picked up his cup, took another drink, then sat back in his chair to wait. He placed the cup on the table, folded his arms, and closed his eyes. He knew what he was doing was not exactly what the council wanted. He was to help these people, to even guide them, but not intervene on their behalf. For the first time in the history of the thirty-six, the number one rule was being challenged further. That rule was to observe and not interfere with the people on any world. You could not help or ever let them know you are from another world. He never liked that rule. The people he met here deserved to have his help and he was determined to give it. He even decided to go with Rae, to help make him king and rebuild his homeworld.

< "They are coming back." >

< "The General?" >

< "Yes, along with the others." >

Reklan's words woke Shaméd from his light sleep. Opening his eyes, he saw the six animals coming toward him. The man out front was the General. He carried himself boldly and long feathers on his helmet swayed in the breeze. His cloak was bright red. Shaméd filled his cup, took a long drink, then put his flask away. He sat there waiting. The men rode up. One man jumped off taking hold of the General's horse. The General looked at Shaméd and slowly and with a great show, dismounted. Taking his gloves off, he stuffed them in his belt. He walked over, and stopped just outside the canopy. He stood there staring at Shaméd, who was still sitting.

"I checked out the helmet. It did belong to my sub General. We tried to contact him and his men. There has been no answer. I have sent a rider to check on them. I will not have an answer for at least two days. Therefore, I will take you at your word that you have stopped them. I demand to know why you are blocking my road, and the meaning of the flyers."

Shaméd stood and motioned to the table and chairs.

"Would you care to come in and rest? I offer you food and drink. I believe that is the custom here in this land when meeting someone for the first time. I will answer all your questions even if you do not except my hospitality."

The General stood there for a moment. He walked in and stopped near the table.

"I will accept your shade but not your food or drink."

Shaméd stepped around the table to within three feet of the General.

"That is fine. To answer your first question, I am here to stop you and your army from invading and making slaves of the people of Kaloon and Kal-aron. They have joined and made an alliance with each other and several other nations. They asked for my help and I have freely given it to them. The offer in the flyers is real. I hope you will be smart and except it. I have no desire in killing you or your men. However, believe me when I say this: if you fight, you will die. You cannot win, because as we speak, your king and his followers are being attacked. A rebellion has begun in your land. The people there are tired of being slaves and living in fear. If you return, you will find a completely different nation. I believe a better one. Do you have any other questions?"

Shaméd watched as the red rose in the General's face. As he looked into the General's mind, he saw and felt nothing but contempt, anger, and hate. The man cared for nothing - he hated everything. In the General's mind he saw this campaign was more than just a battle, it was his way of becoming a king. Shaméd heard his thoughts before they were screamed aloud. Shaméd blocked out the thoughts as the General began to speak.

"You dare to talk to me this way? I am not afraid of one man. Even if he claims to be a wizard. I have twenty priests who have the power to stop you or anyone that stands in my way."

Shaméd turned his back to the General. He stepped back to his chair and sat. He looked up at the General.

"I was not trying to sound like I was talking down to you. I was trying to reason with you. As for your priests? They cannot help you. As you stand here, they have just learned that they cannot speak. If I am pushed, they will suffer even more. And so will you. Go back and think the offer over. If you want I will give you proof of my power. The dry lakebed ten miles from here will be a lake again. The river that once ran below in the ravine is starting to flow again. By midday tomorrow it will be as it was thousands of years ago. When you see it you can give me your answer. I will be right here waiting."

Without a word the General turned away and walked to his horse. When he was mounted, he looked back at Shaméd.

"You are young and arrogant. It will be a pleasure to watch you die. I saw your two pets tossing the rock around. I do not care that you have an ogre and a Titian helping you. I have over seventy-five thousand seasoned warriors. I have the equipment to take the bridge and storm all the cities. Kaloon and Kal-aron and any others who are stupid enough to join them will fall at my feet. They could never gather the men to stop me. Kaloon and Kal-aron combined could only have ten thousand men. I will give you my answer now, wizard. In the morning, we will attack. I will crush you where you sit."

Twisting his animal's head, he kicked and rode off. The five men looked at Shaméd. Their worried expressions did not change as they turned and followed their General.

"Demahs, I have work to do before morning. Do you want to come with me?"

Demahs head came up and he looked at Shaméd.

< "I will go with you. Where are you going?">

"I need to go to the lake. I need to speed it up. Since I told the General the water would be here tomorrow.

Reklan, can you contact Mordock and let him know he and the others can come here and have the food and drink?"

< "I will tell them. I am sure the others will like the ale - they just started cooking dinner.">

Shaméd started walking toward his tent. He saw Smash and Cuchulainn sitting by a large fire talking with the men. Mordock was off to the side stretched out, his arms folded and his eyes closed. Sara was sitting next to Lieutenant Jorge. He still was not sure how it would work out with them. A human and a dragon was not really a good combination.

Chapter Seventeen

The enemy's army began to spread out at first light. Their catapults were spaced fifty feet apart. Their soldiers started lining up.

Shaméd was in front of the trench watching with Lieutenant Jorge. Their men stood on top of the trench looking out at the enemy army.

Shaméd had returned two hours earlier from the lake. It was filling up faster, now. By noon the river below would be flowing as it did many years ago. It would not stop the approaching fight. He knew the General would not care. The General's mind was twisted; he did not care about anyone or anything. He only wanted to kill.

"Lieutenant, you should get your men in place and ready. Keep an eye out for Smash, he might get excited and try to run out. Philip and I told him to behave and do what you said. Smash and Cuchulainn have plenty of rocks. Try to keep them in their trench and have them toss all of the rocks before your men use their guns. Remember their range is only a little bit better than the bows. You will have to let them get close. I will return before the day is over. I will deal with the priests before I leave, that way you will not have to worry about them. Be careful and wait for the signal from Rae, you must not retreat across the bridge too early. If for any reason you cannot make it across, get inside my tent. I am not sure if it will hold all the men, along with Smash and Cuchulainn. However, it will protect you and if needed Reklan can open a portal for you to pass through."

"Do not worry, I won't be a hero. You have told me what to do and I will follow your orders precisely."

Shaméd nodded at the Lieutenant.

"Good. I would not want to have to explain anything to Sara. I will be leaving in a few minutes right after I take care of the priests."

The first rock from the catapult hit a hundred feet from where they were standing. It slammed into the ground. Dirt and dust flew into the air. Shaméd turned and started walking back to his tent - Lieutenant Jorge climbed up the trench wall to his men. He and his men began walking along the top. Once they got to their position the men jumped down inside. Smash and Cuchulainn stood, each one took a rock and tossed it toward the enemy.

Shaméd reached his tent and stopped outside.

"Demahs, you need to go to Rae and Bella. Stay with them until I return."

< *"I want to go with you."*>

"You cannot go. I need you to stay here, to guard Rae, and to make sure Bella stays out of trouble."

< *"He does not need me. He has humans protecting him."*>

"Yes, he does and he even has Bella, but I need you to watch them both. I will be ok, so I need you to stay and protect him. Now please go to his side and watch over him."

Demahs disappeared from Shaméd's shoulder and reappeared in the air flying toward the fortress. Rae was standing on the top, watching. Bella was lying on the wall near him.

Shaméd entered his tent just as the rocks thrown by Smash and Cuchulainn took out one catapult. Inside, he saw Sara, Mordock, Nakobee, and Philip. Philip was the only one eating the food on the table. The others were standing there waiting. As Shaméd walked in, Mordock yelled at Philip.

"Ok, now you can stop eating."

Philip looked over at Mordock as he shoved a piece of meat into his mouth. With his hands free, he stuffed some bread into his pouch.

"Ok. Are we going now or do you still have things to do?"

"One more minute and we will leave. All of you please stand over here in the circle I drew on the ground. Sara, when I step in there you must take hold of my arm. I will be casting a spell that will null all magic within a five-mile radius of this tent. We don't want you to be caught in it."

"What about the others?"

"Your mother, Boone, and all the rest are far away. I informed them what I was going to do."

Sara and the others stepped inside the circle. Shaméd took out the staff, placed it in the center of the tent, and it sank into the ground a few inches. Shaméd held out both of his hands toward the staff. His eyes closed, and the spell began. There were no words spoken out loud. The staff started to glow as one by one, the crystals lit up. Stepping back from the staff, Shaméd looked at them as he stepped within the circle. Sara took hold of his arm and the others moved closer.

"We are ready. All of you must hold on to each other and me. Do not let go. All of you close your eyes. Philip, keep your eyes closed this time."

Shaméd raised his left arm and tapped several crystals on the gauntlet. A light slowly spread up and out, engulfing them. There was a flash and the light was gone, the room was empty except for the staff. It stood in the center of the tent with all its crystal glowing - even the red one.

Shaméd and the others appeared in the middle of a raft, it rocked a little as they each let go of Shaméd. Kinn and his team were around the edge paddling. Kinn called out to Shaméd.

"Just in time. The Dragonfly dropped us off a few minutes ago and is heading back. Please sit down. You are rocking the raft. We will be there in a few minutes."

They sat in the middle of the raft. Nakobee turned to see what looked like a large dragon flying off in the distance. It was gone in seconds. The shore drew closer. As the raft beached, the men jumped off. They pulled it further onto shore into the trees. Without speaking, everyone grabbed their gear and headed inland for the building.

The enemy fired five more rocks toward the trench. One hit the embankment blasting dirt down on the soldiers. Another slammed into the ground on the back side, the last one over shot taking out one of their tents. The men were not happy about just sitting there, but they knew there was nothing they could do until the enemy soldiers came closer.

The sixth rock hit the top of their trench and rolled down inside hitting one of the men. They heard a loud boom; the canons from the fort were now firing. The canon ball hit one of the catapults, smashing it and scattering the men around it.

Smash worked his way over where the boulder landed in the trench. He rolled the boulder up the side and out of the trench. The man who was hit was carried off, but there was no helping him.

The enemies' soldiers were now separated out into twenty groups. The General stood out in front on his steed yelling orders. Two squads of cavalry were over on the right side ready to attack the flank side of the trench. After the catapult was hit, the General waved his arm and one hundred men began charging toward the trench. Waving again, a thousand men ran toward the bridge.

Lieutenant Jorge watched them.

"Wait. They need to pass the boulder marked with yellow. When they reach the one marked with red we can fire."

The advancing soldiers ran by the boulder with yellow. When most of them ran pass the red boulder, Lieutenant Jorge yelled.

"Fire. And do so until there are no more."

Smash threw a rock over his head with great force. It hit a soldier in the chest knocking him down and taking the man behind him, too. Cuchulainn heaved a rock, then two more, at the soldiers heading toward the bridge. Then he jumped out of the trench rushing toward them, his six-foot long sword swinging. Smash saw Cuchulainn head for the bridge. He grabbed his club and followed after him.

The General watched in horror and anger, as he saw the Titian and the Ogre kill all one thousand men before they could get close to the bridge. He yelled for more men to charge the bridge. The General raised and dropped his arm. Within seconds, five thousand men were rushing toward the bridge. During this time he did not notice his men being slaughtered by the men in the trench. When he did look over he saw the devastation. Those not dead were scattered. They were confused as to where to go. He was so furious he was whipping his steed and yelling orders as he moved back and forth along his line. He called for the bugler to sound retreat. It was just in time as his men that were heading for the bridge started dying from the shots being fired from the trenches. As soon as the bugler sounded, those that were not dead started to retreat. The General's men turned around running back faster than they had when they charged. When they all returned, his Lieutenant reported they had lost fifteen hundred men in the attack.

The General bawled out, "Bring the priests out here now!"

As the twenty priests came forward, they stood there with their heads down.

"You will do something about those men over there or I will have all of your heads."

The priests looked up at him in horror. They tried to speak but no words came out. Their mouths worked and worked, but nothing. They stood there waving their hands. One old priest stepped forward, and they all stopped moving. The old priest pointed at five priests who walked over to stand by his side. Then the old priest waved for the others to move back. After they moved a few feet away, the old man held up his hands and began swaying, his mouth moving but no words came out. The five priests started doing the same. After five minutes they stopped, but nothing happened. They looked over at the General. He glared at them, then over at a group of soldiers on his right.

"Kill them. The rest of you filthy priests leave, and think about what will happen to you if you cannot figure out a way to help."

The lieutenant of the soldiers raised his hand. His men drew arrows setting them into their bows. The six priests drew closer to each other, turned their backs, and stood there. When the soldier dropped his arm, the archers fired at them. They fell to the ground dead. The other priests watched in horror, then hurried back to their tent rushing inside.

The catapults began firing, again, aiming at the men in the trench. After each would fire, the enemy would move it forward ten feet. Rocks began hitting closer and more went into the trench.

The men stayed crouched down on the side facing the enemy. Rocks were shot at Shaméd's tent. After the fourth one bounced away, the catapult was turned toward the trench.

The fort kept firing their canons. They took out two more catapults, causing them to stop their advancement and begin drawing them back.

Three hours later, the catapults stopped. The dust began to settle. The men in the trench slowly stood and looked out. There were large boulders all over the ground - many at the base of their trench.

The General moved out front and waved his arm. Soldiers began marching from the right side flanking the trench. They stopped a thousand feet from the trench. After stopping, they began stepping aside making an opening in the middle. More men came running through the opening. Once out front they lined up and drew their bows. A man yelled an order: "Fire!"

Arrows flew up toward the trench. The men inside moved closer and held their shields over their heads. Most of the arrows hit dirt in and around the trench, only a few made it through the shields. Some of the men were hit; Smash was hit five times and he roared out in pain. The Titian stood and drew his sword. He was about to charge when Lieutenant Jorge yelled: "Fire. Take those archers out."

Some of the men dropped their shields and grabbed the rifles. The others kept the shields up to cover both the ones with the rifles and themselves. They moved around getting into better positions. Once they were there, they began firing. Each shot hit an archer with extreme precision. Within seconds there were no more arrows; most of the archers lay dead on the ground. The ones still alive started retreating back behind their soldiers. They held up their shields to protect themselves. It did not work. The bullets from the rifles went through the shields, killing or wounding them. The enemy continued retreating. When they were out of range, Lieutenant Jorge called out again.

"One last volley, aim high and see if you can hit anything."

Those who were holding shields dropped them. They picked up rifles. All of them raised their weapons and fired. They saw a few men fall. They watched as the soldiers moved out of range.

A strange quiet slowly crept over the battleground - the only sounds came from dying men. There were no further attacks.

Lieutenant Jorge stood in the trench trying to figure out what was coming. It was now five hours after the fighting had started. There were four hours of fighting and one hour of both sides just staring at each other.

Lieutenant Jorge had lost eight men. The enemy had lost thousands of men. The field out front of them was littered with their dead and dying. It made him sick inside to see all this death. Then he saw the enemy begin to move forward.

The catapults began firing, not big rocks, but small ones. They rained down inside the trench taking out three men. They were now able to hit with greater accuracy. The men were starting to get worried and frightened. Getting knocked down by rocks and dirt, Lieutenant Jorge stood back up and dusted off the dirt.

"Ok, men. We have stayed here long enough. Take all of your ammo and head for the bridge. We will make our stand over there."

Five more volleys of rocks fell as they packed up to leave. Three large boulders hit the side of the trench caving it in. The men moved out of the way. They grabbed what was left of the ammo and began running down the trench toward the bridge. The canons from the fortress began firing at the catapults. They hit four, taking them out. Now the enemy only had three catapults left.

Twenty feet from the bridge the trench ended. They had stacked boulders along the open area to give them some protection. The soldiers and Lieutenant Jorge exited the trench staying low behind the boulders and ran to the bridge. As they ran across, the Titian stopped. He stood there looking back at the enemy.

The General called out for all of his men to get ready to charge the bridge. He sat there on his horse looking at the bridge. He had won a small victory. The men in the trench with their strange weapons were now running away. They had made it to the bridge and headed for the other side. Only the Titian and the Ogre stood there pretending to guard the bridge. The Titian stood there with his sword and shield, the Ogre with a large club. They would not stand there much longer. The Ogre had over a dozen arrows in him; the Titian just as many.

The General called out; he had a smile on his face. Those close to him were scared when they saw it.

"All archers move forward and fire at those two until they drop."

The archers moved out front of the others. They lined up and soon the sky was filled with arrows. The sky grew dark as the arrows arched closer, blocking out the sun over Smash and Cuchulainn.

Cuchulainn stood there with Smash who was shuffling his feet. He wanted to run. He did not want to die here. His father had told him he had proven his was a man. When he was home his father told the clan he was heir to his father's throne. He had waited a long time for his father's approval. He was in pain and did not want to do this anymore. But he did not want Cuchulainn or the others to think him a coward. He looked around for something to help stop the arrows. Cuchulainn raised his arm up toward the arrows.

"Smash, get behind me and stay close"

Cuchulainn's shield began to grow slowly larger, spreading out covering him and Smash just as the arrows rained down and around them.

Chapter Eighteen

They planned the incursion around the time of day when most of the demons were gone from the island. This gave Shaméd and his group an almost clear way to the building. Slipping by what few demons were there was easy. When they reached the building, they saw three demons guarding the door. One stood near it all the time. The other two walked from the door along the side of the building down to the corner, then back to the door, again. Mordock and Sara took out the two as they were coming back. Atrell ran straight at the demon standing guard at the door. The demon stood there staring at Atrell as he ran toward him.

The large demon tipped his head at the little man coming toward him. He stood there trying to figure out what the little person was doing here on the island. Atrell drew his sword when he was ten feet away and jumped in the air at the demon. The sword went deep into his throat slicing it open, killing him where he stood. The demon fell back and slid down the wall.

Atrell watched as Sara came walking toward him dragging her demon with one hand. She reached out taking hold of the demon he just killed. With one in each hand, she dragged them away taking them into the trees. The others went to help Mordock drag his into the trees.

Shaméd walked up to the door. Pushing it open he stood there waiting. When the others arrived they entered. The door open up to a long hallway, walking down it they came to a junction and stopped.

"Here is where we split up. Kinn, be careful and at the first sign of trouble have Reklan open the mirror gate for you..."

"I know what to do. Remember I have done this many times, mostly before you were born. I will be careful. You remember to do the same."

Smiling, Kinn patted Shaméd on the back. Kinn moved to the right leading his group down the hallway. Shaméd watched for a second before leading his group forward. They walked by many rooms, their doors missing or open. All the rooms were sleeping chambers for the demons. They were filthy and all of them reeked. The further they went the worst the odor. It was becoming hard to breathe as they went further and further.

"These demons are filthier than Ogres. Smash would even hate the smell."

Philip pinched his nose as he moved away from a doorway. Walking around a bend, they came to a blockage. They turned around and went back to the stairwell that they saw before the bend. Stepping inside they saw the way up was blocked from the collapsed wall, they went down.

Going down they stopped and checked three floors. They checked out all the rooms they found before going to the next floor. All the rooms were like the ones above, all were filthy and smelled of demons. On the fourth floor down, they met up with Kinn and his group.

"Did you find anything?" Kinn asked when they met.

"Nothing. And I take it you found nothing."

"Only filth. I will never understand why any creature would live in such filth."

"We are going to the next floor. You might as well join us. We can split up again if needed."

Shaméd headed for the stairwell. Going down to the next floor they split up, each going in the opposite directions. This floor was different in only one way; they could walk all the way around the building back to the stairwell. When Shaméd reached the stairway he saw Kinn and the others. He stopped to wait. Kinn and his group stopped in front of a door. This one was different. The door was shut and locked.

"Shaméd, we found a locked door."

Shaméd and his group walked over. Shaméd tried to open the door then moved away.

"Philip, looks like you are up."

Philip came closer. He dug out his lock picking tools.

"It is about time I had something to do. All this walking about was getting boring."

Philip made short work of the lock and pushed the door open. Shaméd, Kinn, and the others walked in. They all stopped a few feet inside the room and stared. The room was completely empty.

Philip shut the door and stared around the room.

"Looks like no one ever slept in this room."

The others began walking around the room.

The room looked about fifty feet long with the inside wall curving in the shape of the building. Not only was the room empty it was also very clean. There was no dust or dirt anywhere. The only thing they found were two doors on the inside wall one at each end of the room. The door they entered was in the center on the opposite wall.

"This could be interesting. Do we open both to see where they go or only one?"

Kinn called out as he stood near one and Shaméd at the other.

"Might as well open both since we are already here."

Shaméd opened his as Kinn opened the other. They stepped through.

Shaméd stepped out onto a metal walkway, looking left as he went through the door. He saw Kinn step out on another walkway fifty feet away. They looked out over the railing of the walkway and found the center of the building and it was a very large circular room. It was at least three or four hundred feet in diameter. Kinn looked around and then looked over at Shaméd.

"It would seem we go down. Mine goes out from the wall and twists back and forth going almost straight down. Yours looks like a ramp that travels down around the wall and it looks like it passes under this one a few times. Do we race to see who gets to the bottom first?"

Kinn smiled at Shaméd. Shaméd smiled back then waived his hand as he spoke.

"Ok, go."

Kinn started down with the others right behind him. When Atrell came out, he saw Shaméd and his group moving rapidly down the ramp. Looking down he saw the staircase twist creating a small balcony every ten feet. He jumped over, grabbed the side of the railing, and then let go. He began dropping from railing to railing. He passed Kinn and the others. He heard Kinn yell out to stop, but he kept going. Soon he stood on the bottom looking up at the others with a big grin on his face. Rolling his shoulders to loosen them and jumping up and down, he spoke for the first time since coming to this world.

"That felt good. I have not had that much fun in a long time. It was like being home when I was younger jumping from building to building, chasing and playing with the animals."

He began walking and looking around. There were doors every fifteen feet all the way around the large room. Shaméd and his group arrived and a moment later Kinn stepped off his path and walked over to Atrell.

"Atrell! What were you doing? You could have been killed!"

"You and Shaméd wanted to race. Well, we won, thanks to me. As for me being killed, you know very well I cannot die. Ok; I could have gotten hurt, but I didn't. As for what I am doing? Since I did not want to wait for the rest of you, I have been looking around. There are twenty doors, and as you can see, the mirror is here. It is over there - the large thing in the middle of the room. I am not sure how you expect to take it. It is a lot larger than the one in the world room. Or were you and Shaméd thinking of taking it apart?"

"You do not have to be so arrogant. Some of us may live a long time, but we can still die. I was only worried about you. As for your question, I do not believe we are going to dismantle it. Nogar may try to take it through his mirror. I believe it is bigger than this one."

The rest of the team stood around them as they talked. Shaméd walked over to the mirror as he listened to Atrell. He walked around it looking from all angles before speaking.

"This place is clean like the room above - a lot cleaner than the other floors. They must come here to use the mirror. I don't think we have much time left. Start searching the rooms."

They split up and began opening doors. Philip walked up behind Atrell as he was about to open a door.

"Hey, Atrell, I got a question to ask you."

Turning around, Atrell looked down at Philip, holding the door handle.

"What is it, Peck?"

Philip twisted his head up and glared at him.

"First off, I am not a peck. I'm a Hobbit."

"Whatever. What is your question? You heard Shaméd - we don't have all day."

Philip looked up. His mind was racing.

"I heard you tell old pointed ears you cannot die. My question is how do you know? Have you ever died?"

"That was two questions, and yes, I have died many times."

"How can you say you do not die when you just said you died? That is impossible."

"Well, it looks like I'm an impossible being, because I don't really die."

"Have you ever been stabbed in the heart? Or in any other part of your body that could kill you? I am very interested. Can you explain how you don't die?"

Atrell looked around to make sure no one was near. He looked at Philip.

"Ok, Peck, if you must know my history, here it is, fast, and short: I am from a world far from here. I am the last of my people. I outlived the last two by over a couple hundred years before Shaméd who was just a kid back then showed up. He was part of a team that was sent there to explore the world. They found me and brought me back to their world. I have lived on his world and a couple of other worlds for two thousand years. I found out I could not die when I was caught in an explosion and was declared dead. However, in less than a day my body reformed and I was alive again. I scared everyone in the room when I woke up. I laughed when they all jumped and ran out. I have lost body parts and they grow back. Does that answer your question? If not, I don't care. Start searching unless you want to be caught and eaten by these demons."

Atrell opened the door and started to step inside. He heard Philip ask.

"Have you ever lost your head?"

Atrell turned back toward Philip glaring.

"No. I have never lost my head"

"So, you do not know if you cannot die. If you lost your head, you might die. On the other hand, your body might grow a new head. Then again, your head might grow a new body. It would be something if both your head and body grew new parts. You would be twins. That would be something to see - your head and body both growing new parts, you should try it."

Atrell stood there glaring at Philip. Atrell twisted his neck to work out the kinks he was beginning to feel.

"You are one sick and disturbed little peck. Get away from me before I do something that will make the others upset."

Philip was about to speak when he heard Shaméd yell out to him.

"Philip, leave Atrell alone. There are still doors that need to be opened."

Philip shrugged his shoulders and went to the next door. As he was about to open it, he heard the yell from Mordock.

"I found something over here. This room has stuff stacked all over the place."

Mordock stood in the doorway waiting for everyone to get there. When Shaméd arrived, they entered. The room was just what he said. It was full of tables with boxes stacked on them. There were boxes stacked all around the room.

"This might be what we were looking for. All of you spread out and start searching. Philip you come with me, we need to see if we can disconnect the mirror and get it ready to move."

Philip looked at Shaméd. He was not happy about leaving the room. He saw one box that had jewels and what looked like gold coins in it. He knew there could be even more treasures there, and he wanted some. Just as Shaméd was about to call him again, he headed for the door.

It took some time for them to walk around and examine the large mirror. Shaméd found a box like the MA-TED on a table over in a corner. It did not talk and only had buttons and dials. Two long metal ropes ran from the back of it along the floor to a larger box. This box was seven feet high and ten feet long and ten feet wide. There was a door at one end. From that box there were four more metal ropes ranging from two inches to twelve inches in diameter. The metal ropes came out the back and went over to the mirror; they hooked up in the same location as the mirror in the world room.

This mirror was twice the size as the one in the world room and did not have any of the decorations. It was made of metal, shiny in some parts and there was what looked like corrosion along the bottom.

Shaméd stood there looking at it.

<Someone is using this. We need to get it apart and out of here fast. There is no telling if or when that someone will return.>

Shaméd looked over at Philip.

"Philip, I figured out how to take it apart. Can you check to make sure there are no traps? I cannot use any magic. It might set off an alarm."

Philip began searching around. After a few minutes he looked over at Shaméd.

"There are no traps, not even an alarm. Do we start or are we going to get the others to help."

"Go get the others. I will start taking it apart."

Philip headed back to the room as Shaméd bent down and began taking the metal ropes off. Reaching the room, Philip entered and walked over to the box with the jewels and gold. He began filling his pack after dumping out what he did not need. Philip was just closing his pack when Kinn saw him.

"What are you doing here?"

Kinn walked over to Philip. Philip closed his pack put it on his back as he looked up smiling.

"Oh, there you are. Shaméd said he is ready to start taking apart the mirror and sent me in here to get you and the others."

"Why are you looking through these boxes, if you were sent in here to get us?"

"They looked interesting. I found nothing that was important. Are you ready? We should get out there and help."

"Yes, I think we should. Ok, everyone we need to get out there and help take apart the mirror. Atrell, you stay and keep searching. Pick someone to help if you think you need it."

"Hey. I will stay and help."

"I don't need your help, peck, so leave. Ted can stay and help."

Kinn looked at Ted and Meckler as they went back to searching.

"We will call out when we are ready to leave."

Kinn followed the others out. Philip mumbled the whole way. When everyone was gone, Atrell opened the small box he had shut when Kinn called out. Inside he picked up what looked like a metal armband. It was similar to what Shaméd wore on his arm, minus the jewels. It had wires coming from it going to a small box on a belt. Atrell looked around. Ted was facing the other way. He placed everything from the box into his pack. Closing it, he looked around and kept searching.

Shaméd started unhooking the metal ropes when the others showed up. They began rolling up them up and placing them near the large box that Shaméd had moved closer to the mirror. It did not take long to get it all apart and ready to move. Ted and Atrell brought out boxes from the room and placed them with the other stuff. As they placed the last ones on the ground Atrell called out to Shaméd.

"We found a few things that might be of interest."

Shaméd looked at all the items.

"Ok, everyone stand over here. I am going to contact Reklan."

Tapping his amulet, he closed his eyes and spoke.

"Reklan, we are ready. When can we start?'

< *"Nogar is in his room. He has the mirror ready. He just told me he has it lined up to the right side of the mirror."* >

All at once they saw a very large scaly hand come out and take hold of the mirror.

"Ok, let's get this through."

Everyone grabbed the mirror and began pushing. In moments it was gone. Then they started passing the boxes and the rest through. When the last of the items were gone, Shaméd looked around and spoke.

"Ok, people let's get out of here before we get caught. Kinn, get everyone out of here."

Kinn motioned at the two men closest to where the mirror was. The first man took two steps and disappeared. The next man walking right behind him walked all the way to wall. He turned around and looked at Kinn and Shaméd.

"Reklan, what is going on?"

There was no answer. All at once, Shaméd grabbed his head with both hands, bent over, and dropped to his knees. Kinn and Mordock ran to him.

"Shaméd, what's wrong?" They said in unison.

Shaméd dropped his hands, raised his head, and looked around at each one of them.

"I can't hear any of you."

"What do you mean you can't hear us?"

"I mean, I cannot hear any of you mentally. I received a mental blast when I tried to contact Reklan. A scream shot through my mind. It felt like I was being sliced open. Then there was nothing. It was gone, everything *is* gone. I have never been without some sort of voice in my head. We need to leave now. We have been discovered and if we do not move fast we will be caught. We will have to fight our way out of here."

Chapter Nineteen

They all started running toward the stairs and ramp. Kinn was in the lead. Philip was the only one talking.

"Great, we are trapped in the bowels of hell and now we have to run and fight our way out. Does anyone but me know how stupid and impossible that sounds?"

"Don't worry, peck, - stay close to me."

"I am not a peck. Stop calling me one."

Philip ran up behind Atrell and stayed on his heels. Halfway up, Philip started slowing down from the weight in his pack. Shaméd saw him slow down. He reached over and picked Philip up. Twisting him up onto his shoulders, he rode on Shaméd's shoulders the rest of the way up.

Reaching the top, Kinn opened the door and with sword drawn entered the room. Running through the room to the hallway door, Kinn stood waiting. As the others entered, they came over to stand next to him. Shaméd entered and sat Philip down, then walked over to the door. Kinn moved back as Shaméd opened it. Shaméd, with sword and knife in hand, stepped out with Atrell right behind and Philip after him. As the others came out, they heard the sounds. Turning, they saw two demons coming toward them.

"Now the fun begins."

Atrell with his sword and knife in hand ran at the demons. When he got within a few feet he dove into the air, blades out front. Screaming and yelling, his knife hit one and his body hit the other. All three fell to the floor. He was up stabbing and slashing before the demons could move.

When Shaméd and the others arrived, Atrell was standing on top of one demon. Philip walked up and stared at Atrell.

"If you are going to continue running at these guys and fighting them, I most definitely am not staying close to you. You will get me killed."

Atrell's body was covered with demon blood. There was a grin on his face. His eyes had a wild look. He blinked a few times then looked down at Philip.

"Where is your sense of adventure, peck?'

"My sense of adventure is staying alive. You are the one that can't die, I can."

Shaméd called out.

"Ok, people stay together. Philip, you stay in the middle. Mordock, you, and Kinn take up the rear and make sure no one gets behind us. Atrell, since you are having fun, you take the lead."

Everyone but Sara had weapons; even Philip held a pistol in each hand. Mordock walked over to her.

"Do you want one of my swords or knife?"

"No, thank you. I was never any good with them. I am better with my hands and feet."

Mordock watched as Sara walked away. Two more demons came running at them. Atrell jumped back on top of the dead bodies.

Atrell grinned over his shoulder at Shaméd.

"Get the others out of here. I will be right with you as soon as I take care of these."

Shaméd turned back toward the others. Kinn pointed down the hallway.

"The door leading up is back that way. So for now, I guess I lead the way."

Kinn took off at a slow run down the hallway, Mordock two steps behind. Philip shook his head at Atrell, turned, and ran behind Sara as she took off. Everyone was moving away as Shaméd called out to Atrell.

"Try not to take too long. Remember, just because you can't die does not mean they won't have fun trying to kill you, if you get captured."

"Don't worry. That is the last thing I want to happen. I won't let them catch me and I will be right behind you."

He stood there waiting. The demons stopped when they saw he was not running away like the others. They slowly walked closer. Behind the first two were about twenty other demons pushing each other and trying to get in front.

Shaméd caught up to the others at the door to the stairwell. They had stopped to wait for him. Kinn started to enter when they heard a loud explosion. They looked down the hallway where black smoked filled it and was billowing toward them. They heard laughter, then they saw Atrell come running out of the smoke toward them. He was the one laughing.

Everyone entered the stairwell. Atrell entered, slamming the door shut behind him. He was leaning against it when he saw Shaméd standing on the steps looking at him.

"What was that noise?"

"There were more demons coming and I did not want to stay and kill them all. I left them a gift, instead. Something I found back on my world. This is the first time I have been able to put it to good use. You want me to take the lead?"

"Go, we are right behind you."

Atrell moved through the others. Once in front, he ran up the stairs. The others followed. They went up passing three open doors to the other floors. Shaméd stopped at each one, shutting and doing what he could to lock them. As they came up to the main floor, they slowed down when they saw Atrell standing at the top step. As they came close to him, they stopped and stared at the sight in front of them.

The door was lying on the floor and in the door was a very large demon. Half of his body was jammed through. He was thrashing about trying to enter. He growled and swung his left arm trying to reach them.

"If they are all as smart as this one, we won't have any trouble getting out of here."

Atrell jumped forward stabbing at the demon. After several tries to get Atrell, the creature was even more stuck. He kept swinging his arm. Mordock came up beside Atrell.

"Let me see if I can clear the way."

Atrell looked at him, shrugged his shoulders, and stepped back. Mordock reach inside his coat and pulled out a metal rod. He pointed it at the demon. There was a bruuummm sound and a light shot out. Mordock twisted the rod and the light grew larger.

Mordock started toward the demon. The demon screamed when Mordock cut off his left horn, then the right one fell to the floor. The demon was glaring at Mordock. It began screaming and roaring louder. Atrell called out.

"Do you have any idea what it is saying?"

Mordock stopped and looked at Atrell, then jumped back as the demon's hand swept out at him.

"Not a clue. I know twenty different languages and demon is not one of them."

"We do not have much time. The longer we are inside the more difficult it becomes to escape. If you have a plan I think you should hurry."

Shaméd pointed at the demon and Mordock moved in and sliced the demon's arm off. Blood began pouring out of the wound, covering the floor. The beast threw back his head and screeched and finally slid back into the hallway. Mordock rushed in to kill it before it could do more than lean against the wall.

Turning, Mordock faced the other demons that were now in the hallway. He moved toward them to give the others time to get into the hallway. When the demons were close, he attacked, slicing at them. The first two lost hands. They shrieked, turned around, and pushed their way through to the back. The other demons crouched there, glaring. They were not sure what to make of this little creature that could cut off their hands.

Shaméd and the others entered the hallway behind Atrell. Kinn was the last one through the door, he yelled out to Shaméd.

"Shaméd, they are coming up the stairs. We need to get moving."

"This is the only clear way."

Shaméd pointed and Sara led the way with Philip right behind her. The others were close behind. Atrell was still standing there looking at Mordock and his weapon.

"I would really like to have one of those."

"Ask Shaméd. There are only six of them."

"Atrell, I want you to go with the others. We will stop or at least slow these things down and catch up with you in a few minutes."

Shaméd reached down and grabbed the metal rod on his belt. He pressed the button and twisted it. A noise – bruummm came from it.

Shaméd looked at Mordock holding the other weapon. Down the hallway the demons came closer. They were growling as well as glaring at them.

"I forgot about this until I saw you use yours. This is a good place for them."

The demons either got brave or the pushing from behind was too much. The ones in front came rushing at them. The two fought shoulder to shoulder, as the demons came forward. When the last demon fell, Mordock and Shaméd stood there. There were demons lying all over filling the hallway. Without speaking, they both turned and ran down the hallway after the others.

They caught up to the others a few minutes later. They had stopped. They stood in a large room. It was about fifteen feet wide and twenty feet across. The opening on the other side was partly blocked with debris. The ceiling and floor above had long ago caved in. The walls and the ceiling were cracked. They had entered a dead-end and now they were trapped.

They could hear the demons digging the debris away from the other side. Mordock went forward to try to stop the demons from getting in Atrell went with him. Shaméd and Kinn stood facing the hallway opening they just came through. They could hear the demons. They were not moving quickly, but they would be there soon. They could hear them shrieking and snarling as they came forward. The others moved to the middle of the room.

There was a crash and dust rolled across the room as the blocked wall came tumbling in and now lay open. The demons pushed the last bit of debris down toward Mordock and Atrell who jumped back out of the way. The demons in front were being pushed by the ones behind trying to get in.

Mordock and Atrell attacked - they were lucky in one way, the opening was only large enough for one demon to come in at a time.

As the demons died, they were dragged back and others took their place. It seemed as if there would never be an end to them.

The demons coming down the hallway arrived. Shaméd, Kinn, and Ted moved forward with swords in hand. They fought the demons, swords crashing, keeping them from entering the room.

Shaméd's group was getting tired. He could see the exhaustion on their faces and in their bodies. There were just too many demons. Ted and Kinn moved back as

Meckler and Nakobee came in to take their place. Every few minutes they would switch, so they could rest.

Shaméd knew if he could not use his magic soon, the fight would turn in favor of the demons.

Sara called out as she moved between Shaméd and others.

"Move back."

As they moved back the demons stopped when they saw her boldly walk toward them. She backhanded the first demon that came at her. It flew back hitting the wall, its jaw was broken, and it was out cold. The demons, seeing what happened, stopped. Sara stood there alone. She took a step toward the demons, they moved back.

They had heard her tell the others to move back. They saw she was just a small human female. Yet they saw her slam one of their own against the wall. They were confused. She did not even have a weapon.

Sara stood facing them. She took a deep breath, then in one swift movement, as the first demon started to move, she exhaled.

Flames shot down the hallway filling it from wall to wall. The demons in front were hit with the flames and were evaporated. Within seconds demons began shrieking. Those on fire turned to run crashing into the ones behind. All the demons in the hallway were on fire and screaming. They tried to run away.

Sara stopped, coughed, and looked at Shaméd and Kinn, who moved closer to her and stood there grinning.

"Nice. Can you do it again over there?'

Sara walked over to the other side of the room.

"Mordock, step back."

Mordock, then Atrell, moved back as Sara reached the opening. A demon came rushing at her. Doubling up her left fist, she punched it in the face. The demon was driven back though the hole, bowling down the ones trying to enter. Taking a deep breath, she exhaled, again. Flames fill the opening. Demons yelled and screamed from the other side as they burned and tried to run away.

The only sound was from the flames. There were no demons. They could rest for a few minutes. They stood there looking around at each other. They knew they could not keep this up much longer.

"Shaméd, can you use your magic, yet?"

Kinn stood there waiting.

"I have been trying. I cannot bring any spells together. Something is blocking my mind from concentrating. Everything is blurry. I do not dare try to do one. I might get it wrong and we would be in worse trouble."

"I have an idea."

Mordock walked over to the wall. Using the energy weapon he pushed it into the wall. It went in up to the handle.

"What are you doing?"

Shaméd walked up as Mordock began moving the weapon.

"Remember what Jon said? He told us these were not real weapons. They are tools people used to cut into the mountains. If they can cut through the wall we can get out of here."

Slowly he started moving it. He made a complete circle in the wall. He turned off the beam and started to push.

"The wall is four feet thick. The beam is only two. It did not make it all the way. We need to cut some away so we can reach the outer wall."

Shaméd started to use his weapon when they heard a sound. Six demons came rushing down the hallway. Three small ones came through the opening on the other side of the room. The fighting began, again, and within moments more demons were coming down the hallway.

It was easy to keep the large demons back. It was the small ones - they kept dodging in and out, several of them slithered passed to engage Sara and the others. That was where they lost their first man: Ted was fighting two small demons. One sliced his arm the other knocked his weapon from his hand, and pushed him to the ground. The man next to him caught the demon's next full swing - its claws cut him in half. Ted rolled away as Shaméd came over and killed both demons.

There were dead demons all over the floor. The demons in the doorway were pulling the dead back so they could get in. It was slowing them down and making it hard for them to get in. It gave Shaméd's group some protection.

It was like a flood - a demon flood. It looked like no matter how many they killed, there were more to take their place. The hallway was filled with them. One made it passed Kinn and it moved into the room. It stopped in front of Sara who just stood there. He towered over her looking down. His stench was over powering, but Sara blocked it out. She had done it from the beginning, at the very first room. The demon swung his head back and forth trying to figure out why she was not afraid. She just stood there, her hands out in front in a fighting stance. There was fighting all around them and the two just stood there facing each other. The demon gave a loud growl and lunged at her. She drove her right first into the creatures face. The sound of breaking bones was heard. As the creature bellowed in pain, he brought his hands toward his face, and Sara's left hand shot out grabbing a horn on his head. Twisting it, the demon's head went with Sara as she continued to bring it down to the floor. As the demon's head hit the floor, its body followed. Sara let go and jumped up on its chest. She drove her right fist down into the demon's chest, breaking its rib cage and driving the bones into its heart and lungs. The demon let out a gasping sound, then died.

Turning, Sara saw two demons moving after Ted and Philip. She jumped on the back of one demon. Philip moved closer to Ted holding his two pistols out at the demon as it came rushing at him. He fired both guns at the demon. Both shots struck it in the head. It dropped to the floor, dead, sliding forward and pushing Philip against the wall. Philip's heart was pounding in his chest. He had never been this scared. Ted moved closer to him.

With his back to the wall, Philip slid down to floor. He pulled out powder and shot so he could reload his pistols. He had not used them until now and he wanted to be ready if he needed them again. Atrell yelled out.

"This is getting us nowhere. We have to do something. I have three more toys left. I am going to toss one into the hole over there. I will also place one in the wall where Mordock cut the hole. If it works, we will have our own doorway and we can get out of here."

Atrell took out a small bundle from his pack. He twisted off a metal tab and tossed it in the hole. It went off as it rolled along the back of a demon that was crawling through. There was a loud thundering noise: dust, dirt, and debris went flying. When the dust settled the hole was no more. The demons in the hallway stopped. But it lasted for only a second before they attacked, again.

Shaméd, Kinn, Sara, Mordock, and Nakobee rushed forward to keep the demons back and to give Atrell the time he needed.

Atrell moved to the wall. He looked around in the hole that Mordock had made. It was almost a five foot circle and barely three feet into the wall. He saw a crack in the back where Mordock made a couple of slices. He started excavating some of the loose rocks, then he placed his bomb in the wall. He took out a small metal item.

"Everyone, we need to move back as far as we can."

They all rushed back to a corner. The demons followed. The demons were between Shaméd's group and the wall.

Shaméd and Mordock fought the demons keeping them back. Atrell squeezed his hand. There was a loud explosion, the wall cracked open, more dust, and debris went everywhere.

Those closest died at once, those not dead, were within seconds. Mordock made sure of it. A rock had hit Philip in the head. Kinn bent down to help him; he wrapped a cloth around his head to stop the bleeding. As the dust settled, they saw a small opening in the wall. Sunlight was coming through.

"It is a start. I can make it bigger."

"We will keep the demons back. When we get out of here, do me one favor. Do not ever tell Jon about this stuff. He is already too dangerous with what he has."

Atrell and Nakobee climbed over the dead demons and began moving rocks and debris away.

The demons in the hallway slowed down because of the blast. Sara picked up a dead demon and tossed it toward the hallway opening. Then she grabbed another and tossed it at the demons trying to enter. The demons would grab it and throw it behind them. She kept tossing demons.

Sara grabbed and tossed the last dead demon, the demons started to rush in when they heard Atrell yell.

"Ok. It is ready - let's get out of here."

The others moved forward. Kinn was carrying Philip through the hole. Shaméd walked over to Atrell. He held out the energy weapon to him.

"Here, you can use this."

With the weapon in hand, Atrell grinned and jumped toward the demons, slicing and cutting them as he moved. Mordock stepped up beside Shaméd.

"There is something wrong with that man - he likes killing way too much."

"Atrell has always been different. He was alone on his world for a long time with no human contact before we found him."

Mordock turned to help Nakobee fight the demons off to the right. Atrell was keeping the rest away.

The demons were coming slower. They realized they could not get close. The crazy one would cut and slice at them, laughing as he did. Atrell was like a demon in human form. They were beginning to fear him: they would cut the little human and he did not bleed for more than a few seconds.

The others were outside. Shaméd began to leave. He looked back.

"I'm leaving - hurry up."

"Nakobee, Mordock, go. I will be right behind you."

When Nakobee heard Atrell he stabbed the demon he was fighting in the chest, turned off his weapon, and ran. Atrell pulled a small bundle out from his pocket. Mordock saw it and without saying anything, sliced the demon he was fighting across the chest, turned and ran.

Atrell cut a demon in half and pressed the button on the energy weapon turning it off. He raised his arms and let out a long screech. The demons all stopped moving. They were scared of this little human; they stood there watching to see what he was doing.

Atrell looked around at the demons as he took slow steps toward the opening. At the opening he turned his back and ran. The demons screamed and ran after him. As Atrell ran through the opening, he dropped the bundle and squeezed his hand, diving out and hitting the ground. The explosion went off, collapsing the wall on the demons coming after him.

As Atrell rolled on the ground, the dust and debris poured out from the building. He stood and looked back at his handy work as the dust settled.

"That should help. Now can we get out of this infestation?"

He turned took one step, and stopped when he saw the others. He looked down when he heard a noise. Shaméd was on the ground holding his head with both hands. He looked up then stared straight ahead.

In front of them, a thousand feet away, was an impregnable wall of demons. There were thousands of them, all different sizes, and shapes. They all just stood there glowering at them.

"Every demon in all the galaxies and every universe must be here. When Shaméd gets someone mad at him he does a great job."

Atrell waited for someone to answer - no one did.

Sara stepped off to the side, her body began to blur, then a large blue-black dragon appeared. A rumbling growl escaped her dripping maw as she spoke.

"Now I can really fight. I will take them from above and try to make an opening for you."

Sara spread her wings and jumped into the air. Shaméd stopped moaning dropped his hands to the ground; slowly he pushed himself up to a sitting position. He looked out at all the demons.

"So much hate and anger. They almost killed me when I came outside. My mind opened up and I could hear them all. Is everyone out?"

Shaméd stood. He could feel his strength returning. Soon he would be able to fight. Kinn walked over and stood next to Shaméd.

"Since we got out here and after you collapsed, here is what has happened. Ted has lost a lot of blood. I have stopped the bleeding, but if we do not get him help, he will not make it. I could not get any power or energy to heal him inside the building. Out here is just as bad. This island is dead. It has no energy or life force, only rocks and dirt and those things out there. Philip is hurt almost as bad. I

215

stopped the bleeding on his head. He is unconscious. There is a deep cut on his chest and his right hand is crushed. I have him leaning against the building with Ted. He will live but like Ted we must get him out of here. Sara just took off to fight the demons from the air. That being said, we will all be dead if we cannot escape. I have been unable to reach Reklan or anyone."

There was movement among the demons, the ones in front moved back. The air swirled, a flash of light and black smoke appeared in front of the horde. They could see a shape about six feet tall. As the smoke cleared, the shape began growing. Seconds later there stood a demon of such size and stature that all the others looked like children. It was not only the largest creature any of them had ever seen, but also the most gruesome looking. It was red, black, and scaly. The horns on its head twisted up and around three times before going out and up.

Chapter Twenty

Shaméd looked up at the demon. The smoke was fading away, and what stood before them was a fifty foot tall demon. Shaméd called out.

"I presume you are the one called Gormorrah?"

The demon looked around. The demons closest to him moved back and lowered their heads when he looked at them. Then he looked down at Shaméd.

"I have many names. I have as many names as there are worlds with their pathetic life forms that crawl around on them. Gormorrah is the name the creatures here call me."

Shamed looked up,

"It is nice to finally see you. You are a lot shorter than I thought you would be. I believe you are the cause for all the trouble I have been having since coming to this world."

The demon shifted on his feet, bellowing:

"Trouble? You know nothing of trouble. How dare you sneak into my home and steal my most prized possession. I have used the mirror for millions of years and I will have it returned to me at once. If you return it now I may let you and your companions live a few years before killing you."

Shaméd stepped away from the others.

"We stole nothing of yours. The mirror is not yours. I have sent it to a safe place. As for you killing us, my friends and I are not ready to die, so we will have to decline."

The demon bent down, leaning forward. He sniffed the air above and around Shaméd, twisting his head back and forth as if searching for something. He stopped and looked at Shaméd's face then stood straight.

"You! It is you! You are the one who has been causing me all the trouble. Now I feel and smell the power radiating from you. You were the one who chased away my banshees, reducing them to nothing but worthless mist. You are the one who talked the humans and others to join forces to stop my minions. You killed the sea drake, and the Lizarians I sent after you. You diverted the water to refill the river and lake. It was you, who removed Krakdrol from the man-elf. I watched as he was tossed into a sun. I felt the power and life essence of Krakdrol die. You caused those pathetic priests to lose their power. Now they stand there looking like the idiots they are.

I have planned for too many centuries to have someone like you stop me. Do you know how long it took me to twist Krakdrol into hating his siblings? Dragons were one of the first creatures created after us. They have the power that I needed to conquer the creator. I used Krakdrol and his followers for many centuries, causing hate among the lesser beings. I gathered many souls and much power because of him. Now it is gone, and it is because of you.

217

I have plans for you. You took Krakdrol from me, but I will take his brother. I want the staff and its power. I will have it, along with your power, and soul. You are right about me. I have tried many times since you arrived on this world to take the staff and your life. Now that you have invaded my land, I do not have to abide by the stupid rules, rules that were made so many years ago on this world. They have slowed me down but not stopped me. Now I can openly attack you and the others. Once I have the power from the staff, I can take what I want by force. I will not let the rules and forces in the universes stop me or hold me back any longer. For too long, I have been held in check by the rules created at the end of the war. All the power and combined forces of the people on this world or any other world will not stop me once I have your power and that staff. Then I will go after Nogar, himself."

As the demon spoke, Shaméd's strength kept growing stronger. His mind cleared - he was now ready for this creature. He was about to answer the demon, when he heard Reklan.

< *"Shaméd, help is on the way. I was trying to get the mirror closer to you but I could not - there is too much interference. I can only see from far above you. Heather and that old blind dragon said you had to stay and fight. They are bringing reinforcements. Nogar is with them and over a thousand other dragons from that world and others. I do not know the complete story or all the information. This Boone person supplied Nogar and the council with enough evidence to convince them to go there. Something about this demon is the cause of all the trouble. Boone said Gormorrah was behind Red's brother going crazy with hate. He has been causing trouble on other worlds for millions of years. It seems he has used the mirror to send his minions to other worlds, and they have information he was the one that kept moving Krakdrol to other worlds trying to find him a new body."* >

< "Then it would seem we fight. ">

Shaméd held out his hand and closed his eyes. There was a flash and the staff of Rednogording was in his hand. The power radiated from the crystals as they glowed. Shaméd looked up at the demon, pointing the staff.

"I have always been amazed at creatures like you. No matter what the life form, they are always talking and bragging about themselves and what they will do. Your kind must enjoy listening to your own voices. I am glad, however, that you have been rambling on and on. It has given me time to regain my strength. So I'm afraid we will not be surrendering. If however, you wish to surrender, I will accept nothing but total and unrestricted surrender from you and your followers.

There is no way you will ever win. You will never possess the staff. Your time of causing trouble on this world is at an end. I will drive you and your kind back to your own world."

The crystals on the staff began glowing more. A deep blue flash of crackling light shot out toward Gormorrah. It hit the demon in the chest knocking him back. There was a loud roar. Gormorrah stood straight, raised both arms above his head and screamed.

"Kill them all!!!!"

The demons screeched and bellowed as they rushed forward to do his bidding.

Kinn and the others moved away from Shaméd, so they could fight without being in each other's way. Mordock spread his feet to get a better stance, pressed the button on the metal rod and the light shot out. It flickered a few times, then it went out. He looked down at it in his hand.

"What? This cannot happen now. Jon said it would last for a couple of hours."

"He said three hours at high power, six at the low. You have been using it at the high setting. When you get back, yell at him. I am sure he will enjoy the fact he was wrong. For now, all we have to do is hold out - help is on its way."

There was screaming from above. Sara began her attack on the flying demons. Two were tumbling down to the ground. Another was trying to get away from her. She was on its back and they could see flesh falling.

Nakobee had seen what was coming and had begun to prepare for battle. As Shaméd and the demon talked, he stabbed his sword into the ground. He removed his backpack tossing it back against the wall where Philip lay. He pulled out his second sword and stabbed it into the ground. Then he put his arms through the holes of his cloak. After tightening it around his neck and waist, he took hold of his swords and stood there looking toward the horde of demons.

When the demons attacked he called out.

"It is a good day to die. Shaméd, it has been an honor to serve by your side. May we meet in the afterlife and continue our friendship."

"You are not dead yet, my friend. We will live and you and I will go on many more journeys together."

"You two want to concentrate on those things coming at us? Shaméd, how about using some more of that magic you are so good at?"

Shaméd looked over at Kinn. Kinn grinned.

"I have lived a long life. Just do me a favor and if one of these things gets me; make sure I am dead before it starts eating me."

Atrell stood to his right. He reached over and patted Kinn on the shoulder.

"Don't worry, I will make sure."

Atrell ran forward, the energy beam in one hand, his sword in the other. He met the horde of demons before they were halfway to them. The first ones never stood a chance. They died before they could do a thing.

The fight was on and he was killing and maiming demons, yelling, and taunting them as he attacked. Kinn, Mordock, Nakobee, and Shaméd stood there waiting for the demons to get closer. Shaméd held the staff out and five bolts of light shot out, hitting and killing five demons.

The staff began shooting out bolts of light from each crystal, each light causing a different level of damage. The red light caused the most. When it hit a demon, the creature would explode or it would melt into a pile of slime.

The staff kept moving around shooting beams at the demons. Shaméd was not controlling its power - Red was in control. Shaméd was only holding it.

The demons kept coming. Demons were attacking from all three sides, only their backs were protected. The building behind them kept the demons from completely encircling them.

They did not notice the slow down from the demons until they heard the firing of the canons from above. Mordock was the first to look up.

"The dragonfly is here and look, the sky is full of dragons."

Each one took a quick glance up. They saw help had arrived. The group began moving back toward the building because of the pressure from the demons. Only Shaméd stood his ground. He saw the others moving back, so he began maneuvering himself between them and the demons.

Shaméd held the staff in his right hand and held out his left hand. He said some words and a sonic blast shot from the palm of his hand hitting the demons on his left. The beams of energy from the staff began to shoot faster, cutting down demons and slowly pushing them back. Shaméd called out to the others.

"Stay here, I am going to press them back."

The battle in the air was something to see. There were dragons flying around shooting flames and attacking the demons that were in the air. Some dragons swooped down and attacked the demons on the ground. A few dragons had riders, mostly elves. Some of the riders had staffs that fired bolts of energy, others had bows and arrows.

Gormorrah had been standing there just watching. When the dragons showed up he began to fight.

Nogar, Heather, Sara, and Boone were diving in and out attacking demons. After some time, they moved off and concentrated their attacks on Gormorrah. They shot flames and energy bolts at the demon leader.

Boone popped in and out around Gormorrah getting so close that once he landed on the demon's back. Boone dug his front and hind claws deep into the demon's back. He shot a bolt of energy at the back of Gomorrah's head as he let go. He left a burned mark and long deep cuts, and blood running down the demon's back.

Gormorrah was howling and swinging at the dragons attacking him. He grabbed two large demons, holding them by their tails. With one in each hand, he was using them as clubs, swinging them at the dragons as they attacked.

Shaméd stood twenty feet from Gormorrah; the staff had jerked away from his hand and was chasing the demons as it shot blasts of energy at them. Shaméd just stood there. Everything around him disappeared and his eyes glazed over as words were spoken in his mind.

<You can do all things through me, I created you. Ask of me what you want and it shall be.>

He had read those words, or words like them, hundreds of times on many worlds he traveled to. He now understood the references that people made when they said

God, The One, The Trinity, or The Creator - they all meant the same thing. There is only one true God and he created everything. He loves his creations and wants them to live in peace. The creatures in front of Shaméd were the ones who had fought Him long ago and were cast out. He knew what to do.

Shaméd closed his eyes and began to do something he had never done in his life - he prayed.

<God, the creator of all life, I ask for your help in this time of need. Not for me, but for the people Gormarrah has hurt on this world and all the other worlds. I ask you to help me to have the power to stop him here and now.>

Shaméd began to glow.

When Boone flew away after his attack, Gormorrah twisted around to hit whatever was attacking him.

Nogar dove and attacked Gomorrah's now exposed and bleeding back with flames. Nogar turned and flew away as the demon screamed in pain.

Everyone began to move away from Gormorrah because he began to glow. The demons, seeing this, began to run away. His whole body was glowing and all the dragons moved as far back as they could. There was a sudden flash, flames shot out and thunder roared from where Gormorrah stood. There were flames erupting from the ground, burning and killing everything within fifty feet.

The fight was over. Gormorrah was gone. The demons not destroyed began to run or fly away. There were flashes and popping sounds as they blinked and disappeared. Within seconds they, too, were gone.

No one saw Shaméd as he walked out of the fire back toward the building to his friends.

Mordock and the others could hear the cheering from the ship above. Ropes dropped down as the ship came lower. Ted was dead. Somehow, a demon got passed the others and ripped him apart. Nakobee killed the demon as it turned toward Philip.

The only ones left from the team were, Shaméd, Mordock, Atrell, Kinn, Sara, Philip, and Nakobee, and Meckler who went through the mirror. It would be some time before they knew how many died in this battle.

Soon, Shaméd and his group were on the ship heading back to the ravine. The fight was still going on there. Shaméd wanted to get there before the priests could gather their strength. Now that the staff was back with him, some of their power would return. They would not be as powerful since Gormorrah was out of the picture, but they could still cause a lot of harm. He knew Gormorrah was not dead. All he had done was drive him away. Someday somewhere, he would return

A large gold-red dragon came toward the ship. When it was within a hundred feet it shimmered as its wings folded in around its body. A tall blond haired man in gold and black robes hovered in the air. He floated over and landed on the deck next to Shaméd.

"You found a lot of interesting artifacts. Some of them if you can believe it have the Thorns drooling trying to figure out what they are."

The men on the ship stopped what they were doing to see Nogar. None of them had ever seen him. When he showed up, some whispered he was Shaméd's father because they looked so much alike. Captain Stark yelled at them

"You men get back to work. We have a lot to do before we take a break."

The men returned to their stations and continued cleaning and fixing what the demons had wrecked.

Nogar watched them. He turned and placed both hands on the railing looking out over the land.

"I have not been in a battle of this magnitude in many centuries. It almost makes me feel young, and I do mean almost. I hurt in places I have not felt pain for many years. I am impressed with how you handled Gormorrah."

"It was not me, or at least not all of it."

"What do you mean?'

"I think we should talk about it later."

"Very well. For now Gormorrah is gone, he might return so we will put people here to make sure he or his kind never return. I think this island will be a good place for our people to set up a base. I am sure the people of this world will not mind after what we have given them."

"I lost men today. We lost a lot of good people here. There should have been a better way to get this done."

Shaméd's face was sad. The others stood waiting to hear Nogar's answer.

"There was no other way. Some creatures are so evil they only create death. No matter what you do or say or how hard you try to reason with them they force us to fight and kill. It is a fine line we walk so we don't become like them. We can know we are justified in what we do because we are bringing good and freedom to this world. You know the council had to have a very good reason before they let us come here and do this. This creature Gormorrah was so evil he spanned millions of worlds causing so much pain and destruction we had to stop him. We may have lost lives here today, but they will be remembered. You still have work to do here before it is all over. I am leaving. I will have Reklan set up the IDG to let anyone who wants to come here to help you."

"That will be good. I am going to transport back to my tent and try to end this war. I may have to do more than the rules allow. Will there be a problem with that?"

"Shaméd, after today there will be a lot of changes. You do what you think is best for this world and I will back you. So will a lot of others. Kinn, you and Atrell can return home. Reklan has the mirror set up at the bow of the ship."

Kinn and Atrell walked to the bow and disappeared. Nogar nodded at Shaméd, put his hand on the railing, and jumped over. There was a flash and a gold-red dragon appeared. His wings flapped powerfully as he flew toward the other dragons.

Some of the sailors were watching Shaméd. They witnessed him standing face to face with thousands of demons and here he stood with very little blood on his body and no apparent damage.

Shaméd looked at Mordock and Nakobee. They were next to a water barrel cleaning the blood off their bodies.

Shaméd knew Nakobee and Mordock would want to go back with him. He had to return quickly. With the staff in his possession the spell keeping the priests from using their power was gone. He wanted to transport into the middle of the battle. He knew he would not be able to protect them if they came along. He decided to walk over and tell them.

"I need to leave."

Mordock looked up.

"We know. Nakobee told me now that you have the staff the people back there are in trouble. He also said you would want to go straight into battle and we would be in the way, so we decide for you: we will return with the Dragonfly. You go and stop the war."

Shaméd stood there looking at them. He was caught completely off guard. He thought for sure Nakobee would argue.

"Thank you for understanding. I will see you both in two hours. It should take about that long for you to get there."

Shaméd turned and walked to the railing. He stopped when he saw three dragons come flying toward the ship.

<"We know you are going back. We are going to help you.">

The words came from all three. Heather banked right and with two flaps of her wings was gone. Boone also disappeared. Sara did a couple of flips in the air up and over the ship and then disappeared. Shaméd raised the staff. It started to glow, soon covered his body in a soft blue light, then it and he, was gone.

Nakobee and Mordock watched as Shaméd disappeared.

"Don't worry. He will be alright. We will be there before the two hours. Captain Stark told me the ship is almost empty of extra weight. With most of the shot and cannon balls gone, he can have us there in an hour."

Nakobee listened to Mordock as they walked over to the railing. He knew letting Shaméd leave was the right thing to do. It just felt wrong not being there by his side.

"I know. It will be all over when we get there. He will not hold back now. There has been too much death and he has never liked killing."

The two felt the ship pick up speed as soon as Shaméd disappeared. Captain Stark had unfurled all the sails. They stood there looking forward. All they could do now was wait.

Chapter Twenty-One

Shaméd appeared above the bridge. As he floated in the air he saw Cuchulainn, he was lying across Smash. Their bodies were a few feet from the edge of the bridge. There was movement from Smash as Shaméd drifted closer. There had to be over a thousand arrows in the Titian. Cuchulainn's shield lay over Smash's left side and his body was on Smash's right. Cuchulainn had tried to protect Smash.

Shaméd floated over to their bodies, stopping when he was two feet above.

"Smash, do not move. I know you are hurt. I will return to help you as soon as I can."

There was a moaning sound from Smash, then quiet.

Shaméd heard, and then saw, the priests. They were walking forward in an arrow pattern, holding hands and chanting. He raised the staff and slowly floated out toward them. When he was fifteen feet above and in front of them, he called out. They stopped walking and looked up.

"Stop now or die. Gormorrah and his demons have been neutralized. They were beaten and driven into hiding. Gormorrah has abandoned you and all those who follow him. The power you are about to use will kill you if you continue. I give this warning only once. I can and will stop the spell from doing what you intend. I will not stop it from killing you. It is over. There has been enough senseless killing. You will not destroy or harm anymore of these people ever again."

The priests stood there looking up at him. The leader laughed.

"You stopped us once with your little tricks, but we are stronger and more powerful now. Gormorrah has not lost or abandoned us. We all felt his power flow though us. That was how we were able to destroy the Titian and his little friend. Nothing can stop us. We have never felt this much power before. We know it is because we are faithful followers of Gormorrah. You and your followers will all die today for the shame you have caused."

They moved closer raising their hands and with one loud voice, they yelled.

"Gormorrah, we command you to kill and destroy this man and everyone on the other side of the ravine."

Then they began chanting in a low voice. They started to glow red, within seconds they were radiating bright red. A deep red light began expanding. It spread up and out toward Shaméd and the bridge.

Shaméd pointed the staff at the priests while closing his eyes. The blue crystals began to glow.

The blue light grew, spreading out toward the oncoming red light. It engulfed the red light, expanding out, covering it and the surrounding area. Then there was nothing but blue. It grew brighter and became so bright that those watching had to turn and cover their eyes for fear that they would go blind. Then it slowly collapsed down around the priests. There was a flash and then it was gone. A burnt mark was all that was left on the ground where the priests previously stood.

Out of the sky three dragons appeared, diving at the invading army, shooting flames, and energy bolts. They destroyed the weapons and wagons. The soldiers scattered in all directions.

The General was yelling. He started swinging his sword, slashing and killing the men around him who tried to run. As the General was attacking a man, one of his Lieutenants drew his sword and drove it through the side of the General's armor. The General fell dead to the ground. The Lieutenant yelled to his men to follow him as he ran out to a clearing away from the fire and weapons. He and those who followed him tossed their weapons away. He knelt down and placed his hands over his head. Those that followed him did the same. Other soldiers seeing that the ones on the ground were not being harmed began dropping their weapons and moving out into the open. They placed their hands on their heads.

Shaméd floated out toward the now destroyed army. He watched as Heather, Boone, and Sara made two more passes over the enemy, then turned and came back. They dropped down, changing into human form as they landed a few feet from him. Shaméd headed toward them.

"Reklan, send some brandy - lots of it to my tent. I have some friends that are thirsty."

< *"I saw them and have sent word. It will be there in a few moments."* >

As Heather, Boone, and Sara walked over to his tent. Shaméd floated closer to them and called out.

"Go inside. I have sent for some brandy for the three of you."

Sara waved as Heather and Boone entered the tent. Rae's men were running across the bridge, swords drawn. As they came across, the sky filled with more dragons that flew in circles over the enemy soldiers kneeling in the field. Rae and the other leaders came walking across the bridge. Shaméd floated back down to meet them.

As Rae stepped off the bridge he stopped next to Smash and Cuchulainn.

"You men get over here and help me get Smash out from under Cuchulainn. Send a doctor over here."

Ten men, with Rae's help, pulled Cuchulainn off Smash. A doctor came up and started pulling the arrows out. He had two people helping him stop the bleeding.

Rae walked over to Shaméd. He was looking at the burning debris and the enemy soldiers spread out across the open field surrendering to his men.

"I think this was the shortest war I've ever fought in. It was only one day. It seems so strange. They out numbered us ten to one and yet, we won. Of course, when those priests started fighting we thought we were done. They took out four of the canons after killing the Titian and, I thought, the ogre. They began walking toward the bridge on their way to take us all out. It is a good thing you returned. We tossed everything at them and nothing worked. It did a lot of damage to the humans but not them. These weapons could be very dangerous. They will change the way wars and the fighting will be fought on this world.

Are you sure you want to leave this knowledge here for these people?"

"The knowledge was here, we only helped them rediscover it. We can only hope they will not abuse it. I am sure King Kalona, Lord Taloree, and Lord Digdeepest as well as the others can see how letting these weapons out to the world would not be the best thing or the safest for their world. Let's go see if any of the officers are still alive to make the surrender official."

The coalition had gathered around Rae and Shaméd, they had heard everything he said.

"We do understand and will make sure the knowledge is kept secret."

King Kalona spoke up and the others nodded their heads in agreement. They followed Shaméd toward the enemy.

The fires were put out and those that were hurt were taken to large tents set up for treating the wounded. It took two days to clean up and separate the mess of the invading army. After removing all their weapons, they were set free and allowed to walk around on their side without any guards. The officers from the Nanzorban Army met with Rae and the other leaders to work out the surrender agreement. More than three-quarters of the soldiers wanted to stay. They agreed to work the land around the new lake. The ones returning home agreed to swear allegiance to Duke Nactoon and help rebuild Nanzorba.

Kinn and Meckler returned, they were assigned to help the people to rebuild the peace among the nations. Nogar started sending his people to the island of the demons. Over a hundred Thorns were there searching and repairing the buildings. Nogar met with Mordock and asked him to collect and bring his family and any of his people to the island to live and protect it.

On the third day, Philip woke and the first thing he said was "Where is my pack?"

It was a good thing he was strapped down, too. They sent for Kinn. When he arrived he told him he had left it on the island because it was so heavy. When Philip started ranting, Kinn laughed.

"Do not worry. It is under your bed. Shaméd made sure it was brought here and was safe."

Kinn reached under it and dragged it out. He placed it on the bed next to Philip.

"Shaméd wants you to know there is more for you and Smash."

Philip looked up at Kinn when he mentioned Smash.

"Is the big lug ok?"

"He will be fine. He was hit over a hundred times with arrows. If Cuchulainn had not protected him when the last volley of arrows came they both would be dead."

"The Titian protected him?"

"I was told he and Smash were holding off the enemy as the men retreated across the bridge. They were doing very well until the priests regained their power. They killed Cuchulainn. He pushed Smash back and covered him with his body and shield."

"I am sorry to hear he is dead. I thought he was smug and arrogant. He was always picking on Smash and it made me mad."

"He may have been many things but he died protecting a friend. Cuchulainn's family arrived the day after he died. It was an interesting sight as they arrived on a flying ship. It was bigger than the fortress. When it landed ten Titians walked off picked up Cuchulainn, and left. They were here no longer than ten minutes. No one had time to talk to them. In the meantime, you relax and rest. In a few days you will be able to leave here."

Kinn walked away as Philip laid there clutching his pack.

Mordock arrived on the island a week after the war. He brought his family and over two hundred of his people. He used the Dragonfly to go and get them. He said others were on their way and would be there within the month. Word was passed that all of Murdock's people now had a home of their own. Within a year there would be over three thousand of his people living there.

Over the next few months, the Thorns found many items in the building from worlds they never knew existed. It would take many years to find out where the worlds were and how to reach them using the LDG.

A week after the war, Shaméd was sitting in his tent. It was now set up in the small field by the city Kalaron. Prince Japheth offered Shaméd a set of rooms inside the castle, but he had declined. He said he had some work to do, and the isolation would make it easier.

Prince Japheth was going to be crowned King and Shaméd was asked to attend the ceremony. Mordock, Sara, Lieutenant Jorge, and Nakobee were there on the day he was crowned.

Heather was on Rednog helping Nogar and his men with the cloning of Red. They would have a body for him in three to four months. Things were going along faster and better than Shaméd had hoped.

Three months after the war, Shaméd was with Mordock, Sara, and Lieutenant Jorge. They were standing on the beach, the same one where he and the others landed to invade the demon's building. It now belonged to Mordock's people. They stood there looking out over the ocean.

"I am leaving but you have the amulet and at anytime you can contact me. I have to go with Rae to his world and help him be crowned king. Mordock, I hope your family and your people will be happy living on this island."

"I am very happy to be with my wife and children. They and my people are happy. We are free, we have our own land, and we no longer have to hide from the world. Nogar's offer for us to come here and live on this island was a surprise and a blessing. My people will work hard to bring back life to the land. They've agreed to help protect and keep others from discovering the power here."

With Demahs on his shoulders, Shaméd waved. Sara and Lieutenant Jorge stood there holding hands. They waved with their free ones. Shaméd smiled at them - he still was not sure how those two would end up, but for now they were happy.

He turned and disappeared.

In the world room, Ben was working and Jon stood near the table of food, eating. He started talk as soon as Shaméd appeared.

"You know you could have warned me they were going to lock me up. Do you have any idea what they put me through? I was poked, prodded, and things were put into me where things should not be put, at least not willingly."

"If I had told you what was going to happen, you would not have gone. It was for the best. You were infected and now you are safe. It only took two weeks for them to get you better."

"Two weeks? It felt like forever. They were poking and doing all kinds of things to me. They only released me because they ran out of tests to do to me and Rae said he would not return to our world without me. By the way, no one will tell me why we have to go home. Am I being punished for something I did? Are you going to tell me? Or do I have to wait until we get there?"

"You are not being punished. I will tell you. Walk with me - I have to get some things, then we can go meet Rae and the others. We leave in three hours, so we have some time."

As they walked out of the world room Shaméd began telling Jon why after four hundred years why they were going back to his world.

Chapter Twenty -Two

Turning the monitor off, the three children sat there staring at each other. For the last five hours, they had watched and read the history on planet ZMEDWT87. They now understood a little more about their great-grandparents.

Daren, Michelle, and Nasif had asked the MA-TED where they could find Master Elfaren. When they got the information, they left the room and headed down the hallway. Turning a corner, they saw Master Elfaren right where the MA-TED told them he would be, standing in the hallway talking to a couple of students.

Master Elfaren knew the children were looking for him. The MA-TED had informed him so he was waiting for them. When they reached him, they stood there waiting, trying to be patient as he talked to the student. They knew better to interrupt so they stood there trying not to wiggle and waited for him to stop talking. Daren twice tried to interrupt but the other two kept stopping him.

"That is fine. Meet me in the classroom tomorrow and we can talk some more."

The children he was talking with left and Master Elfaren turned and looked at the three others.

"You were looking for me and I presume you wanted to talk with me?"

Daren and Michelle looked at Nasif. He rolled his eyes at them, and took a step closer.

"Yes sir, we finished reading what happened on world *ZMEDWT873*. What we want to know is what happened to Lord Shaméd. We know about the five missions he had after that one where he came to our world and helped our great-grandfathers. What we cannot find is when, how, and what happened to him during and after he moved the world Rednog. We know he disappeared for five of this planet's years, but there seems to be no record of it anywhere. Can you tell us why?"

Master Elfaren stood there looking at them. When it looked like they were about to speak, he raised his hand.

"Yes, I can. Walk with me to my office. On the way I will tell you some of it and then I will see about giving the three of you access to the hidden files."

Master Elfaren started walking and the three followed.

"After Lord Shaméd went with your grandfathers to your world, he returned here to Rednog and with the help of Red, Nogar's father, they moved the world. That was when he disappeared. Everyone knows that - but what most people do not know is where he went. He was teleported through space and time to a place called Earth. It is your people's homeworld. He went to a time very far in the past of your ancestors. We are not sure what sent him there - we just know he did. It took us five of our years to track and find him. Of course we would not have been able to find him if not for Ann. When we found him, he had spent one year on Earth. He met some people and started working on ways to find his way back. He lost a lot of his memories, so that made it harder for him."

They reached the door to Master Elfaren's office. Reaching for the handle, he started talking again.

"Come inside and I will give you access so you can read the events of his time on Earth, and I will tell you things about Lord Shaméd that most others do not know.

Entering the room, the three looked around. They saw floor to ceiling bookshelves filled with books and scrolls. A table with a small MA-TED and four chairs was all there was in the room.

"Sit and I will tell you what happened."

Master Elfaren sat in his chair and moved close to the small MA-TED.

"MA-TED, I am granting access to the hidden files of Lord Shaméd to Daren, Michelle, and Nasif. Please let them read it once. They are not to have any copy or transcript. When they are done, reseal the file."

Sitting back, Master Elfaren moved his chair so he could look at the three children.

"After, Lord Shaméd returned he went on twenty more missions. The last one is where he found his people. By his people, I mean to say his race. We knew for years his DNA was an unknown. Until we found his people's world we did not know if they existed anymore. Now here is what you will not read in the history records. After finding the world, we found they were in some ways more advanced than the Thorns or any of us. They live on five worlds and their culture is very advanced. They may be as advanced as the ones that created the MA-TED. They have spaceflight better than the Thorns, and their history is very long. Their lifespan is longer than any other race of beings - longer than the Thorns and Elf's. We believe they can live as long as the dragons. We think this because we found Lord Shaméd's father. A few years after finding his people, Lord Shaméd moved there to live. He took with him his wife, Terrine and their two children. Terrine's son, Téral stayed here a few years to finish his training. Later, he left to visit with Shaméd and Terrine. He ended up staying there. The last time I spoke with Shaméd he told me they were doing well and Terrine had twins, so now they have four children. They have become very popular on their world because most people there have only been able to have two children. So now, you know more about Lord Shaméd. You can now leave and read about him on earth."

The three sat there not moving. Michelle looked at the boys then leaned forward.

"Master Elfaren, how could Lord Shaméd's father still be alive? Why have we never met any of these people and…"

"You have met them. You just do not know you have. They live in secret, they move from world to world watching and studying the people. They do this because they can and because after many years of being an aggressive race, they discovered that they were the ones who should be the caretakers. They now work with the Thorns giving them what they learn - remember they live a long time. Shaméd's father is alive but very old. He is not allowed to leave their world. When he was young, he led a group of others and they went across the cosmos to other worlds trying to conquer them. Eventually they were tracked down and stopped. Those who were not killed were brought back and punished. Now go and read the story about Shaméd on earth."

They stood and Daren and Michelle turned to leave, Nasif stood there looking at Master Elfaren.

"Sir, could we have access to the events of our great-grandparents when they returned to our world? We know our world history, but I believe there are some things left out."

Master Elfaren placed his finger in the book he had just opened. He looked up at Nasif as the other two stopped and looked back.

"Yes, you can. MA-TED, you can give them access to their great-grandparents' files. However, limit it to only Jym, Jon, and Rae, and let them see only what pertains to the time on their homeworld. They are not allowed to see anything that is classified, secret, or top secret. Now will you leave, so I can get back to work?"

238

"Thank you. And good day, Master Elfaren."

The three turned and walked out of the room. Master Elfaren sat there with a smile on his face.

"You know these three might be as much trouble as Jym, Jon, and Rae."

"They were not that much trouble."

"Not that much trouble? Jon was always trying to take me apart and arguing with me on his experiments."

"Jon kept you busy and you liked arguing with him. Most of those you deal with, and I include myself, do not argue with you. We know you have access to more data and know more than all of us, so we trust you. Jon always wanted to know more. As for Jym and Rae, they were interesting for being human. I have some work to do. Let me know when they are finished. It will give me time to find them something more to do."

Master Elfaren opened his book, leaned back in his chair, and started to read.

Other books by

TJ Boyer and Elizabeth Ajamie-Boyer

The Quest: Book One:
The Journey: Book Two:
The Rescue: Book Three:
The War: Book Four:
The Reluctant King: Book Five
Invasion: Book Six
Vanished: Book Seven
Nakobee: Book Eight
Atrell: Book Nine
The World Rednog and the Thorns: Book Ten
Nogar the Golden Dragon: Book Eleven

Books by Elizabeth Ajamie-Boyer and TJ Boyer

Death at Hell's Canyon Quarry-A Murder Mystery

Books by Elizabeth Ajamie-Boyer

Memories of War
And Freedom to the Prisoners
My Soul Awaits
Death in Hells Canyon Quarry
Miriam Attalla, An Emigrant's Story
Cheyenne on Her mind

All books are available on Kindle and Amazon
https://mirrorgatechronicles.wordpress.com/

Our web site is:
https://mirrorgatechronicles.wordpress.com/

Made in the USA
Middletown, DE
09 September 2023